SERPENTS IN EDEN

SERPENTS IN EDEN

COUNTRYSIDE CRIMES

EDITED AND INTRODUCED BY
MARTIN EDWARDS

BRITISH LIBRARY

First published in 2016 by
The British Library
96 Euston Road
London NW1 2DB

Introduction and notes copyright © 2016 Martin Edwards

Cataloguing in Publication Data
A catalogue record for this book is available from the British Library

ISBN 978 0 7123 5794 4

Typeset by IDSUK (DataConnection) Ltd
Printed and bound by CPI Group (UK) Ltd, Croydon, CR0 4YY

CONTENTS

INTRODUCTION

One of the most famous conversations in the literature of crime fiction takes place in Arthur Conan Doyle's story "The Copper Beeches". Sherlock Holmes and Dr Watson are travelling by train to Winchester on a lovely spring day, and the delights of the passing scenery move the good doctor to raptures. Holmes, that old spoilsport, shakes his head gravely: "You look at these scattered houses, and you are impressed by their beauty ... I look at them, and the only thought that comes to me is a feeling of their isolation and of the impunity with which crime may be committed there ... They always fill me with a certain horror. It is my belief, Watson, founded upon my experience, that the lowest and vilest alleys in London do not present a more dreadful record of sin than does the smiling and beautiful countryside ... Think of the deeds of hellish cruelty, the hidden wickedness which may go on, year in, year out, in such places, and none the wiser."

This memorable passage helps to explain why the appeal of crime in the countryside is both intense and enduring. More than half a century later, W.H. Auden went so far as to say, in his essay "The Guilty Vicarage" that he found it "very difficult, for example, to read [a detective story] that is not set in rural England." This sounds rather extreme, but for Auden, there was an ideal milieu for crime and mystery: "Nature should reflect its human inhabitants, *i.e.*, it should be the Great Good Place; for the more Eden-like it is, the greater the contradiction of murder. The country is preferable to the town ..."

Auden was writing at a time when "the Golden Age of Murder" in detective fiction was drawing to a close. Agatha Christie had led the way in popularising the rural English whodunit novel (although she also set many of her stories in exotic foreign locations) with enduringly popular books such as *The Murder of Roger Ackroyd* and *The Murder at the Vicarage*. In his survey of the genre *Snobbery with Violence*, a crime writer of a later generation, Colin Watson, coined the term Mayhem Parva to convey the typical setting of this kind of story.

For Watson, Mayhem Parva was located in the south of England, and had "an inn with reasonable accommodation for itinerant detectives, a village institute, a library, and shops – including a chemist's where weed-killer and hair dye might be conveniently bought ... there would be a good bus service for the keeping of suspicious appointments in the nearby town..." Watson regarded Mayhem Parva as "a mythical kingdom ... It was derived in part from the ways and values of a society that had begun to fade away from the very moment of the shots at Sarajevo..."

Watson's portrayal is a caricature of Golden Age fiction, though like many caricatures, it contains more than a grain of truth. He acknowledged the durability of the appeal of the rural whodunit, but nevertheless under estimated it, perhaps because he failed fully to understand it. More than a quarter of a century after *Snobbery with Violence* was published, *Midsomer Murders,* based on novels written by Caroline Graham, arrived on the television screens. At the time of writing the series is still going strong, with more than one hundred episodes screened. Midsomer has become a Mayhem

Parva for the twenty-first century, with a homicide *per capita* rate outstripping those of many an urban ghetto.

Just as *Midsomer Murders* has been watched around the world, so Agatha Christie's books (and the TV series, films, and other adaptations they spawned) continue to enjoy global success, even half a century after her death. Detective stories set in the heart of the countryside remain remarkably popular, as has been illustrated by the success of several titles in the British Library's Crime Classics, such as three books by the previously neglected John Bude: *The Cornish Coast Murder*, *The Lake District Murder*, and *The Sussex Downs Murder*.

Serpents in Eden celebrates the rural British mystery by bringing together an eclectic mix of short crime stories written over, very roughly, half a century. Conan Doyle is represented, as are such major figures as G.K. Chesterton and Margery Allingham. Famous in their day were such authors as R. Austin Freeman, H.C. Bailey, and Anthony Berkeley. M. McDonnell Bodkin and Herbert Jenkins were rather less renowned. At different times, and in different ways, they all explored the possibilities of crime in the countryside in lively fashion, and sometimes with great ingenuity.

The Berkeley story included here is especially noteworthy, as it was unpublished during his lifetime, and thereafter appeared in a privately produced book so rare that even the British Library did not have a copy. By way of contrast, only in recent years has the real, and rather surprising, identity of the author of "Inquest" become known. She was, in fact, the step-daughter of P.G. Wodehouse, and she originally published the story under the unlikely pen-name "Loel Yeo". One of many pleasures afforded by the invitation to put this anthology together has been the chance to give credit where it is due – and to ensure that this enjoyable story, from an author whose promise as a crime writer was sadly never fulfilled, is finally credited to Leonora Wodehouse.

Martin Edwards

www.martinedwardsbooks.com

THE BLACK DOCTOR

Arthur Conan Doyle

Arthur Conan Doyle (1859–1930) will forever be remembered as the creator of Sherlock Holmes, but his literary achievements were many and varied. His work included historical and science fiction, tales about boxing and pirates, and stories of terror and the supernatural. His disenchantment with being typecast as Holmes' creator led him to kill off the great detective at the Reichenbach Falls, so that he could focus on other areas of writing, but Holmes' popularity was so great that pressure to revive him ultimately proved irresistible.

Holmes does not feature in this relatively unfamiliar tale, which first appeared in the *Strand Magazine* in 1898, prior to the detective's return in *The Hound of the Baskervilles*. Set in a village in the north west of England, it is a mystery story which displays those touches of the macabre and exotic that distinguish Conan Doyle's better work. It also boasts a murder trial which gives rise to a splendid sensation in court.

*　*　*　*　*

Bishop's Crossing is a small village lying ten miles in a south-westerly direction from Liverpool. Here in the early seventies there settled a doctor named Aloysius Lana. Nothing was known locally either of his antecedents or of the reasons which had prompted him to come to this Lancashire hamlet. Two facts only were certain about him; the one that he had gained his medical qualification with some distinction at Glasgow; the other that he came undoubtedly of a tropical race, and was so dark that he might almost have had a strain of the Indian in his composition. His predominant features were, however, European, and he possessed a stately courtesy and carriage which suggested a Spanish extraction. A swarthy skin, raven-black hair, and dark, sparkling eyes under a pair of heavily-tufted brows made a strange contrast to the flaxen or chestnut rustics of England, and the newcomer was soon known as 'The Black Doctor of Bishop's Crossing.' At first it was a term of ridicule and reproach; as the years went on it became a title of honour which was familiar to the whole country-side, and extended far beyond the narrow confines of the village.

For the newcomer proved himself to be a capable surgeon and an accomplished physician. The practice of that district had been in the hands of Edward Rowe, the son of Sir William Rowe, the Liverpool consultant, but he had not inherited the talents of his father, and Dr Lana, with his advantages of presence and of manner, soon beat him out of the field. Dr Lana's social success was as rapid as his professional. A remarkable surgical cure in the case of the Hon. James Lowry, the second son of Lord Belton, was the means of introducing him to county society, where he became a favourite through the charm of his conversation and the elegance of his manners. An absence of antecedents and of relatives is sometimes an aid rather than an impediment to social advancement, and the distinguished individuality of the handsome doctor was its own recommendation.

His patients had one fault—and one fault only—to find with him. He appeared to be a confirmed bachelor. This was the more remarkable since the house which he occupied was a large one, and it was known that his success in practice had enabled him to save considerable sums. At first the local matchmakers were continually coupling his name with one or other of the eligible ladies, but as years passed and Dr Lana remained unmarried, it came to be generally understood that for some reason he must remain a bachelor. Some even went so far as to assert that he was already married, and that it was in order to escape the consequence of an early misalliance that he had buried himself at Bishop's Crossing. And, then, just as the matchmakers had finally given him up in despair, his engagement was suddenly announced to Miss Frances Morton, of Leigh Hall.

Miss Morton was a young lady who was well known upon the country-side, her father, James Haldane Morton, having been the Squire of Bishop's Crossing. Both her parents were, however, dead, and she lived with her only brother, Arthur Morton, who had inherited the family estate. In person Miss Morton was tall and stately, and she was famous for her quick, impetuous nature and for her strength of character. She met Dr Lana at a garden-party, and a friendship, which quickly ripened into love, sprang up between them. Nothing could exceed their devotion to each other. There was some discrepancy in age, he being thirty-seven, and she twenty-four; but, save in that one respect, there was no possible objection to be found with the match. The engagement was in February, and it was arranged that the marriage should take place in August.

Upon the 3rd of June Dr Lana received a letter from abroad. In a small village the postmaster is also in a position to be the gossip-master, and Mr Bankley, of Bishop's Crossing, had many of the secrets of his neighbours in his possession. Of this particular letter he remarked only that it was in a curious envelope, that it was in a man's handwriting, that the postscript was Buenos Aires, and the stamp of the Argentine Republic. It was the first letter which he had ever known Dr Lana to have from abroad, and this was the reason why his attention was particularly called to it before he handed it to the local postman. It was delivered by the evening delivery of that date.

Next morning—that is, upon the 4th of June—Dr Lana called upon Miss Morton, and a long interview followed, from which he was observed to return in a state of great agitation. Miss Morton remained in her room all that day, and her maid found her several times in tears. In the course of a week it was an open secret to the whole village that the engagement was at an end, that Dr Lana had behaved shamefully to the young lady, and that Arthur Morton, her brother, was talking of horse-whipping him. In what particular respect the doctor had behaved badly was unknown—some surmised one thing and some another; but it was observed, and taken as the obvious sign of a guilty conscience, that he would go for miles round rather than pass the windows of Leigh Hall, and that he gave up attending morning service upon Sundays where he might have met the young lady. There was an advertisement also in the *Lancet* as to the sale of a practice which mentioned no names, but which was thought by some to refer to Bishop's Crossing, and to mean that Dr Lana was thinking of abandoning the scene of his success. Such was the position of affairs when, upon the evening of Monday, June 21st, there came a fresh development which changed what had been a mere village scandal into a tragedy which arrested the attention of the whole nation. Some detail is necessary to cause the facts of that evening to present their full significance.

The sole occupants of the doctor's house were his housekeeper, an elderly and most respectable woman, named Martha Woods, and a young servant—Mary Pilling. The coachman and the surgery-boy slept out. It was the custom of the doctor to sit at night in his study, which was next to the surgery in the wing of the house which was farthest from the servants' quarters. This side of the house had a door of its own for the convenience of patients, so that it was possible for the doctor to admit and receive a visitor there without the knowledge of anyone. As a matter of fact, when patients came late it was quite usual for him to let them in and out by the surgery entrance, for the maid and the housekeeper were in the habit of retiring early.

On this particular night Martha Woods went into the doctor's study at half-past nine, and found him writing at his desk. She bade him good night, sent the maid to bed, and then occupied herself until a quarter to eleven in household matters. It was striking eleven upon the hall clock when she went to her own room. She had been there about a quarter of an hour or twenty minutes when she heard a cry or call, which appeared to come from within the house. She waited some time, but it was not repeated. Much alarmed, for the sound was loud and urgent, she put on a dressing-gown, and ran at the top of her speed to the doctor's study.

'Who's there?' cried a voice, as she tapped at the door.

'I am here, sir—Mrs Woods.'

'I beg that you will leave me in peace. Go back to your room this instant!' cried the voice, which was, to the best of her belief, that of her master. The tone was so harsh and so unlike her master's usual manner, that she was surprised and hurt.

'I thought I heard you calling, sir,' she explained, but no answer was given to her. Mrs Woods looked at the clock as she returned to her room, and it was then half-past eleven.

At some period between eleven and twelve (she could not be positive as to the exact hour) a patient called upon the doctor and was unable to get any reply from him. This late visitor was Mrs Madding, the wife of the village grocer, who was dangerously ill of typhoid fever. Dr Lana had asked her to look in the last thing and let him know how her husband was progressing. She observed that the light was burning in the study, but having knocked several times at the surgery door without response, she concluded that the doctor had been called out, and so returned home.

There is a short, winding drive with a lamp at the end of it leading down from the house to the road. As Mrs Madding emerged from the gate a man was coming along the footpath. Thinking that it might be Dr Lana returning from some professional visit, she waited for him, and was surprised to see that it was Mr Arthur Morton, the young squire. In the light of the lamp she observed that his manner was excited, and that he carried in his hand a heavy hunting-crop. He was turning in at the gate when she addressed him.

'The doctor is not in, sir,' said she.

'How do you know that?' he asked harshly.

'I have been to the surgery door, sir.'

'I see a light,' said the young squire, looking up the drive. 'That is in his study, is it not?'

'Yes, sir; but I am sure that he is out.'

'Well, he must come in again,' said young Morton, and passed through the gate while Mrs Madding went upon her homeward way.

At three o'clock that morning her husband suffered a sharp relapse, and she was so alarmed by his symptoms that she determined to call the doctor without delay. As she passed through the gate she was surprised to see someone lurking among the laurel bushes. It was certainly a man, and to the best of her belief Mr Arthur Morton. Preoccupied with her own troubles, she gave no particular attention to the incident, but hurried on upon her errand.

When she reached the house she perceived to her surprise that the light was still burning in the study. She therefore tapped at the surgery door. There was no answer. She repeated the knocking several times without effect. It appeared to her to be unlikely that the doctor would either go to bed or go out leaving so brilliant a light behind him, and it struck Mrs Madding that it was possible that he might have dropped asleep in his chair. She tapped at the study window, therefore, but without result. Then, finding that there was an opening between the curtain and the woodwork, she looked through.

The small room was brilliantly lighted from a large lamp on the central table, which was littered with the doctor's books and instruments. No one was visible, nor did she see anything unusual, except that in the farther shadow thrown by the table a dingy white glove was lying upon the carpet. And then suddenly, as her eyes became more accustomed to the light, a boot emerged from the other end of the shadow, and she realized, with a thrill of horror, that what she had taken to be a glove was the hand of a man, who was prostrate upon the floor. Understanding that something terrible had occurred, she rang at the front door, roused Mrs Woods, the housekeeper, and the two women made their way into the study, having first dispatched the maidservant to the police-station.

At the side of the table, away from the window, Dr Lana was discovered stretched upon his back and quite dead. It was evident that he had been subjected to violence, for one of his eyes was blackened and there were marks of bruises about his face and neck. A slight thickening and swelling of his features appeared to suggest that the cause of his death had been strangulation. He was dressed in his usual professional clothes, but wore cloth slippers, the soles of which were perfectly clean. The carpet was marked all over, especially on the side of the door, with traces of dirty boots, which were presumably left by the murderer. It was evident that someone had entered by the surgery door, had killed the doctor, and had then made his escape unseen. That the assailant was a man was certain, from the size of the footprints and from the nature of the injuries. But beyond that point the police found it very difficult to go.

There were no signs of robbery, and the doctor's gold watch was safe in his pocket. He kept a heavy cash-box in the room, and this was discovered to be locked but empty. Mrs Woods had an impression that a large sum was usually kept there, but the doctor had paid a heavy corn bill in cash only that very day, and it was conjectured that it was to this and not to a robber that the emptiness of the box was due. One thing in the room was missing—but that one thing was suggestive. The portrait of Miss Morton, which had always stood upon the side-table, had been taken from its frame, and carried off. Mrs Woods had observed it there when she waited upon her employer that evening, and now it was gone. On the other hand, there was picked up from the floor a green eye-patch, which the housekeeper could not remember to have seen before. Such a patch might, however, be in the possession of a doctor, and there was nothing to indicate that it was in any way connected with the crime.

Suspicion could only turn in one direction, and Arthur Morton, the young squire, was immediately arrested. The evidence against him was circumstantial, but damning. He was devoted to his sister, and it was shown that since the rupture between her and Dr Lana he had been heard again and again to express himself in the most vindictive terms towards her former lover. He had, as stated, been seen somewhere about eleven o'clock entering the doctor's drive with a hunting-crop in his hand. He had then, according to the theory of the police, broken in upon the doctor, whose exclamation of fear or of anger had been loud enough to attract the attention of Mrs Woods. When Mrs Woods descended, Dr Lana had made up his mind to talk it over with his visitor, and had, therefore, sent his housekeeper back to her room. This conversation had lasted a long time, had become more and more fiery, and had ended by a personal struggle, in which the doctor lost his life. The fact, revealed by a *post-mortem*, that his heart was much diseased—an ailment quite unsuspected during his life—would make it possible that death might in his case ensue from injuries which would not be fatal to a healthy man. Arthur Morton had then removed his sister's photograph, and had made his way homeward, stepping aside into the laurel bushes to avoid Mrs Madding at the gate. This was the theory of the prosecution, and the case which they presented was a formidable one.

On the other hand, there were some strong points for the defence. Morton was high-spirited and impetuous, like his sister, but he was respected and liked by everyone, and his frank and honest nature seemed to be incapable of such a crime. His own explanation was that he was anxious to have a conversation with Dr Lana about some urgent family matters (from first to last he refused even to mention the name of his sister). He did not attempt to deny that this conversation would probably have been of an unpleasant nature. He had heard from a patient that the doctor was out, and he therefore waited until about three in the morning for his return, but as he had seen nothing of him up to that hour, he had given it up and had returned home. As to his death, he knew no more about it than the constable who arrested him. He had formerly been an intimate friend of the deceased man; but circumstances, which he would prefer not to mention, had brought about a change in his sentiments.

There were several facts which supported his innocence. It was certain that Dr Lana was alive and in his study at half-past eleven o'clock. Mrs Woods was prepared to swear that it was at that hour that she had heard his voice. The friends of the prisoner contended that it was probable that at that time Dr Lana was not alone. The sound which had originally attracted the attention of the housekeeper, and her master's unusual impatience that she should leave him in peace, seemed to point to that. If this were so then it appeared to be probable that he had met his end between the moment when the housekeeper heard his voice and the time when Mrs Madding made her first call and found it impossible to attract his attention. But if this were the time of his death, then it was certain that Mr Arthur Morton could not be guilty, as it was *after* this that she had met the young squire at the gate.

If this hypothesis were correct, and someone was with Dr Lana before Mrs Madding met Mr Arthur Morton, then who was this someone, and what motives had he for wishing evil to the doctor? It was universally admitted that if the friends of the accused could throw light upon this, they would have gone a long way towards establishing his innocence. But in the meanwhile it was open to the public to say—as they did say—that there was no proof that anyone had been there at all except the young squire; while, on the other hand, there was ample proof that his motives in going were of a sinister kind. When Mrs Madding called, the doctor might have retired to his room, or he might, as she thought at the time, have gone out and returned afterwards to find Mr Arthur Morton waiting for him. Some of the supporters of the accused laid stress upon the fact that the photograph of his sister Frances, which had been removed from the doctor's room, had not been found in her brother's possession. This argument, however, did not count for much, as he had ample time before his arrest to burn it or to destroy it. As to the only positive evidence in the case—the muddy footmarks upon the floor—they were so blurred by the softness of the carpet that it was impossible to make any trustworthy deduction from them. The most that could be said was that their appearance was not inconsistent with the theory that they were made by the accused, and it was further shown that his boots were very muddy upon that night. There had been a heavy shower in the afternoon, and all boots were probably in the same condition.

Such is a bald statement of the singular and romantic series of events which centred public attention upon this Lancashire tragedy. The unknown origin of the doctor, his curious and distinguished personality, the position of the man who was accused of the murder, and the love affair which had preceded the crimes all combined to make the affair one of those dramas which absorb the whole interest of a nation. Throughout the three kingdoms men discussed the case of the Black Doctor of Bishop's Crossing, and many were the theories put forward to explain the facts; but it may safely be said that among them all there was not one which prepared the minds of the public for the extraordinary sequel, which caused so much excitement upon the first day of the trial, and came to a climax upon the second. The long files of the *Lancaster Weekly* with their report of the case lie before me as I write, but I must content myself with a synopsis of the case up to the point when, upon the evening of the first day, the evidence of Miss Frances Morton threw a singular light upon the case.

Mr Porlock Carr, the counsel for the prosecution, had marshalled his facts with his usual skill, and as the day wore on, it became more and more evident how difficult was the task which

Mr Humphrey, who had been retained for the defence, had before him. Several witnesses were put up to swear to the intemperate expressions which the young squire had been heard to utter about the doctor, and the fiery manner in which he resented the alleged ill-treatment of his sister. Mrs Madding repeated her evidence as to the visit which had been paid late at night by the prisoner to the deceased, and it was shown by another witness that the prisoner was aware that the doctor was in the habit of sitting up alone in this isolated wing of the house, and that he had chosen this very late hour to call because he knew that his victim would then be at his mercy. A servant at the squire's house was compelled to admit that he had heard his master return about three that morning, which corroborated Mrs Madding's statement that she had seen him among the laurel bushes near the gate upon the occasion of her second visit. The muddy boots and an alleged similarity in the footprints were duly dwelt upon, and it was felt when the case for the prosecution had been presented that, however circumstantial it might be, it was none the less so complete and so convincing, that the fate of the prisoner was sealed, unless something quite unexpected should be disclosed by the defence. It was three o'clock when the prosecution closed. At half-past four, when the court rose, a new and unlooked-for development had occurred. I extract the incident, or part of it, from the journal which I have already mentioned, omitting the preliminary observations of the counsel.

'Considerable sensation was caused in the crowded court when the first witness called for the defence proved to be Miss Frances Morton, the sister of the prisoner. Our readers will remember that the young lady had been engaged to Dr Lana, and that it was his anger over the sudden termination of this engagement which was thought to have driven her brother to the perpetration of this crime. Miss Morton had not, however, been directly implicated in the case in any way, either at the inquest or at the police-court proceedings, and her appearance as the leading witness for the defence came as a surprise upon the public.

Miss Frances Morton, who was a tall and handsome brunette, gave her evidence in a low but clear voice, though it was evident throughout that she was suffering from extreme emotion. She alluded to her engagement to the doctor, touched briefly upon its termination, which was due, she said, to personal matters connected with his family, and surprised the court by asserting that she had always considered her brother's resentment to be unreasonable and intemperate. In answer to a direct question from her counsel, she replied that she did not feel that she had any grievance whatever against Dr Lana, and that in her opinion he had acted in a perfectly honourable manner. Her brother, on an insufficient knowledge of the facts, had taken another view, and she was compelled to acknowledge that, in spite of her entreaties, he had uttered threats of personal violence against the doctor, and had, upon the evening of the tragedy, announced his intention of 'having it out with him.' She had done her best to bring him to a more reasonable frame of mind, but he was very headstrong where his emotions or prejudices were concerned.

Up to this point the young lady's evidence had appeared to make against the prisoner rather than in his favour. The questions of her counsel, however, soon put a very different light upon the matter, and disclosed an unexpected line of defence.

Mr Humphrey: Do you believe your brother to be guilty of this crime?

The Judge: I cannot permit that question, Mr Humphrey. We are here to decide upon questions of fact—not of belief.

Mr Humphrey: Do you know that your brother is not guilty of the death of Doctor Lana?

Miss Morton: Yes.

Mr Humphrey: How do you know it?

Miss Morton: Because Dr Lana is not dead.

There followed a prolonged sensation in court, which interrupted the cross-examination of the witness.

Mr Humphrey: And how do you know, Miss Morton, that Dr Lana is not dead?

Miss Morton: Because I have received a letter from him since the date of his supposed death.

Mr Humphrey: Have you this letter?

Miss Morton: Yes, but I should prefer not to show it.

Mr Humphrey: Have you the envelope?

Miss Morton: Yes, it is here.

Mr Humphrey: What is the post-mark?

Miss Morton: Liverpool.

Mr Humphrey: And the date?

Miss Morton: June the 22nd.

Mr Humphrey: That being the day after his alleged death. Are you prepared to swear to this handwriting, Miss Morton?

Miss Morton: Certainly.

Mr Humphrey: I am prepared to call six other witnesses, my lord, to testify that this letter is in the writing of Doctor Lana.

The Judge: Then you must call them to-morrow.

Mr Porlock Carr (counsel for the prosecution): In the meantime, my lord, we claim possession of this document, so that we may obtain expert evidence as to how far it is an imitation of the handwriting of the gentleman whom we still confidently assert to be deceased. I need not point out that the theory so unexpectedly sprung upon us may prove to be a very obvious device adopted by the friends of the prisoner in order to divert this inquiry. I would draw attention to the fact that the young lady must, according to her own account, have possessed this letter during the proceedings at the inquest and at the police-court. She desires us to believe that she permitted these to proceed, although she held in her pocket evidence which would at any moment have brought them to an end.

Mr Humphrey: Can you explain this, Miss Morton?

Miss Morton: Dr Lana desired his secret to be preserved.

Mr Porlock Carr: Then why have you made this public?

Miss Morton: To save my brother.

A murmur of sympathy broke out in court, which was instantly suppressed by the Judge.

The Judge: Admitting this line of defence, it lies with you, Mr Humphrey, to throw a light upon who this man is whose body has been recognized by so many friends and patients of Dr Lana as being that of the doctor himself.

A Juryman: Has anyone up to now expressed any doubt about the matter?

Mr Porlock Carr: Not to my knowledge.

Mr Humphrey: We hope to make the matter clear.
The Judge: Then the court adjourns until to-morrow.'

This new development of the case excited the utmost interest among the general public. Press comment was prevented by the fact that the trial was still undecided, but the question was everywhere argued as to how far there could be truth in Miss Morton's declaration, and how far it might be a daring ruse for the purpose of saving her brother. The obvious dilemma in which the missing doctor stood was that if by any extraordinary chance he was not dead, then he must be held responsible for the death of this unknown man, who resembled him so exactly, and who was found in his study. This letter which Miss Morton refused to produce was possibly a confession of guilt, and she might find herself in the terrible position of only being able to save her brother from the gallows by the sacrifice of her former lover. The court next morning was crammed to overflowing, and a murmur of excitement passed over it when Mr Humphrey was observed to enter in a state of emotion, which even his trained nerves could not conceal, and to confer with the opposing counsel. A few hurried words—words which left a look of amazement upon Mr Porlock Carr's face—passed between them, and then the counsel for the defence, addressing the Judge, announced that, with the consent of the prosecution, the young lady who had given evidence upon the sitting before would not be recalled.

The Judge: But you appear, Mr Humphrey, to have left matters in a very unsatisfactory state.

Mr Humphrey: Perhaps, my lord, my next witness may help to clear them up.

The Judge: Then call your next witness.

Mr Humphrey: I call Dr Aloysius Lana.

The learned counsel has made many telling remarks in his day, but he has certainly never produced such a sensation with so short a sentence. The court was simply stunned with amazement as the very man whose fate had been the subject of so much contention appeared bodily before them in the witness-box. Those among the spectators who had known him at Bishop's Crossing saw him now, gaunt and thin, with deep lines of care upon his face. But in spite of his melancholy bearing and despondent expression, there were few who could say that they had ever seen a man of more distinguished presence. Bowing to the judge, he asked if he might be allowed to make a statement, and having been duly informed that whatever he said might be used against him, he bowed once more, and proceeded:

'My wish,' said he, 'is to hold nothing back, but to tell with perfect frankness all that occurred upon the night of the 21st of June. Had I known that the innocent had suffered, and that so much trouble had been brought upon those whom I love best in the world, I should have come forward long ago; but there were reasons which prevented these things from coming to my ears. It was my desire that an unhappy man should vanish from the world which had known him, but I had not forseen that others would be affected by my actions. Let me to the best of my ability repair the evil which I have done.

'To anyone who is acquainted with the history of the Argentine Republic the name of Lana is well known. My father, who came of the best blood of old Spain, filled all the highest offices of the State, and would have been President but for his death in the riots of San Juan. A brilliant career might have been open to my twin brother Ernest and myself had it not been for financial losses which made it necessary that we should earn our own living. I apologize, sir, if these details appear to be irrelevant, but they are a necessary introduction to that which is to follow.

'I had, as I have said, a twin brother named Ernest, whose resemblance to me was so great that even when we were together people could see no difference between us. Down to the smallest detail we were exactly the same. As we grew older this likeness became less marked because our expression was not the same, but with our features in repose the points of difference were very slight.

'It does not become me to say too much of one who is dead, the more so as he is my only brother, but I leave his character to those who knew him best. I will only say—for I *have* to say it—that in my early manhood I conceived a horror of him, and that I had good reason for the aversion which filled me. My own reputation suffered from his actions, for our close resemblance caused me to be credited with many of them. Eventually, in a peculiarly disgraceful business, he contrived to throw the whole odium upon me in such a way that I was forced to leave the Argentine for ever, and to seek a career in Europe. The freedom from his hated presence more than compensated me for the loss of my native land. I had enough money to defray my medical studies at Glasgow, and I finally settled in practice at Bishop's Crossing, in the firm conviction that in that remote Lancashire hamlet I should never hear of him again.

'For years my hopes were fulfilled, and then at last he discovered me. Some Liverpool man who visited Buenos Aires put him upon my track. He had lost all his money, and he thought that he would come over and share mine. Knowing my horror of him, he rightly thought that I would be willing to buy him off. I received a letter from him saying that he was coming. It was at a crisis in my own affairs, and his arrival might conceivably bring trouble, and even disgrace, upon some whom I was especially bound to shield from anything of the kind. I took steps to insure that any evil which might come should fall on me only, and that'—here he turned and looked at the prisoner—'was the cause of conduct upon my part which has been too harshly judged. My only motive was to screen those who were dear to me from any possible connection with scandal or disgrace. That scandal and disgrace would come with my brother was only to say that what had been would be again.

'My brother arrived himself one night not very long after my receipt of the letter. I was sitting in my study after the servants had gone to bed, when I heard a footstep upon the gravel outside, and an instant later I saw his face looking in at me through the window. He was a clean-shaven man like myself, and the resemblance between us was still so great that, for an instant, I thought it was my own reflection in the glass. He had a dark patch over his eye, but our features were absolutely the same. Then he smiled in a sardonic way which had been a trick of his from his boyhood, and I knew that he was the same brother who had driven me from my native land, and brought disgrace upon what had been an honourable name. I went to the door and I admitted him. That would be about ten o'clock that night.

'When he came into the glare of the lamp, I saw at once that he had fallen upon very evil days. He had walked from Liverpool, and he was tired and ill. I was quite shocked by the expression upon his face. My medical knowledge told me that there was some serious internal malady. He had been drinking also, and his face was bruised as the result of a scuffle which he had had with some sailors. It was to cover his injured eye that he wore this patch, which he removed when he entered the room. He was himself dressed in a pea-jacket and flannel shirt, and his feet were bursting through his boots. But his poverty had only made him more savagely vindictive towards me. His hatred rose to the height of a mania. I had been rolling in money in England, according to his account, while he had been starving in South America. I cannot describe to you the threats which he uttered or the insults which he poured upon me. My impression is, that hardships and debauchery had unhinged his reason. He paced about the room like a wild beast, demanding drink, demanding money, and all in the foulest language. I am a hot-tempered man, but I thank God that I am able to say that I remained master of myself, and that I never raised a hand against him. My coolness only irritated him the more. He raved, he cursed, he shook his fists in my face, and then suddenly a horrible spasm passed over his features, he clapped his hand to his side, and with a loud cry he fell in a heap at my feet. I raised him up and stretched him upon the sofa, but no answer came to my exclamations, and the hand which I held in mine was cold and clammy. His diseased heart had broken down. His own violence had killed him.

'For a long time I sat as if I were in some dreadful dream, staring at the body of my brother. I was aroused by the knocking of

Mrs Woods, who had been disturbed by that dying cry. I sent her away to bed. Shortly afterwards a patient tapped at the surgery door, but as I took no notice, he or she went off again. Slowly and gradually as I sat there a plan was forming itself in my head in the curious automatic way in which plans do form. When I rose from my chair my future movements were finally decided upon with-out my having been conscious of any process of thought. It was an instinct which irresistibly inclined me towards one course.

'Ever since that change in my affairs to which I have alluded, Bishop's Crossing had become hateful to me. My plans of life had been ruined, and I had met with hasty judgments and unkind treatment where I had expected sympathy. It is true that any dan-ger of scandal from my brother had passed away with his life; but still, I was sore about the past, and felt that things could never be as they had been. It may be that I was unduly sensitive, and that I had not made sufficient allowance for others, but my feel-ings were as I describe. Any chance of getting away from Bishop's Crossing and of everyone in it would be most welcome to me. And here was such a chance as I could never have dared to hope for, a chance which would enable me to make a clean break with the past.

'There was this dead man lying upon the sofa, so like me that save for some little thickness and coarseness of the features there was no difference at all. No one had seen him come and no one would miss him. We were both clean-shaven, and his hair was about the same length as my own. If I changed clothes with him, then Dr Aloysius Lana would be found lying dead in his study, and there would be an end of an unfortunate fellow, and of a blighted career. There was plenty of ready money in the room, and this I could carry away with me to help me to start once more in some other land. In my brother's clothes I could walk by night unobserved as far as Liverpool, and in that great seaport I would soon find some means of leaving the country. After my lost hopes, the humblest existence where I was unknown was far preferable, in my estimation, to a practice, however successful, in Bishop's Crossing, where at any moment I might come face to face with those whom I should wish, if it were possible, to forget. I determined to effect the change.

'And I did so. I will not go into particulars, for the recollection is as painful as the experience; but in an hour my brother lay, dressed down to the smallest detail in my clothes, while I slunk out by the surgery door, and taking the back path which led across some fields, I started off to make the best of my way to Liverpool, where I arrived the same night. My bag of money and a certain portrait were all I carried out of the house, and I left behind me in my hurry the shade which my brother had been wearing over his eye. Everything else of his I took with me.

'I give you my word, sir, that never for one instant did the idea occur to me that people might think that I had been murdered, nor did I imagine that anyone might be caused serious danger through this stratagem by which I endeavoured to gain a fresh start in the world. On the contrary, it was the thought of relieving others from the burden of my presence which was always uppermost in my mind. A sailing vessel was leaving Liverpool that very day for Corunna, and in this I took my passage, thinking that the voyage would give me time to recover my balance, and to consider the future. But before I left my resolution softened. I bethought me that there was one person in the world to whom I would not cause an hour of sadness. She would mourn me in her heart, however harsh and unsympathetic her relatives might be. She understood and appreciated the motives upon which I had acted, and if the rest of her family condemned me, she, at least, would not forget. And so I sent her a note under the seal of secrecy to save her from a baseless grief. If under the pressure of events she broke that seal, she has my entire sympathy and forgiveness.

'It was only last night that I returned to England, and during all this time I have heard nothing of the sensation which my supposed death had caused, nor of the accusation that Mr Arthur Morton had been concerned in it. It was in a late evening paper that I read an account of the proceedings of yesterday, and I have come this morning as fast as an express train could bring me to testify to the truth.'

Such was the remarkable statement of Dr Aloysius Lana which brought the trial to a sudden termination. A subsequent investigation corroborated it to the extent of finding out the vessel in which his brother Ernest Lana had come over from South America. The ship's doctor was able to testify that he had complained of a weak heart during the voyage, and that his symptoms were consistent with such a death as was described.

As to Dr Aloysius Lana, he returned to the village from which he had made so dramatic a disappearance, and a complete reconciliation was effected between him and the young squire, the latter having acknowledged that he had entirely misunderstood the other's motives in withdrawing from his engagement. That another reconciliation followed may be judged from a notice extracted from a prominent column in the *Morning Post*:

'A marriage was solemnized upon September 19th, by the Rev Stephen Johnson, at the parish church of Bishop's Crossing, between Aloysius Xavier Lana, son of Don Alfredo Lana, formerly Foreign Minister of the Argentine Republic, and Frances Morton, only daughter of the late James Morton, J.P., of Leigh Hall, Bishop's Crossing, Lancashire.'

MURDER BY PROXY

M. McDonnell Bodkin

Matthias McDonnell Bodkin (1850–1933) was an Irish lawyer whose first book, published pseudonymously in 1890, rejoiced in the title *Poteen Punch, Strong, Hot, and Sweet: Being a Succession of Irish After-Dinner Stories*. A couple of years later, he was elected to Parliament, and the experience of three years as an MP, as well as his time as a barrister and judge, contributed to a book of reminiscences he published about his life in the law and in politics.

When Conan Doyle lost his enthusiasm for writing about Sherlock Holmes in the 1890s, Bodkin was one of many authors who tried, with varying degrees of success, to fill the void. He created Paul Beck ("the Rule of Thumb Detective") and then Dora Myrl ("the Lady Detective") and proceeded to marry them off; in due course, the fruit of their union also turned to sleuthing in *Young Beck: A Chip of the Old Block* (1912). This story shows Beck senior at his best.

* * * * *

At two o'clock precisely on that sweltering 12th of August, Eric Neville, young, handsome, *debonair*, sauntered through the glass door down the wrought-iron staircase into the beautiful, old-fashioned garden of Berkly Manor, radiant in white flannel, with a broad-brimmed Panama hat perched lightly on his glossy black curls, for he had just come from lazing in his canoe along the shadiest stretches of the river, with a book for company.

The back of the Manor House was the south wall of the garden, which stretched away for nearly a mile, gay with blooming flowers and ripening fruit. The air, heavy with perfume, stole softly through all the windows, now standing wide open in the sunshine, as though the great house gasped for breath.

When Eric's trim, tan boot left the last step of the iron staircase it reached the broad gravelled walk of the garden. Fifty yards off the head gardener was tending his peaches, the smoke from his pipe hanging like a faint blue haze in the still air that seemed to quiver with the heat. Eric, as he reached him, held out a petitionary hand, too lazy to speak.

Without a word the gardener stretched for a huge peach that was striving to hide its red face from the sun under narrow ribbed leaves, plucked it as though he loved it, and put it softly in the young man's hand.

Eric stripped off the velvet coat, rose-coloured, green, and amber, till it hung round the fruit in tatters, and made his sharp, white teeth meet in the juicy flesh of the ripe peach.

BANG!

The sudden shock of sound close to their ears wrenched the nerves of the two men; one dropped his peach, and the other his pipe. Both stared about them in utter amazement.

'Look there, sir,' whispered the gardener, pointing to a little cloud of smoke oozing lazily through a window almost directly over their head, while the pungent spice of gunpowder made itself felt in the hot air.

'My uncle's room,' gasped Eric. 'I left him only a moment ago fast asleep on the sofa.'

He turned as he spoke, and ran like a deer along the garden walk, up the iron steps, and back through the glass door into the house, the old gardener following as swiftly as his rheumatism would allow.

Eric crossed the sitting-room on which the glass door opened, went up the broad, carpeted staircase four steps at a time, turned sharply to the right down a broad corridor, and burst straight through the open door of his uncle's study.

Fast as he had come, there was another before him. A tall, strong figure, dressed in light tweed, was bending over the sofa where, a few minutes before, Eric had seen his uncle asleep.

Eric recognized the broad back and brown hair at once.

'John,' he cried, 'John, what is it?'

His cousin turned to him a handsome, manly face, ghastly pale now even to the lips.

'Eric, my boy,' he answered falteringly, 'this is too awful. Uncle has been murdered—shot stone dead.'

'No, no; it cannot be. It's not five minutes since I saw him quietly sleeping,' Eric began. Then his eyes fell on the still figure on the sofa, and he broke off abruptly.

Squire Neville lay with his face to the wall, only the outline of his strong, hard features visible. The charge of shot had entered at the base of the skull, the grey hair was all dabbled with blood, and the heavy, warm drops still fell slowly on to the carpet.

'But who can have ...' Eric gasped out, almost speechless with horror.

'It must have been his own gun,' his cousin answered. 'It was lying there on the table, to the right, barrel still smoking, when I came in.'

'It wasn't suicide—was it?' asked Eric, in a frightened whisper.

'Quite impossible, I should say. You see where he is hit.'

'But it was so sudden. I ran the moment I heard the shot, and you were before me. Did you see anyone?'

'Not a soul. The room was empty.'

'But how could the murderer escape?'

'Perhaps he leapt through the window. It was open when I came in.'

'He couldn't do that, Master John.' It was the voice of the gardener at the door. Me and Master Eric was right under the window when the shot came.'

'Then how in the devil's name did he disappear, Simpson?'

'It's not for me to say, sir.'

John Neville searched the room with eager eyes. There was no cover in it for a cat. A bare, plain room, panelled with brown oak, on which hung some guns and fishing-rods—old fashioned for the most part, but of the finest workmanship and material. A small bookcase in the corner was the room's sole claim to be called 'a study'. The huge leather-covered sofa on which the corpse lay, a massive round table in the centre of the room, and a few heavy chairs completed the furniture. The dust lay thick on everything, the fierce sunshine streamed in a broad band across the room. The air was stifling with the heat and the acrid smoke of gunpowder.

John Neville noticed how pale his young cousin was. He laid his hand on his shoulder with the protecting kindness of an elder brother.

'Come, Eric,' he said softly, 'we can do no good here.'

'We had best look round first, hadn't we, for some clue?' asked Eric, and he stretched his hand towards the gun; but John stopped him.

'No, no,' he cried hastily, 'we must leave things just as we find them. I'll send a man to the village for Wardle and telegraph to London for a detective.'

He drew his young cousin gently from the room, locked the door on the outside and put the key in his pocket.

'Who shall I wire to?' John Neville called from his desk with pencil poised over the paper, to his cousin, who sat at the library table with his head buried in his hands. 'It will need be a sharp man—one who can give his whole time to it.'

'I don't know any one. Yes, I do. That fellow with the queer name that found the Duke of Southern's opal—Beck. That's it. Thornton Crescent, W.C., will find him.'

John Neville filled in the name and address to the telegram he had already written—

'Come at once. Case of murder. Expense no object. John Neville, Berkly Manor, Dorset.'

Little did Eric guess that the filling in of that name was to him a matter of life or death.

John Neville had picked up a time-table and rustled through the leaves. 'Hard lines, Eric,' he said, 'do his best, he cannot get here before midnight. But here's Wardle already, anyhow; that's quick work.'

A shrewd, silent man was Wardle, the local constable, who now came briskly up the broad avenue; strong and active too, though well over fifty years of age.

John Neville met him at the door with the news. But the groom had already told of the murder.

'You did the right thing to lock the door, sir,' said Wardle, as they passed into the library where Eric still sat apparently unconscious of their presence, 'and you wired for a right good man. I've worked with this here Mr Beck before now. A pleasant man and a lucky one. "No hurry, Mr Wardle," he says to me, "and no fuss. Stir nothing. The things about the corpse have always a story of their own if they are let tell it, and I always like to have the first quiet little chat with them myself".'

So the constable held his tongue and kept his hands quiet and used his eyes and ears, while the great house buzzed with gossip. There was a whisper here and a whisper there, and the whispers patched themselves into a story. By slow degrees dark suspicion settled down and closed like a cloud round John Neville.

Its influence seemed to pass in some strange fashion through the closed doors of the library. John began pacing the room restlessly from end to end.

After a little while the big room was not big enough to hold his impatience. He wandered out aimlessly, as it seemed, from one room to another; now down the iron steps to gaze vacantly at the window of his uncle's room, now past the locked door in the broad corridor.

With an elaborate pretence of carelessness Wardle kept him in sight through all his wanderings, but John Neville seemed too self-absorbed to notice it.

Presently he returned to the library. Eric was there, still sitting with his back to the door, only the top of his head showing over the high chair. He seemed absorbed in thought or sleep, he sat so still.

But he started up with a quick cry, showing a white, frightened face, when John touched him lightly on the arm.

'Come for a walk in the grounds, Eric?' he said. 'This waiting and watching and doing nothing is killing work; I cannot stand it much longer.'

'I'd rather not, if you don't mind,' Eric answered wearily, 'I feel completely knocked over.'

'A mouthful of fresh air would do you good, my poor boy; you do look done up.'

Eric shook his head.

'Well, I'm off,' John said.

'If you leave me the key, I will give it to the detective, if he comes.'

'Oh, he cannot be here before midnight, and I'll be back in an hour.'

As John Neville walked rapidly down the avenue without looking back, Wardle stepped quietly after, keeping him well in view.

Presently Neville turned abruptly in amongst the woods, the constable still following cautiously. The trees stood tall and well apart, and the slanting sunshine made lanes of vivid green through the shade. As Wardle crossed between Neville and the sun his shadow fell long and black on the bright green.

John Neville saw the shadow move in front of him and turned sharp round and faced his pursuer.

The constable stood stock still and stared.

'Well, Wardle, what is it? Don't stand there like a fool fingering your baton! Speak out, man—what do you want of me?'

'You see how it is, Master John,' the constable stammered out, 'I don't believe it myself. I've known you twenty-one years—since you were born, I may say—and I don't believe it, not a blessed word of it. But duty is duty, and I must go through with it; and facts is facts, and you and he had words last night, and Master Eric found you first in the room when...'

John Neville listened, bewildered at first. Then suddenly, as it seemed to dawn on him for the first time that he *could* be suspected of this murder, he kindled a sudden hot blaze of anger.

He turned fiercely on the constable. Broad-chested, strong limbed, he towered over him, terrible in his wrath; his hands clenched, his muscles quivered, his strong white teeth shut tight as a rat-trap, and a reddish light shining at the back of his brown eyes.

'How dare you! how dare you!' he hissed out between his teeth, his passion choking him.

He looked dangerous, that roused young giant, but Wardle met his angry eyes without flinching.

'Where's the use, Master John?' he said soothingly. 'It's main hard on you, I know. But the fault isn't mine, and you won't help yourself by taking it that way.'

The gust of passion appeared to sweep by as suddenly as it arose. The handsome face cleared and there was no trace of anger in the frank voice that answered. 'You are right, Wardle, quite right. What is to be done next? Am I to consider myself under arrest?'

'Better not, sir. You've got things to do a prisoner couldn't do handy, and I don't want to stand in the way of your doing them. If you give me your word it will be enough.'

'My word for what?'

'That you'll be here when wanted.'

'Why, man, you don't think I'd be fool enough—innocent or guilty—to run away. My God! run away from a charge of murder!'

'Don't take on like that, sir. There's a man coming from London that will set things straight, you'll see. Have I your word?'

'You have my word.'

'Perhaps you'd better be getting back to the house, sir. There's a deal of talking going on amongst the servants. I'll keep out of the way, and no one will be the wiser for anything that has passed between us.'

Half-way up the avenue a fast-driven dog-cart overtook John Neville, and pulled up so sharply that the horse's hoofs sent the coarse gravel flying. A stout, thick-set man, who up to that had been in close chat with the driver, leapt out more lightly than could have been expected from his figure.

'Mr John Neville, I presume? My name is Beck—Mr Paul Beck.'

'Mr Beck! Why, I thought you couldn't have got here before midnight.'

'Special train,' Mr Beck answered pleasantly. 'Your wire said "Expense no object". Well, time is an object, and comfort is an object too, more or less, in all these cases; so I took a special train, and here I am. With your permission, we will send the trap on and walk to the house together. This seems a bad business, Mr Neville. Shot dead, the driver tells me. Any one suspected?'

'I'm suspected.' The answer broke from John Neville's lips almost fiercely.

Mr Beck looked at him for a minute with placid curiosity, without a touch of surprise in it.

'How do you know that?'

'Wardle, the local constable, has just told me so to my face. It was only by way of a special favour he refrained from arresting me then and there.'

Mr Beck walked on beside John Neville ten or fifteen paces before he spoke again.

'Do you mind,' he said, in a very insinuating voice, 'telling me exactly why you are suspected?'

'Not in the very least.'

'Mind this,' the detective went on quickly, 'I give you no caution and make you no pledge. It's my business to find out the truth. If you think the truth will help you, then you ought to help me. This is very irregular, of course, but I don't mind that. When a man is charged with a crime there is, you see, Mr Neville, always one witness who knows whether he is guilty or not. There is very often only that one. The first thing the British law does by way of discovering the truth is to close the mouth of the only witness that knows it. Well, that's not my way. I like to give an innocent man a chance to tell his own story, and I've no scruple in trapping a guilty man if I can.'

He looked John Neville straight in the eyes as he spoke.

The look was steadily returned. 'I think I understand. What do you want to know? Where shall I begin?'

'At the beginning. What did you quarrel with your uncle about yesterday?'

John Neville hesitated for a moment, and Mr Beck took a mental note of his hesitation.

'I didn't quarrel with him. He quarrelled with me. It was this way: There was a bitter feud between my uncle and his neighbour, Colonel Peyton. The estates adjoin, and the quarrel was about some shooting. My uncle was very violent—he used to call Colonel Peyton "a common poacher". Well, I took no hand in the row. I was rather shy when I met the Colonel for the first time after it, for I knew my uncle had the wrong end of the stick. But the Colonel spoke to me in the kindest way. "No reason why you and I should cease to be friends, John," he said. "This is a foolish business. I would give the best covert on my estate to be out of it. Men cannot fight duels in these days, and gentlemen cannot scold like fishwives. But I don't expect people will call me a coward because I hate a row."

' "Not likely," I said.

'The Colonel, you must know, had distinguished himself in a dozen engagements, and has the Victoria Cross locked up in a drawer of his desk. Lucy once showed it to me. Lucy is his only daughter, and he is devoted to her. Well, after that, of course, the Colonel and I kept on good terms, for I liked him, and I like going there and all that. But our friendship angered my uncle. I had been going to the Grange pretty often of late, and my uncle heard of it. He spoke to me in a very rough fashion of Colonel Peyton and his daughter at dinner last night, and I stood up for them.

' "By what right, you insolent puppy," he shouted, "do you take this upstart's part against me?"

' "The Peytons are as good a family as our own, sir," I said—that was true—"and as for right, Miss Lucy Peyton has done me the honour of promising to be my wife."

'At that he exploded in a very tempest of rage. I cannot repeat his words about the Colonel and his daughter. Even now, though he lies dead yonder, I can hardly forgive them. He swore he would never see or speak to me again if I disgraced myself by such a marriage. "I cannot break the entail," he growled, "worse luck. But I can make you a beggar while I live, and I shall live forty years to spite you. The poacher can have you a bargain for all I care. Go, sell yourself as dearly as you can, and live on your wife's fortune as soon as you please."

'Then I lost my temper, and gave him a bit of my mind.'

'Try and remember what you said; it's important.'

'I told him that I cast his contempt back in his face; that I loved Lucy Peyton, and that I would live for her, and die for her, if need be.'

'Did you say "it was a comfort he could not live for ever"? You see the story of your quarrel has travelled far and near. The driver told me of it. Try and remember—did you say that?'

'I think I did. I'm sure I did now, but I was so furious I hardly knew what I said. I certainly never meant...'

'Who was in the room when you quarrelled?'

'Only Cousin Eric and the butler.'

'The butler, I suppose, spread the story?'

'I suppose so. I'm sure Cousin Eric never did. He was as much pained at the scene as myself. He tried to interfere at the time, but his interference only made my uncle more furious.'

'What was your allowance from your uncle?'

'A thousand a year.'

'He had power to cut it off, I suppose?'

'Certainly.'

'But he had no power over the estate. You were heir-apparent under the entail, and at the present moment you are owner of Berkly Manor?'

'That is so; but up to the moment you spoke I assure you I never even remembered…'

'Who comes next to you in the entail?'

'My first cousin, Eric. He is four years younger than I am.'

'After him?'

'A distant cousin. I scarcely know him at all; but he has a bad reputation, and I know my uncle and he hated each other cordially.'

'How did your uncle and your cousin hit it off?'

'Not too well. He hated Eric's father—his own youngest brother—and he was sometimes rough on Eric. He used to abuse the dead father in the son's presence, calling him cruel and treacherous, and all that. Poor Eric had often had a hard time of it. Uncle was liberal to him so far as money went—as liberal as he was to me— had him to live at the Manor and denied him nothing. But now and again he would sting the poor lad by a passionate curse or a bitter sneer. In spite of all, Eric seemed fond of him.'

'To come now to the murder; you saw your uncle no more that night, I suppose?'

'I never saw him alive again.'

'Do you know what he did next day?'

'Only by hearsay.'

'Hearsay evidence is often first-class evidence, though the law doesn't think so. What did you hear?'

'My uncle was mad about shooting. Did I tell you his quarrel with Colonel Peyton was about the shooting? He had a grouse moor rented about twelve miles from here, and he never missed the first day. He was off at cock-shout with the head gamekeeper, Lennox. I was to have gone with him, but I didn't of course. Contrary to his custom he came back about noon and went straight to his study. I was writing in my own room and heard his heavy step go past the door. Later on Eric found him asleep on the great leather couch in his study. Five minutes after Eric left I heard the shot and rushed into his room.'

'Did you examine the room after you found the body?'

'No. Eric wanted to, but I thought it better not. I simply locked the door and put the key in my pocket till you came.'

'Could it have been suicide?'

'Impossible, I should say. He was shot through the back of the head.'

'Had your uncle any enemies that you know of?'

'The poachers hated him. He was relentless with them. A fellow once shot at him, and my uncle shot back and shattered the man's leg. He had him sent to hospital first and cured, and then prosecuted him straight away, and got him two years.'

'Then you think a poacher murdered him?' Mr Beck said blandly.

'I don't well see how he could. I was in my own room on the same corridor. The only way to or from my uncle's room was past my door. I rushed out the instant I heard the shot, and saw no one.'

'Perhaps the murderer leapt through the window?'

'Eric tells me that he and the gardener were in the garden almost under the window at the time.'

'What's your theory, then, Mr Neville?'

'I haven't got a theory.'

'You parted with your uncle in anger last night?'

'That's so.'

'Next day your uncle is shot, and you are found—I won't say caught—in his room the instant afterwards.'

John Neville flushed crimson; but he held himself in and nodded without speaking.

The two walked on together in silence.

They were not a hundred yards from the great mansion—John Neville's house—standing high above the embowering trees in the glow of the twilight, when the detective spoke again.

'I'm bound to say, Mr Neville, that things look very black against you, as they stand. I think that constable Wardle ought to have arrested you.'

'It's not too late yet,' John Neville answered shortly, 'I see him there at the corner of the house and I'll tell him you said so.'

He turned on his heel, when Mr Beck called quickly after him: 'What about that key?'

John Neville handed it to him without a word. The detective took it as silently and walked on to the entrance and up the great stone steps alone, whistling softly.

Eric welcomed him at the door, for the driver had told of his coming.

'You have had no dinner, Mr Beck?' he asked courteously.

'Business first; pleasure afterwards. I had a snack in the train. Can I see the gamekeeper, Lennox, for five minutes alone?'

'Certainly, I'll send him to you in a moment here in the library.'

Lennox, the gamekeeper, a long-limbed, high-shouldered, elderly man, shambled shyly into the room, consumed by nervousness in the presence of a London detective.

'Sit down, Lennox, sit down,' said Mr Beck kindly. The very sound of his voice, homely and good-natured, put the man at ease. 'Now, tell me, why did you come home so soon from the grouse this morning?'

'Well, you see, sir, it was this ways. We were two hours hout when the Squire, 'e says to me, "Lennox," 'e says, "I'm sick of this fooling. I'm going 'ome."'

'No sport?'

'Birds wor as thick as blackberries, sir, and lay like larks.'

'No sportsman, then?'

'Is it the Squire, sir?' cried Lennox, quite forgetting his shyness in his excitement at this slur on the Squire. 'There wasn't a better sportsman in the county—no, nor as good. Real, old-fashioned style, 'e was. "Hang your barnyard shooting," 'e'd say when they'd ask him to go kill tame pheasants. 'E put up 'is own birds with 'is own dogs, 'e did. 'E'd as soon go shooting without a gun very near as without a dog any day. Aye and 'e stuck to 'is old "Manton" muzzle-loader to the last. "'Old it steady, Lennox," 'ed say to me oftentimes, "and point it straight. It will hit harder and further than any of their telescopes, and it won't get marked with rust if you don't clean it every second shot."

' "Easy to load, Squire," the young men would say, cracking up their hammerless breech-loaders.

' "Aye," he'd answer them back, "and spoil your dog's work. What's the good of a dog learning to 'down shot,' if you can drop in your cartridges as quick as a cock can pick corn."

'A dead shot the Squire was, too, and no mistake, sir, if he wasn't flurried. Many a time I've seen him wipe the eyes of gents who thought no end of themselves with that same old muzzle-loader that shot hisself in the long run. Many a time I seen...'

'Why did he turn his back on good sport yesterday?' asked Mr Beck, cutting short his reminiscences.

'Well, you see, it was scorching hot for one thing, but that wasn't it, for the infernal fire would not stop the Squire if he was on for sport. But he was in a blazing temper all the morning, and temper tells more than most anything on a man's shooting. When Flora sprung a pack—she's a young dog, and the fault wasn't hers either—for she came down the wind on them—but the Squire had the gun to his shoulder to shoot her. Five minutes after she found another pack and set like a stone. They got up as big as haycocks and as lazy as crows, and he missed right and left—never touched a feather—a thing I haven't seen him do since I was a boy.

' "It's myself I should shoot, not the dog," he growled and he flung me the gun to load. When I'd got the caps on and had shaken the powder into the nipples, he ripped out an oath that 'e'd have no more of it. 'E walked right across country to where the trap was. The birds got up under his feet, but divil a shot he'd fire, but drove straight 'ome.

'When we got to the 'ouse I wanted to take the gun and fire it off, or draw the charges. But 'e told me to go to…, and carried it up loaded as it was to his study, where no one goes unless they're sent for special. It was better than an hour afterwards I heard the report of the "Manton"; I'd know it in a thousand. I ran for the study as fast as…'

Eric Neville broke suddenly into the room, flushed and excited.

'Mr Beck,' he cried, 'a monstrous thing has happened. Wardle, the local constable, you know, has arrested my cousin on a charge of wilful murder of my uncle.'

Mr Beck, with his eyes intent on the excited face, waved a big hand soothingly.

'Easy,' he said, 'take it easy, Mr Neville. It's hurtful to your feelings, no doubt; but it cannot be helped. The constable has done no more than his duty. The evidence is very strong, as you know, and in such cases it's best for all parties to proceed regularly.'

'You can go,' he went on, speaking to Lennox, who stood dumbfounded at the news of John Neville's arrest, staring with eyes and mouth wide open.

Then turning again very quietly to Eric: 'Now, Mr Neville, I would like to see the room where the corpse is.'

The perfect flaccidity of his manner had its effect upon the boy, for he was little more than a boy, calming his excitement as oil smooths troubled water.

'My cousin has the key,' he said, 'I will get it.'

'There is no need,' Mr Beck called after him, for he was half-way out of the room on his errand: 'I've got the key if you will be good enough to show me the room.'

Mastering his surprise, Eric showed him upstairs, and along the corridor to the locked door. Half unconsciously, as it seemed, he was following the detective into the room, when Mr Beck stopped him.

'I know you will kindly humour me, Mr Neville,' he said, 'but I find that I can look closer and think clearer when I'm by myself. I'm not exactly shy you know, but it's a habit I've got.'

He closed the door softly as he spoke, and locked it on the inside, leaving the key in the lock.

The mask of placidity fell from him the moment he found himself alone. His lips tightened, and his eyes sparkled, and his muscles seemed to grow rigid with excitement, like a sporting dog's when he is close upon the game.

One glance at the corpse showed him that it was not suicide. In this, at least, John Neville had spoken the truth.

The back of the head had literally been blown in by the charge of heavy shot at close quarters. The grey hair was clammy and matted, with little white angles of bone protruding. The dropping of the blood had made a black pool on the carpet, and the close air of the room was foetid with the smell of it.

The detective walked to the table where the gun, a handsome, old-fashioned muzzle loader, lay, the muzzle still pointed at the corpse. But his attention was diverted by a water-bottle, a great globe of clear glass quite full, and perched on a book a little distance from the gun, and between it and the window. He took it from the table and tested the water with the tip of his tongue. It had a curious insipid, parboiled taste, but he detected no foreign flavour in it. Though the room was full of dust there was almost none on the cover of the book where the water-bottle stood, and Mr Beck noticed a gap in the third row of the bookcase where the book had been taken.

After a quick glance round the room Mr Beck walked to the window. On a small table there he found a clear circle in the thick dust. He fitted the round bottom of the water-bottle to this circle and it covered it exactly. While he stood by the window he caught sight of some small scraps of paper crumbled up and thrown into a corner. Picking them up and smoothing them out he found they were curiously drilled with little burnt holes. Having examined the holes minutely with his magnifying glass, he slipped these scraps folded on each other into his waistcoat pocket.

From the window he went back to the gun. This time he examined it with the minutest care. The right barrel he found had been recently discharged, the left was still loaded. Then he made a startling discovery. *Both barrels were on half cock.* The little bright copper cap twinkled on the nipple of the left barrel, from the right nipple the cap was gone.

How had the murderer fired the right barrel without a cap? How and why did he find time in the midst of his deadly work to put the cock back to safety?

Had Mr Beck solved this problem? The grim smile deepened on his lips as he looked, and there was an ugly light in his eyes that boded ill for the unknown assassin. Finally he carried the gun to the window and examined it carefully through a magnifying glass. There was a thin dark line, as if traced with the point of a red-hot needle, running a little way along the wood of the stock and ending in the right nipple.

Mr Beck put the gun back quietly on the table. The whole investigation had not taken ten minutes. He gave one look at the still figure on the couch, unlocked the door, locking it after him, and walked out through the corridor, the same cheerful imperturbable Mr Beck that had walked into it ten minutes before.

He found Eric waiting for him at the head of the stairs. 'Well?' he said when he saw the detective.

'Well,' replied Mr Beck, ignoring the interrogation in his voice, 'when is the inquest to be? That's the next thing to be thought of; the sooner the better.'

'To-morrow, if you wish. My cousin John sent a messenger to Mr Morgan, the coroner. He lives only five miles off, and he has promised to be here at twelve o'clock to-morrow. There will be no difficulty in getting a jury in the village.'

'That's right, that's all right,' said Mr Beck, rubbing his hands, 'the sooner and the quieter we get those preliminaries over the better.'

'I have just sent to engage the local solicitor on behalf of my cousin. He's not particularly bright, I'm afraid, but he's the best to be had on a short notice.'

'Very proper and thoughtful on your part—very thoughtful indeed. But solicitors cannot do much in such cases. It's the evidence we have to go by, and the evidence is only too plain, I'm afraid. Now, if you please,' he went on more briskly, dismissing the disagreeable subject, as it were, with a wave of his hand, 'I'd be very glad of that supper you spoke about.'

Mr Beck supped very heartily on a brace of grouse—the last of the dead man's shooting—and a bottle of ripe Burgundy. He was in high good-humour, and across 'the walnuts and the wine' he told Eric some startling episodes in his career, which seemed to divert the young fellow a little from his manifest grief for his uncle and anxiety for his cousin.

Meanwhile John Neville remained shut close in his own room, with the constable at the door.

The inquest was held at half-past twelve next day in the library.

The Coroner, a large, red-faced man, with a very affable manner, had got to his work promptly.

The jury 'viewed the body' steadily, stolidly, with a kind of morose delectation in the grim spectacle.

In some unaccountable way Mr Beck constituted himself a master of the ceremonies, a kind of assessor to the court.

'You had best take the gun down,' he said to the Coroner as they were leaving the room.

'Certainly, certainly,' replied the Coroner.

'And the water-bottle,' added Mr Beck.

'There is no suspicion of poison, is there?'

'It's best not to take anything for granted,' replied Mr Beck sententiously.

'By all means if you think so,' replied the obsequious Coroner. 'Constable, take the water-bottle down with you.'

The large room was filled with the people of the neighbourhood, mostly farmers from the Berkly estate and small shopkeepers from the neighbouring village.

A table had been wheeled to the top of the room for the Coroner, with a seat at it for the ubiquitous local newspaper correspondent. A double row of chairs were set at the right hand of the table for the jury.

The jury had just returned from viewing the body when the crunch of wheels and hoofs was heard on the gravel of the drive, and a two-horse phaeton pulled up sharp at the entrance.

A moment later there came into the room a handsome, soldier-like man, with a girl clinging to his arm, whom he supported with tender, protecting fondness that was very touching. The girl's face was pale, but wonderfully sweet and winsome; cheeks with the faint, pure flush of the wild rose, and eyes like a wild fawn's.

No need to tell Mr Beck that here were Colonel Peyton and his daughter. He saw the look—shy, piteous, loving—that the girl gave John Neville as she passed close to the table where he sat with his head buried in his hands; and the detective's face darkened for a moment with a stern purpose, but the next moment it resumed its customary look of good-nature and good-humour.

The gardener, the gamekeeper, and the butler were briefly examined by the Coroner, and rather clumsily cross-examined by Mr Waggles, the solicitor whom Eric had thoughtfully secured for his cousin's defence.

As the case against John Neville gradually darkened into grim certainty, the girl in the far corner of the room grew white as a lily, and would have fallen but for her father's support.

'Does Mr John Neville offer himself for examination?' said the Coroner, as he finished writing the last word of the butler's deposition describing the quarrel of the night before.

'No, sir,' said Mr Waggles. 'I appear for Mr John Neville, the accused, and we reserve our defence.'

'I really have nothing to say that hasn't been already said,' added John Neville quietly.

'Mr Neville,' said Mr Waggles pompously, 'I must ask you to leave yourself entirely in my hands.'

'Eric Neville!' called out the Coroner. 'This is the last witness, I think.'

Eric stepped in front of the table and took the Bible in his hand. He was pale, but quiet and composed, and there was an unaffected grief in the look of his dark eyes and in the tone of his soft voice that touched every heart—except one.

He told his story shortly and clearly. It was quite plain that he was most anxious to shield his cousin. But in spite of this, perhaps because of this, the evidence went horribly against John Neville.

The answers to questions criminating his cousin had to be literally dragged from him by the Coroner.

With manifest reluctance he described the quarrel at dinner the night before.

'Was your cousin very angry?' the Coroner asked.

'He would not be human if he were not angry at the language used.'

'What did he say?'

'I cannot remember all he said.'

'Did he say to your uncle: "Well, you will not live for ever"?'

No answer.

'Come, Mr Neville, remember you are sworn to tell the truth.'

In an almost inaudible whisper came the words: 'He did.'

'I'm sorry to pain you, but I must do my duty. When you heard the shot you ran straight to your uncle's room, about fifty yards, I believe?'

'About that.'

'Whom did you find there bending over the dead man?'

'My cousin. I am bound to say he appeared in the deepest grief.'

'But you saw no one else?'

'No.'

'Your cousin is, I believe, the heir to Squire Neville's property; the owner I should say now?'

'I believe so.'

'That will do; you can stand down.'

This interchange of question and answer, each one of which seemed to fit the rope tighter and tighter round John Neville's neck, was listened to with hushed eagerness by the room full of people.

There was a long, deep drawing-in of breath when it ended. The suspense seemed over, but not the excitement.

Mr Beck rose as Eric turned from the table, quite as a matter of course, to question him.

'You say you *believe* your cousin was your uncle's heir—don't you *know* it?'

Then Mr Waggles found his voice.

'Really, sir,' he broke out, addressing the Coroner, 'I must protest. This is grossly irregular. This person is not a professional gentleman. He represents no one. He has no *locus standi* in court at all.'

No one knew better than Mr Beck that technically he had no title to open his lips; but his look of quiet assurance, his calm assumption of unmistakable right, carried the day with the Coroner.

'Mr Beck,' he said, 'has, I understand, been brought down specially from London to take charge of this case, and I shall certainly not stop him in any question he may desire to ask.'

'Thank you, sir,' said Mr Beck, in the tone of a man whose clear right has been allowed. Then again to the witness: 'Didn't you know John Neville was next heir to Berkly Manor?'

'I know it, of course.'

'And if John Neville is hanged you will be the owner?'

Every one was startled at the frank brutality of the question so blandly asked. Mr Waggles bobbed up and down excitedly; but Eric answered, calmly as ever:

'That's very coarsely and cruelly put.'

'But it's true?'

'Yes, it's true.'

'We will pass from that. When you came into the room after the murder, did you examine the gun?'

'I stretched out my hand to take it, but my cousin stopped me. I must be allowed to add that I believe he was actuated, as he said, by a desire to keep everything in the room untouched. He locked the door and carried off the key. I was not in the room afterwards.'

'Did you look closely at the gun?'

'Not particularly.'

'Did you notice that both barrels were at half cock?'

'No.'

'Did you notice that there was no cap on the nipple of the right barrel that had just been fired?'

'Certainly not.'

'That is to say you did not notice it?'

'Yes.'

'Did you notice a little burnt line traced a short distance on the wood of the stock towards the right nipple?'

'No.'

Mr Beck put the gun into his hand.

'Look close. Do you notice it now?'

'I can see it now for the first time.'

'You cannot account for it, I suppose?'

'No.'

'Sure?'

'Quite sure.'

All present followed this strange, and apparently purposeless cross-examination with breathless interest, groping vainly for its meaning.

The answers were given calmly and clearly, but those that looked closely saw that Eric's nether lip quivered, and it was only by a strong effort of will that he held his calmness.

Through the blandness of Mr Beck's voice and manner a subtle suggestion of hostility made itself felt, very trying to the nerves of the witness.

'We will pass from that,' said Mr Beck again. 'When you went into your uncle's room before the shot why did you take a book from the shelf and put it on the table?'

'I really cannot remember anything about it.'

'Why did you take the water-bottle from the window and stand it on the book?'

'I wanted a drink.'

'But there was none of the water drunk.'

'Then I suppose it was to take it out of the strong sun.'

'But you set it in the strong sun on the table?'

'Really I cannot remember those trivialities.' His self-control was breaking down at last.

'Then we will pass from that,' said Mr Beck a third time.

He took the little scraps of paper with the burnt holes through them from his waistcoat pocket, and handed them to the witness.

'Do you know anything about these?'

There was a pause of a second. Eric's lips tightened as if with a sudden spasm of pain. But the answer came clearly enough:

'Nothing whatever.'

'Do you ever amuse yourself with a burning glass?'

This seemingly simple question was snapped suddenly at the witness like a pistol-shot.

'Really, really,' Mr Waggles broke out, 'this is mere trifling with the Court.'

'That question does certainly seem a little irrelevant, Mr Beck,' mildly remonstrated the Coroner.

'Look at the witness, sir,' retorted Mr Beck sternly. 'He does not think it irrelevant.'

Every eye in court was turned on Eric's face and fixed there.

All colour had fled from his cheeks and lips; his mouth had fallen open, and he stared at Mr Beck with eyes of abject terror.

Mr Beck went on remorselessly: 'Did you ever amuse yourself with a burning glass?'

No answer.

'Do you know that a water-bottle like this makes a capital burning glass?'

Still no answer.

'Do you know that a burning glass has been used before now to touch off a cannon or fire a gun?'

Then a voice broke from Eric at last, as it seemed in defiance of his will; a voice unlike his own—loud, harsh, hardly articulate; such a voice might have been heard in the torture chamber in the old days when the strain on the rack grew unbearable.

'You devilish bloodhound!' he shouted. 'Curse you, curse you, you've caught me! I confess it—I was the murderer!' He fell on the ground in a fit.

'And you made the sun your accomplice!' remarked Mr Beck, placid as ever.

THE FAD OF THE FISHERMAN

G.K. CHESTERTON

Gilbert Keith Chesterton (1874–1936) was, among other accomplishments, a theologian, critic, and journalist, but today he is most widely remembered as a writer of detective stories. He was also the first President of the Detection Club. Above all, his name is associated with Father Brown, the modest priest and amateur sleuth who has in recent years been played on television by Mark Williams in stories adapted very freely indeed from the originals.

The popularity of Father Brown has meant that Chesterton's other work in the detective genre has been under-estimated, and his other detectives (such as Horne Fisher) overshadowed. This story – which opens with a characteristic Chestertonian paradox – is not only entertaining but also a good illustration of the author's interest in politics and hostility towards corrupt capitalists.

*   *   *   *   *

A THING can sometimes be too extraordinary to be remembered. If it is clean out of the course of things, and has apparently no causes and no consequences, subsequent events do not recall it; and it remains only a subconscious thing, to be stirred by some accident long after. It drifts apart like a forgotten dream; and it was in the hour of many dreams, at daybreak and very soon after the end of dark, that such a strange sight was given to a man sculling a boat down a river in the West Country. The man was awake; indeed, he considered himself rather wide awake, being a rising political journalist named Harold March, on his way to interview various political celebrities in their country seats. But the thing he saw was so inconsequent that it might have been imaginary. It simply slipped past his mind and was lost in later and utterly different events; nor did he even recover the memory, till he had long afterwards discovered the meaning.

Pale mists of morning lay on the fields and the rushes along one margin of the river; along the other side ran a wall of dark red brick almost overhanging the water. He had shipped his oars and was drifting for a moment with the stream, when he turned his head and saw that the monotony of the long brick wall was broken by a bridge; rather an elegant, eighteenth century sort of bridge, with little columns of white stone turning grey. There had been floods and the river still stood very high, with dwarfish trees waist deep in it, and rather a narrow arc of white dawn gleamed under the curve of the bridge.

As his own boat went under the dark archway he saw another boat coming towards him, rowed by a man as solitary as himself. His posture prevented much being seen of him; but as he neared the bridge he stood up in the boat and turned round. He was already so close to the dark entry, however, that his whole figure was black against the morning light; and March could see nothing of his face except the ends of two long whiskers or moustaches that gave something sinister to the silhouette, like the horns in the wrong place. Even these details March would never have noticed but for what happened in the same instant. As the man came under the low bridge he made a leap at it and hung, with his legs dangling, letting the boat float away from under him. March had a momentary vision of two black kicking legs; then of one black kicking leg, and then of nothing except the eddying stream and the long perspective of the wall. But whenever he thought of it again, long afterwards when he understood the story in which it figured, it was always fixed in that one fantastic shape; as if those wild legs were a grotesque graven ornament of the bridge itself, in the manner of a gargoyle. At the moment he merely passed staring down the stream. He could see no flying figure on the bridge, so it must have already fled; but he was half conscious of some faint significance in the fact that among the trees round the bridge-head opposite the wall he saw a lamp-post, and, beside the lamp-post, the broad blue back of an unconscious policeman.

Even before reaching the shrine of his political pilgrimage he had many other things to think of besides the odd incident of the bridge; for the management of a boat by a solitary man was not always easy even on such a solitary stream. And, indeed, it was only by an unforeseen accident that he was solitary. The boat had been purchased and the whole expedition planned in conjunction with a friend, who had at the last moment been forced to alter all his arrangements. Harold March was to have travelled with his friend Horne Fisher on that inland voyage to Willowood Place, where the Prime Minister was a guest at the moment. More and more people were hearing of Harold March; for his striking political articles were opening to him the doors of larger and larger salons; but he had never met the Prime Minister yet. Scarcely anybody among the general public had ever heard of Horne Fisher; but he had known the Prime Minister all his life. For these reasons, had the two taken the projected journey together, March might have been slightly disposed to hasten it and Fisher vaguely content to lengthen it out. For Fisher was one of those people who are born knowing the Prime Minister. The knowledge seemed to have no very exhilarant effect; and in his case bore some resemblance to being born tired. Horne Fisher was a tall, fair man, with a bald brow and a listless manner; and it was seldom that he expressed irritation in any warmer form than that of weariness. But he was distinctly annoyed to receive, just as he was doing a little light packing of fishing tackle and cigars for the journey, a telegram from Willowood asking him to come down at once by train, as the Prime Minister had to leave that night. Fisher knew that his friend the journalist could not possibly start till the next day; and he liked his friend the journalist, and had looked forward to a few days on the river. He did not particularly like or dislike the Prime Minister; but he intensely disliked the alternative of a few hours in the train. Nevertheless, he accepted Prime Ministers as he accepted railway trains; as part of a system which he at least was not the revolutionist sent on earth to destroy. So he telephoned to March asking him, with many apologetic curses and faint damns, to take the boat down the river as arranged, that they might meet at Willowood by the time appointed. Then he went outside and hailed a taxicab to take him to the railway station. There he paused at the bookstall to add to his light luggage a number of cheap murder stories, which he read with great pleasure, and without any premonition that he was about to walk into as strange a story in real life.

A little before sunset he arrived with his light suitcase in his hand before the gate of the long riverside gardens of Willowood

Place, one of the smaller seats of Sir Isaac Hook, the master of much shipping and many newspapers. He entered by the gate giving on the road, at the opposite side to the river; but there was a mixed quality in all that watery landscape which perpetually reminded a traveller that the river was near. White gleams of water would shine suddenly like swords or spears in the green thickets; and even in the garden itself, divided into courts and curtained with hedges and high garden trees, there hung everywhere in the air the music of water. The first of the green courts which he entered appeared to be a somewhat neglected croquet lawn, in which was a solitary young man playing croquet against himself. Yet he was not an enthusiast for the game, thus snatching a moment's practice; and his sallow but well-featured face looked rather sullen than otherwise. He was only one of those young men who cannot support the burden of consciousness unless they are doing something, and whose conceptions of doing something are limited to a game of some kind. He was dark and well dressed in a light holiday fashion, and Fisher recognized him at once as a young man named James Bullen, called for some unknown reason Bunker. He was the nephew of Sir Isaac. But, what was much more important at the moment, he was also the private secretary of the Prime Minister.

"Hallo, Bunker," observed Horne Fisher. "You're the sort of man I wanted to see. Has your chief come down yet?"

"He's only staying for dinner," replied Bullen, with his eye on the yellow ball. "He's got a great speech to-morrow at Birmingham, and he's going straight through to-night. He's motoring himself there; driving the car, I mean. It's the one thing he's really proud of."

"You mean you're staying here with your uncle, like a good boy?" replied Fisher. "But what will he do at Birmingham without the epigrams whispered to him by his brilliant secretary?"

"Don't you start ragging me," said the young man called Bunker. "I'm only too glad not to go trailing after him. He doesn't know a thing about maps or money or hotels or anything, and I have to dance about like a courier. As for my uncle, as I'm supposed to come into the estate it's only decent to be here sometimes."

"Very proper," replied the other. "Well, I shall see you later on"; and crossing the lawn he passed out through a gap in the hedge.

He was walking across the lawn towards the landing-stage on the river, and still felt all around him, under the dome of golden evening, an old-world savour and reverberation in that river-haunted garden. The next square of turf which he crossed seemed at first sight quite deserted, till he saw in the twilight of trees in one corner of it a hammock, and in the hammock a man, reading a newspaper and swinging one leg over the edge of the net. Him also he hailed by name, and the man slipped to the ground and strolled forward. It seemed fated that he should feel something of the past in the accidents of that place; for the figure might well have been an Early Victorian ghost revisiting the ghosts of the croquet hoop and mallets. It was the figure of an elderly man with long whiskers that looked almost fantastic; and a quaint and careful cut of collar and cravat. Having been a fashionable dandy forty years ago he had managed to preserve the dandyism while ignoring the fashions. A white top hat lay beside the *Morning Post* in the hammock behind him. This was the Duke of Westmoreland, the relic of a family really some centuries old—and the antiquity was not heraldry but history. Nobody knew better than Fisher how rare such noblemen are in fact, and how numerous in fiction. But whether the duke owed the general respect he enjoyed to the genuineness of his pedigree or to the fact that he owned a vast amount of very valuable property, was a point about which Mr. Fisher's opinion might have been more interesting to discover.

"You were looking so comfortable," said Fisher, "that I thought you must be one of the servants. I'm looking for somebody to take this bag of mine. I haven't brought a man down, as I came away in a hurry."

"Nor have I, for that matter," replied the duke with some pride. "I never do. If there's one animal alive I loathe it's a valet. I learnt to dress myself at an early age, and was supposed to do it decently. I may be in my second childhood, but I've not got so far as being dressed like a child."

"The Prime Minister hasn't brought a valet, he's brought a secretary instead," observed Fisher. "Devilish inferior job. Didn't I hear that Harker was staying down here?"

"He's over there on the landing-stage," replied the duke indifferently, and resumed the study of the *Morning Post.*

Fisher made his way beyond the last green wall of the garden on to a sort of towing-path looking on the river and a wooded island opposite. There indeed he saw a lean dark figure with a stoop almost like that of a vulture; a posture well known in the law courts as that of Sir John Harker, the Attorney-General. His face was lined with headwork, for alone among the three idlers in the garden he was a man who had made his own way; and round his bald brow and hollow temples clung dull red hair quite flat like plates of copper.

"I haven't seen my host yet," said Horne Fisher in a slightly more serious tone than he had used to the others. "But I suppose I shall meet him at dinner."

"You can see him now, but you can't meet him," answered Harker.

He nodded his head towards one end of the island opposite, and looking steadily in the same direction the other guest could see the dome of a bald head and the top of a fishing-rod, both equally motionless, rising out of the tall undergrowth against the background of the stream beyond. The fisherman seemed to be seated against the stump of a tree and facing towards the other bank, so that his face could not be seen, but the shape of his head was unmistakable.

"He doesn't like to be disturbed when he's fishing," continued Harker. "It's a sort of fad of his to eat nothing but fish; and he's very proud of catching his own. Of course he's all for simplicity, like so many of these millionaires. He likes to come in saying he's worked for his daily food like a labourer."

"Does he explain how he blows all the glass and stuffs all the upholstery?" asked Fisher, "and makes all the silver forks, and grows all the grapes and peaches, and designs all the patterns on the carpets? I've always heard he was a busy man."

"I don't think he mentioned it," answered the lawyer. "What is the meaning of this social satire?"

"Well, I am a trifle tired," said Fisher, "of the Simple Life and the Strenuous Life as lived by our little set. We're all really dependent in nearly everything, and we all make a fuss about being independent in something. The Prime Minister prides himself on doing without a chauffeur, but he can't do without a factotum and jack-of-all-trades; and poor old Bunker has to play the part of a universal genius, which God knows he was never meant for. The duke prides himself on doing without a valet; but for all that, he must give a lot of people an infernal lot of trouble to collect such extraordinary old clothes as he wears. He must have them looked up in the British Museum or excavated out of the tombs. That white hat alone must require a sort of expedition fitted out to find it, like the North Pole. And here we have old Hook pretending to produce his own fish when he couldn't produce his own fish-knives or fish-forks to eat it with. He may be simple about simple things like food, but you bet he's luxurious about luxurious things, especially little things. I don't include you; you've worked too hard to enjoy playing at work."

"I sometimes think," said Harker, "that you conceal a horrid secret of being useful sometimes. Haven't you come down here to see Number One before he goes on to Birmingham?"

Horne Fisher answered in a lower voice: "Yes; and I hope to be lucky enough to catch him before dinner. He's got to see Sir Isaac about something just afterwards."

"Hallo," exclaimed Harker, "Sir Isaac's finished his fishing. I know he prides himself on getting up at sunrise and going in at sunset."

The old man on the island had indeed risen to his feet, facing round and showing a bush of grey beard with rather small sunken features but fierce eyebrows and keen choleric eyes.

Carefully carrying his fishing tackle he was already making his way back to the mainland across a bridge of flat stepping-stones a little way down the shallow stream; then he veered round, coming towards his guests and civilly saluting them. There were several fish in his basket, and he was in a good temper.

"Yes," he said, acknowledging Fisher's polite expression of surprise, "I get up before anybody else in the house, I think. The early bird catches the worm."

"Unfortunately," said Harker, "it is the early fish that catches the worm."

"But the early man catches the fish," replied the old man gruffly.

"But from what I hear, Sir Isaac, you are the late man, too," interposed Fisher. "You must do with very little sleep."

"I never had much time for sleeping," answered Hook, "and I shall have to be the late man to-night anyhow. The Prime Minister wants to have a talk, he tells me. And all things considered I think we'd better be dressing for dinner."

Dinner passed off that evening without a word of politics and little enough but ceremonial trifles. The Prime Minister, Lord Merivale, who was a long slim man with curly grey hair, was gravely complimentary to his host about his success as a fisherman, and the skill and patience he displayed; the conversation flowed like the shallow stream through the stepping-stones.

"It wants patience to wait for fish, no doubt," said Sir Isaac, "and skill to play them, but I'm generally pretty lucky with them."

"Does a big fish ever break the line and get away?" inquired the politician with respectful interest.

"Not the sort of line I use," answered Hook with satisfaction. "I rather specialize in tackle, as a matter of fact. If he were strong enough to do that, he'd be strong enough to pull me into the river."

"A great loss to the community," said the Prime Minister bowing.

Fisher had listened to all these futilities with inward impatience, waiting for his own opportunity, and when their host rose he sprang to his feet with an alertness he rarely showed. He managed to catch Lord Merivale before Sir Isaac bore him off for the final interview. He had only a few words to say, but he wanted to get them said.

He said in a low voice as he opened the door for the Premier: "I have seen Montmirail; he says that unless we protest immediately on behalf of Denmark, Sweden will certainly seize the ports."

Lord Merivale nodded.

"I'm just going to hear what Hook has to say about it," he said.

"I imagine," said Fisher with a faint smile, "that there is very little doubt what he will say about it."

Merivale did not answer but lounged gracefully towards the library, whither his host had already preceded him. The rest drifted towards the billiard-room; Fisher merely remarking to the lawyer: "They won't be long. We know they're practically in agreement."

"Hook entirely supports the Prime Minister," assented Harker.

"Or the Prime Minister entirely supports Hook," said Horne Fisher; and began idly to knock the balls about on the billiard-table.

Horne Fisher came down next morning in a late and leisurely fashion, as was his reprehensible habit; he had evidently no appetite for catching worms. But the other guests seemed to have felt a similar indifference, and they helped themselves to breakfast from the sideboard at intervals during the hours verging upon lunch. So that it was not many hours later when the first sensation of that strange day came upon them. It came in the form of a young man with light hair and a candid expression who came sculling down the river and disembarked at the landing-stage. It was in fact no other than Mr. Harold March, the journalistic friend of Mr. Fisher, whose journey had begun far away up the river in the earliest hours of that day. He arrived late in the afternoon, having stopped for tea in a large riverside town, and he had a pink evening paper sticking out of his pocket. He fell on the riverside garden like a quiet and well-behaved thunderbolt; but he was a thunderbolt without knowing it.

The first exchange of salutations and introductions was commonplace enough, and consisted indeed of the inevitable repetition of excuses for the eccentric seclusion of the host. He had gone fishing again, of course, and must not be disturbed till the appointed hour, though he sat within a stone's throw of where they stood.

"You see it's his only hobby," observed Harker apologetically, "and after all it's his own house; and he's very hospitable in other ways."

"I'm rather afraid," said Fisher in a lower voice, "that it's becoming more of a mania than a hobby. I know how it is when a man of that age begins to collect things, if it's only collecting those rotten little river fish. You remember Talbot's uncle with his toothpicks, and poor old Buzzy and the waste of cigar ashes. Hook has done a lot of big things in his time—the great deal in the Swedish timber trade and the Peace Conference at Chicago—but I doubt whether he cares now for any of those big things as he cares for those little fish."

"Oh, come, come," protested the Attorney-General. "You'll make Mr. March think he has come to call on a lunatic. Believe me, Hook only does it for fun like any other sport; only he's of the kind that takes his fun sadly. But I bet if there were big news about fish all or shipping he would drop his fun and his timber right."

"Well, I wonder," said Horne Fisher, looking sleepily at the island in the river.

"By the way, is there any news of anything?" asked Harker of Harold March. "I see you've got an evening paper; one of those enterprising evening papers that come out in the morning."

"The beginning of Lord Merivale's Birmingham speech," replied March, handing him the paper. "It's only a paragraph, but it seems to me rather good."

Harker took the paper, flapped and refolded it, and looked at the stop-press news. It was, as March had said, only a paragraph. But it was a paragraph that had a peculiar effect on Sir John Harker. His lowering brows lifted with a flicker and his eyes blinked, and for a moment his leathery jaw was loosened. He looked in some odd fashion like a very old man. Then, hardening his voice and handing the paper to Fisher without a tremor, he simply said:

"Well, here's a chance for the bet. You've got your big news to disturb the old man's fishing."

Horne Fisher was looking at the paper, and over his more languid and less expressive features a change also seemed to pass. Even that little paragraph had two or three large headlines, and his eye encountered "Sensational Warning to Sweden," and "We Shall Protest."

"What the devil," he said, and his words softened first to a whisper and then a whistle.

"We must tell old Hook at once or he'll never forgive us," said Harker. "He'll probably want to see Number One instantly, though it may be too late now. I'm going across to him at once; I bet I'll make him forget his fish, anyhow." And turning his back he made his way hurriedly along the riverside to the causeway of flat stones.

March was staring at Fisher in amazement at the effect his pink paper had produced.

"What does it all mean?" he cried. "I always supposed we should protest in defence of the Danish ports, for their sakes and our own. What is all this botheration about Sir Isaac and the rest of you? Do you think it bad news?"

"Bad news!" repeated Fisher, with a sort of soft emphasis beyond expression.

"Is it as bad as all that?" asked his friend at last.

"As bad as all that," repeated Fisher. "Why, of course, it's as good as it can be. It's great news. It's glorious news. That's where the devil of it comes in, to knock us all silly. It's admirable. It's inestimable. It is also quite incredible."

He gazed again at the grey and green colours of the island and the river, and his rather dreary eye travelled slowly round to the hedges and the lawns.

"I felt this garden was a sort of dream," he said, "and I suppose I must be dreaming. But there is grass growing and water moving, and something impossible has happened."

Even as he spoke the dark figure with a stoop like a vulture appeared in the gap of the hedge just above him.

"You have won your bet," said Harker in a harsh and almost croaking voice. "The old fool cares for nothing but fishing. He cursed me and told me he would talk no politics."

"I thought it might be so," said Fisher modestly. "What are you going to do next?"

"I shall use the old idiot's telephone, anyhow," replied the lawyer. "I must find out exactly what has happened. I've got to speak for the Government myself to-morrow." And he hurried away towards the house.

In the silence that followed, a very bewildering silence so far as March was concerned, they saw the quaint figure of the Duke of Westmoreland, with his white hat and whiskers, approaching them across the garden. Fisher instantly stepped towards him with the pink paper in his hand, and with a few words pointed out the apocalyptic paragraph. The duke, who had been walking slowly, stood quite still, and for some seconds he looked like a tailor's dummy standing and staring outside some antiquated shop. Then March heard his voice, and it was high and almost hysterical.

"But he must see it, he must be made to understand. It cannot have been put to him properly." Then, with a certain recovery of fullness and even pomposity in the voice: "I shall go and tell him myself."

Among the queer incidents of that afternoon March always remembered something almost comical about the clear picture of the old gentleman in his wonderful white hat carefully stepping from stone to stone across the river, like a figure crossing the traffic in Piccadilly. Then he disappeared behind the trees of the island, and March and Fisher turned to meet the Attorney-General, who was coming out of the house with a visage of grim assurance.

"Everybody is saying," he said, "that the Prime Minister has made the greatest speech of his life. Peroration and loud and pro-longed cheers. Corrupt financiers and heroic peasants. We will not desert Denmark again."

Fisher nodded and turned away towards the towing-path, where he saw the duke returning with a rather dazed expression. In answer to questions he said in a husky and confidential voice:

"I really think our poor friend cannot be himself. He refused to listen; he—ah—suggested that I might frighten the fish."

A keen ear might have detected a murmur from Mr. Fisher on the subject of a white hat, but Sir John Harker struck in more decisively.

"Fisher was quite right. I didn't believe it myself; but it's quite clear that the old fellow is fixed on this fishing notion by now. If the house caught fire behind him he would hardly move till sunset."

Fisher had continued his stroll towards the higher embanked ground of the towing-path, and he now swept a long and search-ing gaze, not towards the island but towards the distant wooded heights that were the walls of the valley. An evening sky as clear as that of the previous day was settling down all over the dim land-scape, but towards the west it was now red rather than gold; there was scarcely any sound but the monotonous music of the river. Then came the sound of a half stifled exclamation from Horne Fisher, and Harold March looked up at him in wonder.

"You spoke of bad news," said Fisher. "Well, there is really bad news now. I am afraid this is a bad business."

"What bad news do you mean?" asked his friend, conscious of something strange and sinister in his tone.

"The sun has set," answered Fisher.

He went on with the air of one conscious of having said something fatal: "We must get somebody to go across whom he will really listen to. He may be mad, but there's method in his madness. There nearly always is method in madness. It's what drives men mad, being methodical. And he never goes on sitting there after sunset, with the whole place getting dark. Where's his nephew? I believe he's really fond of his nephew."

"Look," cried March abruptly, "why, he's been across already. There he is coming back."

And looking up the river once more they saw, dark against the sunset reflections, the figure of James Bullen stepping hastily and rather clumsily from stone to stone. Once he slipped on a stone with a slight splash. When he rejoined the group on the bank his olive face was unnaturally pale.

The other four men had already gathered on the same spot and almost simultaneously were calling out to him: "What does he say now?"

"Nothing. He says—nothing."

Fisher looked at the young man steadily for a moment; then he started from his immobility and, making a motion to March to follow him, himself strode down to the river crossing. In a few moments they were on the little beaten track that ran round the wooded island, to the other side of it where the fisherman sat. Then they stood and looked at him without a word.

Sir Isaac Hook was still sitting propped up against the stump of the tree, and that for the best of reasons. A length of his own infallible fishing-line was twisted and tightened twice round his throat, and then twice round the wooden prop behind him. The leading investigator ran forward and touched the fisherman's hand; and it was as cold as a fish.

"The sun has set," said Horne Fisher in the same terrible tone, "and he will never see it rise again."

Ten minutes afterwards the five men shaken by such a shock were again together in the garden, looking at each other with white but watchful faces. The lawyer seemed the most alert of the group; he was articulate if somewhat abrupt.

"We must leave the body as it is and telephone for the police," he said. "I think my own authority will stretch to examining the servants and the poor fellow's papers, to see if there is anything that concerns them. Of course none of you gentlemen must leave this place."

Perhaps there was something in his rapid and rigorous legality that suggested the closing of a net or trap. Anyhow young Bullen suddenly broke down; or perhaps blew up, for his voice was like an explosion in the silent garden.

"I never touched him," he cried. "I swear I had nothing to do with it!"

"Who said you had?" demanded Harker, with a hard eye. "Why do you cry out before you're hurt?"

"Because you all look at me like that," cried the young man angrily. "Do you think I don't know you're always talking about my damned debts and expectations?"

Rather to March's surprise, Fisher had drawn away from this first collision, leading the duke with him to another part of the garden. When he was out of ear-shot of the others he said with a curious simplicity of manner:

"Westmoreland, I am going straight to the point."

"Well?" said the other, staring at him stolidly.

"You had a motive for killing him," said Fisher.

The duke continued to stare, but he seemed unable to speak.

"I hope you had a motive for killing him," continued Fisher mildly. "You see, it's rather a curious situation. If you had a motive for murdering, you probably didn't murder. But if you hadn't any motive, why, then perhaps you did."

"What on earth are you talking about?" demanded the duke violently.

"It's quite simple," said Fisher. "When you went across he was either alive or dead. If he was alive, it might be you who killed him, or why should you have held your tongue about his death? But if he was dead, and you had a reason for killing him, you might have held your tongue for fear of being accused."

Then after a silence he added abstractedly:

"Cyprus is a beautiful place, I believe. Romantic scenery and romantic people. Very intoxicating for a young man."

The duke suddenly clenched his hands and said thickly: "Well, I had a motive."

"Then you're all right," said Fisher, holding out his hand with an air of huge relief. "I was pretty sure you wouldn't really do it; you had a fright when you saw it done, as was only natural. Like a bad dream come true, wasn't it?"

While this curious conversation was passing Harker had gone into the house, disregarding the demonstrations of the sulky nephew, and came back presently with a new air of animation and a sheaf of papers in his hand.

"I've telephoned for the police," he said, stopping to speak to Fisher, "but I think I've done most of their work for them. I believe I've found out the truth. There's a paper here——"

He stopped, for Fisher was looking at him with a singular expression, and it was Fisher who spoke next:

"Are there any papers that are not there, I wonder. I mean that are not there now."

After a pause he added: "Let us have the cards on the table. When you went through his papers in such a hurry, Harker, weren't you looking for something to—to make sure it shouldn't be found?"

Harker did not turn a red hair on his hard head, but he looked at the other out of the corners of his eyes.

"And I suppose," went on Fisher smoothly, "that is why you told us lies about having found Hook alive. You knew there was something to show that you might have killed him, and you didn't dare tell us he was killed. But believe me, it's much better to be honest now."

Harker's haggard face suddenly lit up as if with infernal flames.

"Honest!" he cried, "it's not so damned fine of you fellows to be honest! You're all born with silver spoons in your mouths, and then you swagger about with everlasting virtue because you haven't got other people's spoons in your pockets. But I was born in a Pimlico lodging-house and I had to make my spoon, and there'd be plenty to say I only spoilt a horn or an honest man. And if a struggling man staggers a bit over the line in his youth in the lower parts of the law, which are pretty dingy, anyhow, there's always some old vampire to hang on to him all his life for it."

"Guatemalan Golcondas, wasn't it?" said Fisher sympathetically.

Harker suddenly shuddered. Then he said:

"I believe you must know everything, like God Almighty."

"I know too much," said Horne Fisher, "and all the wrong things."

The other three men were drawing nearer to them, but before they came too near Harker said in a voice that had recovered all its firmness:

"Yes, I did destroy a paper, but I really did find a paper, too, and I believe that it clears us all."

"Very well," said Fisher in a louder and more cheerful tone, "let us all have the benefit of it."

"On the very top of Sir Isaac's papers," explained Harker, "there was a threatening letter from a man named Hugo. It threatens to kill our unfortunate friend very much in the way that he was actually killed. It is a wild letter, full of taunts—you can see it for yourselves—but it makes a particular point of poor Hook's habit of fishing from the island. Above all the man professes to be writing from a boat. And since we alone went across to him"—and he smiled in a rather ugly fashion—"the crime must have been committed by a man passing in a boat."

"Why, dear me," cried the duke, with something almost amounting to animation. "Why, I remember the man called Hugo quite well. He was a sort of body-servant and bodyguard of Sir Isaac; you see, Sir Isaac was in some fear of assault. He was—he was not very popular with several people. Hugo was discharged after some row or other; but I remember him well. He was a great big Hungarian fellow with great moustaches that stood out on each side of his face——"

A door opened in the darkness of Harold March's memory, or rather oblivion, and showed a shining landscape like that of a lost dream. It was rather a waterscape than a landscape, a thing of flooded meadows and low trees and the dark archway of a bridge. And for one instant he saw again the man with moustaches like dark horns leap up on to the bridge and disappear.

"Good heavens," he cried, "why, I met the murderer this morning."

Horne Fisher and Harold March had their day on the river after all, for the little group broke up when the police arrived. They declared that the coincidence of March's evidence had cleared the whole company and clinched the case against the flying Hugo. Whether that Hungarian fugitive would ever be caught appeared to Horne Fisher to be highly doubtful nor can it be pretended that he displayed any very demoniac detective energy in the matter, as he leaned back in the boat cushions smoking and watching the swaying reeds slide past.

"It was a very good notion to hop up on to the bridge," he said. "An empty boat means very little; he hasn't been seen to land on either bank, and he's walked off the bridge without walking on to it, so to speak. He's got twenty-four hours start, his moustaches will disappear, and then he will disappear. I think there is every hope of his escape."

"Hope?" repeated March, and stopped sculling for an instant.

"Yes, hope," repeated the other. "To begin with, I'm not going to be exactly consumed with Corsican revenge because somebody has killed Hook. Perhaps you may guess by this time what Hook was. A damned blood-sucking blackmailer was that simple, strenuous, self-made captain of industry. He had secrets against nearly everybody; one against poor old Westmoreland about an early marriage in Cyprus that might have put the duchess in a queer position, and one against Harker about some flutter with his client's money when he was a young lawyer. That's why they went to pieces when they found him murdered, of course. They felt as if they'd done it in a dream. But I admit I have another reason for not wanting our Hungarian friend actually hanged for the murder."

"And what is that?" asked his friend.

"Only that he didn't commit the murder," answered Fisher.

Harold March laid down the oars and let the boat drift for a moment.

"Do you know, I was half expecting something like that," he said. "It was quite irrational, but it was hanging about in the atmosphere like thunder in the air."

"On the contrary, it's finding Hugo guilty that's irrational," replied Fisher. "Don't you see that they're condemning him for the very reason for which they acquit everybody else? Harker and Westmoreland were silent because they found him murdered, and knew there were papers that made them look like the murderers. Well, so did Hugo find him murdered, and so did Hugo know there was a paper that would make him look like the murderer. He had written it himself the day before."

"But in that case," said March frowning, "at what sort of unearthly hour in the morning was the murder really committed? It was barely daylight when I met him at the bridge, and that's some way above the island."

"The answer is very simple," replied Fisher. "The crime was not committed in the morning. The crime was not committed on the island."

March stared at the shining water without replying, but Fisher resumed like one who had been asked a question.

"Every intelligent murder involves taking advantage of some one uncommon feature in a common situation. The feature here was the fancy of old Hook for being the first man up every morning, his fixed routine as an angler, and his annoyance at being disturbed. The murderer strangled him in his own house after dinner on the night before, carried his corpse, with all his fishing tackle, across the stream in the dead of night, tied him to the tree, and left him there under the stars. It was a dead man who sat fishing there all day. Then the murderer went back to the house, or rather to the garage, and went off in his motor-car. The murderer drove his own motor-car."

Fisher glanced at his friend's face and went on: "You look horrified, and the thing is horrible. But other things are horrible, too. If some obscure man had been hag-ridden by a blackmailer, and had his family life ruined, you wouldn't think the murder of his persecutor the most inexcusable of murders. Is it any worse when a whole great nation is set free as well as a family?

"By this warning to Sweden we shall probably prevent war and not precipitate it, and save many thousand lives rather more valuable than the life of that viper. Oh, I'm not talking sophistry or seriously justifying the thing but the slavery that held him and his country was a thousand times less justifiable. If I'd really been sharp I should have guessed it from his smooth, deadly smiling at dinner that night. Do you remember I told you of that silly talk about how old Isaac could always play his fish? In a pretty hellish sense he was a fisher of men."

Harold March took the oars and began to row again.

"I remember," he said, "and about how a big fish might break the line and get away."

THE GENUINE TABARD

E.C. BENTLEY

Edmund Clerihew Bentley (1875–1956) met G.K. Chesterton when they were both pupils at St Paul's School, and the pair became lifelong friends. When Chesterton died, Bentley succeeded him as President of the Detection Club. Bentley was a journalist, and invented the "clerihew" verse form which bears his middle name, but he is remembered best today for making an outstanding contribution to detective fiction. His debut novel, *Trent's Last Case*, set the template for the ingenious whodunit, so popular during the "Golden age of murder" between the wars.

Philip Trent, the gentlemanly artist and amateur detective who appeared in the novel, was – despite its title – simply too popular a character to be abandoned. Bentley wrote a series of short stories about him, and eventually a second novel, *Trent's Own Case*, co-written with H. Warner Allen. He never repeated the extraordinary success of his crime writing debut, but this neat little mystery is one of his most enjoyable tales.

* * * * *

IT was quite by chance, at a dinner-party given by the American Naval Attaché, that Philip Trent met the Langleys, who were visiting Europe for the first time. During the cocktail-time, before dinner was served, he had gravitated towards George D. Langley, because he was the finest-looking man in the room—tall, strongly-built, carrying his years lightly, pink of face, with vigorous, massive features and thick grey hair.

They had talked about the Tower of London, the Cheshire Cheese, and the Zoo, all of which the Langleys had visited that day. Langley, so the Attaché had told Trent, was a distant relative of his own; he had made a large fortune manufacturing engineers' drawing-office equipment, was a prominent citizen of Cordova, Ohio, the headquarters of his business, and had married a Schuyler. Trent, though not sure what a Schuyler was, gathered that it was an excellent thing to marry, and this impression was confirmed when he found himself placed next to Mrs. Langley at dinner.

Mrs. Langley always went on the assumption that her own affairs were the most interesting subject of conversation; and as she was a vivacious and humorous talker and a very handsome and good-hearted woman, she usually turned out to be right. She informed Trent that she was crazy about old churches, of which she had seen and photographed she did not know how many in France, Germany, and England. Trent, who loved thirteenth-century stained glass, mentioned Chartres, which Mrs. Langley said, truly enough, was too perfect for words. He asked if she had been to Fairford in Gloucestershire. She had; and that was, she declared with emphasis, the greatest day of all their time in Europe; not because of the church, though that was certainly lovely, but because of the treasure they had found that afternoon.

Trent asked to be told about this; and Mrs. Langley said that it was quite a story. Mr. Gifford had driven them down to Fairford in his car. Did Trent know Mr. Gifford—W. N. Gifford, who lived at the Suffolk Hotel? He was visiting Paris just now. Trent ought to meet him, because Mr. Gifford knew everything there was to know about stained glass, and church ornaments, and brasses, and antiques in general. They had met him when he was sketching some traceries in Westminster Abbey, and they had become great friends. He had driven them about to quite a few places within reach of London. He knew all about Fairford, of course, and they had a lovely time there.

On the way back to London, after passing through Abingdon, Mr. Gifford had said it was time for a cup of coffee, as he always did around five o'clock; he made his own coffee, which was excellent, and carried it in a thermos. They slowed down, looking for a good place to stop, and Mrs. Langley's eye was caught by a strange name on a signpost at a turning off the road—something Episcopi. She knew that meant bishops, which was interesting; so she asked Mr. Gifford to halt the car while she made out the weather-beaten lettering. The sign said "Silcote Episcopi ½ mile."

Had Trent heard of the place? Neither had Mr. Gifford. But that lovely name, Mrs. Langley said, was enough for her. There must be a church, and an old one; and anyway she would love to have Silcote Episcopi in her collection. As it was so near, she asked Mr. Gifford if they could go there so she could take a few snaps while the light was good, and perhaps have coffee there.

They found the church, with the parsonage near by, and a village in sight some way beyond. The church stood back of the church-yard, and as they were going along the footpath they noticed a grave with tall railings round it; not a standing-up stone but a flat one, raised on a little foundation. They noticed it because, though it was an old stone, it had not been just left to fall into decay, but had been kept clean of moss and dirt, so you could make out the inscription, and the grass around it was trim and tidy. They read Sir Rowland Verey's epitaph; and Mrs. Langley—so she assured Trent—screamed with joy.

There was a man trimming the churchyard boundary hedge with shears, who looked at them, she thought, suspiciously when she screamed. She thought he was probably the sexton; so she assumed a winning manner, and asked him if there was any objection to her taking a photograph of the inscription on the stone. The man said that he didn't know as there was; but maybe she ought to ask vicar, because it was his grave, in a manner of speaking. It was vicar's great-grandfather's grave, that was; and he always had it kep' in good order. He would be in the church now, very like, if they had a mind to see him.

Mr. Gifford said that in any case they would have a look at the church, which he thought might be worth the trouble. He observed that it was not very old—about mid-seventeenth century, he would say—a poor little kid church, Mrs. Langley commented with gay sarcasm. In a place so named, Mr. Gifford said, there had probably been a church for centuries farther back; but it might have been burnt down, or fallen into ruin, and replaced by this building. So they went into the church; and at once Mr. Gifford had been delighted with it. He pointed out how the pulpit, the screen, the pews, the glass, the organ-case in the west gallery, were all of the same period. Mrs. Langley was busy with her camera when a pleasant-faced man of middle age, in clerical attire, emerged from the vestry with a large book under his arm.

Mr. Gifford introduced himself and his friends as a party of chance visitors who had been struck by the beauty of the church and had ventured to explore its interior. Could the vicar tell them anything about the armorial glass in the nave windows? The vicar could and did; but Mrs. Langley was not just then interested in any family history but the vicar's own, and soon she broached the subject of his great-grandfather's gravestone.

The vicar, smiling, said that he bore Sir Rowland's name, and had felt it a duty to look after the grave properly, as this was the only Verey to be buried in that place. He added that the living was in the gift of the head of the family, and that he was the third Verey to be vicar of Silcote Episcopi in the course of two hundred years. He said that Mrs. Langley was most welcome to take a photograph of the stone, but he doubted if it could be done successfully with a hand-camera from over the railings—and of course, said Mrs. Langley, he was perfectly right. Then the vicar asked if she would like to have a copy of the epitaph, which he could write for her if they would all come over to his house, and his wife would give them some tea; and at this, as Trent could imagine, they were just tickled to death.

"But what was it, Mrs. Langley, that delighted you so much about the epitaph?" Trent asked. "It seems to have been about a Sir Rowland Verey—that's all I have been told so far."

"I was going to show it to you," Mrs. Langley said, opening her hand-bag. "Maybe you will not think it so precious as we do. I have had a lot of copies made, to send to friends at home." She unfolded a small typed sheet, on which Trent read what follows:

Within this Vault are interred
the Remains of
Lt.-Gen. Sir Rowland Edmund Verey,

Garter Principal King of Arms,
Gentleman Usher of the Black Rod
and
Clerk of the Hanaper,
who departed this Life
on the 2nd May 1795
in the 73rd Year of his Age
calmly relying
on the Merits of the Redeemer
for the Salvation of
his Soul.
Also of Lavinia Prudence,
Wife of the Above,
who entered into Rest
on the 12th March 1799
in the 68th Year of her Age.
She was a Woman of fine Sense
genteel Behaviour,
prudent Oeconomy
and
great Integrity.
"This is the Gate of the Lord:
The Righteous shall enter into it."

"You have certainly got a fine specimen of that style," Trent observed. "Nowadays we don't run to much more, as a rule, than 'in loving memory,' followed by the essential facts. As for the titles, I don't wonder at your admiring them; they are like the sound of trumpets. There is also a faint jingle of money, I think. In Sir Rowland's time, Black Rod's was probably a job worth having; and though I don't know what a Hanaper is, I do remember that its Clerkship was one of the fat sinecures that made it well worth while being a courtier."

Mrs. Langley put away her treasure, patting the bag with affection. "Mr. Gifford said the Clerk had to collect some sort of legal fees for the Crown, and that he would draw maybe seven or eight thousand pounds a year for it, paying another man two or three hundred for doing the actual work. Well, we found the vicarage just perfect—an old house with everything beautifully mellow and personal about it. There was a long oar hanging on the wall in the hall, and when I asked about it the vicar said he had rowed for All Souls College when he was at Oxford. His wife was charming, too. And now listen! While she was giving us tea, and her husband was making a copy of the epitaph for me, he was talking about his ancestor, and he said the first duty that Sir Rowland had to perform after his appointment as King of Arms was to proclaim the Peace of Versailles from the steps of the Palace of St. James's. Imagine that, Mr. Trent!"

Trent looked at her uncertainly. "So they had a Peace of Versailles all that time ago."

"Yes, they did," Mrs. Langley said, a little tartly. "And quite an important Peace, at that. We remember it in America, if you don't. It was the first treaty to be signed by the United States, and in that treaty the British Government took a licking, called off the war, and recognized our independence. Now when the vicar said that about his ancestor having proclaimed peace with the United States, I saw George Langley prick up his ears; and I knew why.

"You see, George is a collector of Revolution pieces, and he has some pretty nice things, if I do say it. He began asking questions; and the first thing anybody knew, the vicaress had brought down the old King of Arm's tabard and was showing it off. You know what a tabard is, Mr. Trent, of course. Such a lovely garment! I fell for it on the spot, and as for George, his eyes stuck out like a crab's. That wonderful shade of red satin, and the Royal Arms embroidered in those stunning colours, red and gold and blue and silver, as you don't often see them.

"Presently George got talking to Mr. Gifford in a corner, and I could see Mr. Gifford screwing up his mouth and shaking his head; but George only stuck out his chin, and soon after, when the vicaress was showing off the garden, he got the vicar by himself and talked turkey.

"Mr. Verey didn't like it at all, George told me; but George can be a very smooth worker when he likes, and at last the vicar had to allow that he was tempted, what with having his sons to start in the world, and the income tax being higher than a cat's back, and the death duties and all. And finally he said yes. I won't tell you or anybody what George offered him, Mr. Trent, because George swore me to secrecy; but, as he says, it was no good acting like a piker in this kind of a deal, and he could sense that the vicar wouldn't stand for any bargaining back and forth. And anyway, it was worth every cent of it to George, to have something that no other curio-hunter possessed. He said he would come for the tabard next day and bring the money in notes, and the vicar said very well, then we must all three come to lunch, and he would have a paper ready giving the history of the tabard over his signature. So that was what we did; and the tabard is in our suite at the Greville, locked in a wardrobe, and George has it out and gloats over it first thing in the morning and last thing at night."

Trent said with sincerity that no story of real life had ever interested him more. "I wonder," he said, "if your husband would let me have a look at his prize. I'm not much of an antiquary, but I am interested in heraldry, and the only tabards I have ever seen were quite modern ones."

"Why, of course," Mrs. Langley said. "You make a date with him after dinner. He will be delighted. He has no idea of hiding it under a bushel, believe me!"

The following afternoon, in the Langley's sitting-room at the Greville, the tabard was displayed on a coat-hanger before the thoughtful gaze of Trent, while its new owner looked on with a pride not untouched with anxiety.

"Well, Mr. Trent," he said. "How do you like it? You don't doubt this is a genuine tabard, I suppose?"

Trent rubbed his chin. "Oh yes, it's a tabard. I have seen a few before, and I have painted one, with a man inside it, when Richmond Herald wanted his portrait done in the complete get-up. Everything about it is right. Such things are hard to come by. Until recent times, I believe, a herald's tabard remained his property, and stayed in the family, and if they got hard up they might perhaps sell it privately, as this was sold to you. It's different now—so Richmond Herald told me. When a herald dies, his tabard goes back to the College of Arms, where he got it from."

Langley drew a breath of relief. "I'm glad to hear you say my tabard is genuine. When you asked me if you could see it, I got the impression you thought there might be something phoney about it."

Mrs. Langley, her keen eyes on Trent's face, shook her head. "He thinks so still, George, I believe. Isn't that so, Mr. Trent?"

"Yes, I am sorry to say it is. You see, this was sold to you as a particular tabard, with an interesting history of its own; and when Mrs. Langley described it to me, I felt pretty sure that you had been swindled. You see, she had noticed nothing odd about the Royal Arms. I wanted to see it just to make sure. It certainly did not belong to Garter King of Arms in the year 1783."

A very ugly look wiped all the benevolence from Langley's face, and it grew several shades more pink. "If what you say is true, Mr. Trent, and if that old fraud was playing me for a sucker, I will get him jailed if it's my last act. But it certainly is hard to believe—a preacher—and belonging to one of your best families—settled in that lovely, peaceful old place, with his flock to look after and everything. Are you really sure of what you say?"

"What I know is that the Royal Arms on this tabard are all wrong."

An exclamation came from the lady. "Why, Mr. Trent, how you talk! We have seen the Royal Arms quite a few times, and they are just the same as this—and you have told us it is a genuine tabard, anyway. I don't get this at all."

"I must apologize," Trent said unhappily, "for the Royal Arms. You see, they have a past. In the fourteenth century Edward III. laid claim to the Kingdom of France, and it took a hundred years of war to convince his descendants that that claim wasn't practical politics. All the same, they went on including the lilies of France in the Royal Arms, and they never dropped them until the beginning of the nineteenth century."

"Mercy!" Mrs. Langley's voice was faint.

"Besides that, the first four Georges and the fourth William were Kings of Hanover; so until Queen Victoria came along, and could not inherit Hanover because she was a female, the Arms of the House of Brunswick were jammed in along with our own. In fact, the tabard of the Garter King of Arms in the year when he proclaimed the peace with the United States of America was a horrible mess of the leopards of England, the lion of Scotland, the harp of Ireland, the lilies of France, together with a few more lions, and a white horse, and some hearts, as worn in Hanover. It was a fairly tight fit for one shield, but they managed it somehow—and you can see that the Arms on this tabard of yours are not nearly such a bad dream as that. It is a Victorian tabard—a nice, gentlemanly coat, such as no well-dressed herald should be without."

Langley thumped the table. "Well, I intend to be without it, anyway, if I can get my money back."

"We can but try," Trent said. "It may be possible. But the reason why I asked to be allowed to see this thing, Mr. Langley, was that I thought I might be able to save you some unpleasantness. You see, if you went home with your treasure, and showed it to people, and talked about its history, and it was mentioned in the newspapers, and then somebody got inquiring into its authenticity, and found out what I have been telling you, and made it public—well, it wouldn't be very nice for you."

Langley flushed again, and a significant glance passed between him and his wife.

"You're damn right, it wouldn't," he said. "And I know the name of the buzzard who would do that to me, too, as soon as I had gone the limit in making a monkey of myself. Why, I would lose the money twenty times over, and then a bundle, rather than have that happen to me. I am grateful to you, Mr. Trent—I am indeed. I'll say frankly that at home we aim to be looked up to socially, and we judged that we would certainly figure if we brought this dog-goned thing back and had it talked about. Gosh! When I think— but never mind that now. The thing is to go right back to that old crook and make him squeal. I'll have my money out of him, if I have to use a can-opener."

Trent shook his head. "I don't feel very sanguine about that, Mr. Langley. But how would you like to run down to his place tomorrow with me and a friend of mine, who takes an interest in affairs of this kind, and who would be able to help you if any one can?"

Langley said, with emphasis, that that suited him.

The car which called for Langley next morning did not look as if it belonged, but did belong, to Scotland Yard; and the same could be said of its dapper chauffeur. Inside was Trent, with a black-haired, round-faced man whom he introduced as Superintendent Owen. It was at his request that Langley, during the journey, told with as much detail as he could recall the story of his acquisition of the tabard, which he had hopefully brought with him in a suitcase.

A few miles short of Abingdon the chauffeur was told to go slow. "You tell me it was not very far this side of Abingdon,

Mr. Langley, that you turned off the main road," the superintendent said. "If you will keep a look-out now, you might be able to
point out the spot."

Langley stared at him. "Why, doesn't your man have a map?"

"Yes; but there isn't any place called Silcote Episcopi on his
map."

"Nor," Trent added, "on any other map. No, I am not suggesting
that you dreamed it all; but the fact is so."

Langley, remarking shortly that this beat him, glared out of the
window eagerly; and soon he gave the word to stop. "I am pretty
sure this is the turning," he said. "I recognize it by these two hay-
stacks in the meadow, and the pond with osiers over it. But there
certainly was a signpost there, and now there isn't one. If I was not
dreaming then, I guess I must be now." And as the car ran swiftly
down the side-road he went on, "Yes; that certainly is the church
on ahead—and the covered gate, and the graveyard—and there is
the vicarage, with the yew trees and the garden and everything.
Well, gentlemen, right now is when he gets what is coming to him,
I don't care what the name of the darn place is."

"The name of the darn place on the map," Trent said, "is
Oakhanger."

The three men got out and passed through the lychgate.

"Where is the gravestone?" Trent asked.

Langley pointed. "Right there." They went across to the
railed-in grave, and the American put a hand to his head. "I must
be nuts!" he groaned. "I *know* this is the grave—but it says that
here is laid to rest the body of James Roderick Stevens, of this
parish."

"Who seems to have died about thirty years after Sir Rowland Verey," Trent remarked, studying the inscription; while the superintendent gently smote his thigh in an ecstasy of silent admiration. "And now let us see if the vicar can throw any light on the subject."

They went on to the parsonage; and a dark-haired, bright-faced girl, opening the door at Mr. Owen's ring, smiled recognizingly at Langley. "Well, you're genuine, anyway!" he exclaimed. "Ellen is what they call you, isn't it? And you remember me, I see. Now I feel better. We would like to see the vicar. Is he at home?"

"The canon came home two days ago, sir," the girl said, with a perceptible stress on the term of rank. "He is down in the village now; but he may be back any minute. Would you like to wait for him?"

"We surely would," Langley declared positively; and they were shown into the large room where the tabard had changed hands.

"So he has been away from home?" Trent asked. "And he is a canon, you say?"

"Canon Maberley, sir; yes, sir, he was in Italy for a month. The lady and gentleman who were here till last week had taken the house furnished while he was away. Me and cook stayed on to do for them."

"And did that gentleman—Mr. Verey—do the canon's duty during his absence?" Trent inquired with a ghost of a smile.

"No, sir; the canon had an arrangement with Mr. Giles, the vicar of Cotmore, about that. The canon never knew that Mr. Verey was a clergyman. He never saw him. You see, it was Mrs. Verey who came to see over the place and settled everything; and it seems she never mentioned it. When we told the canon, after they had gone, he was quite took aback. 'I can't make it out at all,' he says. 'Why should he conceal it?' he says. 'Well, sir,' I says, 'they was very nice people, anyhow, and the friends they had to see them here was very nice, and their chauffeur was a perfectly respectable man,' I says."

Trent nodded. "Ah! They had friends to see them."

The girl was thoroughly enjoying this gossip. "Oh yes, sir. The gentleman as brought you down, sir"—she turned to Langley—"he brought down several others before that. They was Americans too, I think."

"You mean they didn't have an English accent, I suppose," Langley suggested dryly.

"Yes, sir; and they had such nice manners, like yourself," the girl said, quite unconscious of Langley's confusion, and of the grins covertly exchanged between Trent and the superintendent, who now took up the running.

"This respectable chauffeur of theirs—was he a small, thin man with a long nose, partly bald, always smoking cigarettes?"

"Oh yes, sir; just like that. You must know him."

"I do," Superintendent Owen said grimly.

"So do I!" Langley exclaimed. "He was the man we spoke to in the churchyard."

"Did Mr. and Mrs. Verey have any—er—ornaments of their own with them?" the superintendent asked.

Ellen's eyes rounded with enthusiasm. "Oh yes, sir—some lovely things they had. But they was only put out when they had friends coming. Other times they was kept somewhere in Mr. Verey's bedroom, I think. Cook and me thought perhaps they was afraid of burglars."

The superintendent pressed a hand over his stubby moustache. "Yes, I expect that was it," he said gravely. "But what kind of lovely things do you mean? Silver—china—that sort of thing?"

"No, sir; nothing ordinary, as you might say. One day they had out a beautiful goblet, like, all gold, with little figures and patterns worked on it in colours, and precious stones, blue and green and white, stuck all round it—regular dazzled me to look at, it did."

"The Debenham Chalice!" exclaimed the superintendent.

"Is it a well-known thing, then, sir?" the girl asked.

"No, not at all," Mr. Owen said. "It is an heirloom—a private family possession. Only we happen to have heard of it."

"Fancy taking such things about with them," Ellen remarked. "Then there was a big book they had out once, lying open on that table in the window. It was all done in funny gold letters on yellow paper, with lovely little pictures all round the edges, gold and silver and all colours."

"The Murrane Psalter!" said Mr. Owen. "Come, we're getting on."

"And," the girl pursued, addressing herself to Langley, "there was that beautiful red coat with the arms on it, like you see on a half-crown. You remember they got it out for you to look at, sir; and when I brought in the tea it was hanging up in front of the tallboy."

Langley grimaced. "I believe I do remember it," he said, "now you remind me."

"There is the canon coming up the path now," Ellen said, with a glance through the window. "I will tell him you gentlemen are here."

She hurried from the room, and soon there entered a tall, stooping old man with a gentle face and the indescribable air of a scholar.

The superintendent went to meet him.

"I am a police officer, Canon Maberley," he said. "I and my friends have called to see you in pursuit of an official inquiry in connection with the people to whom your house was let last month. I do not think I shall have to trouble you much, though, because your parlourmaid has given us already most of the information we are likely to get, I suspect."

"Ah! That girl," the canon said vaguely. "She has been talking to you, has she? She will go on talking for ever, if you let her. Please sit down, gentlemen. About the Vereys—ah yes! But surely there was nothing wrong about the Vereys? Mrs. Verey was quite a nice, well-bred person, and they left the place in perfectly good order. They paid me in advance, too, because they live in New Zealand, as she explained, and know nobody in London. They were on a visit to England, and they wanted a temporary home in the heart of the country, because that is the real England, as she said. That was so sensible of them, I thought—instead of flying to the grime and turmoil of London, as most of our friends from overseas do. In a way, I was quite touched by it, and I was glad to let them have the vicarage."

The superintendent shook his head. "People as clever as they are make things very difficult for us, sir. And the lady never mentioned that her husband was a clergyman, I understand."

"No, and that puzzled me when I heard of it," the canon said. "But it didn't matter, and no doubt there was a reason."

"The reason was, I think," Mr. Owen said, "that if she had mentioned it, you might have been too much interested, and asked questions which would have been all right for a genuine parson's wife, but which she couldn't answer without putting her foot in it. Her husband could do a vicar well enough to pass with laymen, especially if they were not English laymen. I am sorry to say, canon, that your tenants were impostors. Their name was certainly not Verey, to begin with. I don't know who they are—I wish I did—they are new to us and they have invented a new method. But I can tell you what they are. They are thieves and swindlers."

The canon fell back in his chair. "Thieves and swindlers!" he gasped.

"And very talented performers too," Trent assured him. "Why, they have had in this house of yours part of the loot of several country-house burglaries which took place last year, and which puzzled the police because it seemed impossible that some of the things taken could ever be turned into cash. One of them was a herald's tabard, which Superintendent Owen tells me had been worn by the father of Sir Andrew Ritchie. He was Maltravers Herald in his day. It was taken when Sir Andrew's place in Lincolnshire was broken into, and a lot of very valuable jewellery was stolen. It was dangerous to try to sell the tabard in the open market, and it was worth little, anyhow, apart from any associations it might have. What they did was to fake up a story about the tabard which might appeal to an American purchaser, and, having found a victim, to induce him to buy it. I believe he parted with quite a large sum."

"The poor simp!" growled Langley.

Canon Maberley held up a shaking hand. "I fear I do not understand," he said. "What had their taking my house to do with all this?"

"It was a vital part of the plan. We know exactly how they went to work about the tabard; and no doubt the other things were got rid of in very much the same way. There were four of them in the gang. Besides your tenants, there was an agreeable and cultured person—I should think a man with real knowledge of antiquities and objects of art—whose job was to make the acquaintance of wealthy people visiting London, gain their confidence, take them about to places of interest, exchange hospitality with them, and finally get them down to this vicarage. In this case it was made to appear as if the proposal to look over your church came from the visitors themselves. They could not suspect anything. They were attracted by the romantic name of the place on a signpost up there at the corner of the main road."

The canon shook his head helplessly. "But there is no signpost at that corner."

"No, but there was one at the time when they were due to be passing that corner in the confederate's car. It was a false signpost, you see, with a false name on it—so that if anything went wrong, the place where the swindle was worked would be difficult to trace. Then, when they entered the churchyard their attention was attracted by a certain gravestone with an inscription that interested them. I won't waste your time by giving the whole story— the point is that the gravestone, or rather the top layer which had been fitted on to it, was false too. The sham inscription on it was meant to lead up to the swindle, and so it did."

The canon drew himself up in his chair. "It was an abominable act of sacrilege!" he exclaimed. "The man calling himself Verey——"

"I don't think," Trent said, "it was the man calling himself Verey who actually did the abominable act. We believe it was the fourth member of the gang, who masqueraded as the Vereys' chauffeur— a very interesting character. Superintendent Owen can tell you about him."

Mr. Owen twisted his moustache thoughtfully. "Yes; he is the only one of them that we can place. Alfred Coveney, his name is; a man of some education and any amount of talent. He used to be a stage-carpenter and property-maker—a regular artist, he was. Give him a tub of papier-mâché, and there was nothing he couldn't model and colour to look exactly like the real thing. That was how the false top to the gravestone was made, I've no doubt. It may have been made to fit on like a lid, to be slipped on and off as required. The inscription was a bit above Alf, though—I expect it was Gifford who drafted that for him, and he copied the lettering from other old stones in the churchyard. Of course the fake signpost was Alf's work too—stuck up when required, and taken down when the show was over.

"Well, Alf got into bad company. They found how clever he was with his hands, and he became an expert burglar. He has served two terms of imprisonment. He is one of a few who have always been under suspicion for the job at Sir Andrew Ritchie's place, and the other two when the chalice was lifted from Eynsham Park and the Psalter from Lord Swanbourne's house. With what they collected in this house and the jewellery that was taken in all three burglaries, they must have done very well indeed for themselves; and by this time they are going to be hard to catch."

Canon Maberley, who had now recovered himself somewhat, looked at the others with the beginnings of a smile. "It is a new experience for me," he said, "to be made use of by a gang of criminals. But it is highly interesting. I suppose that when these confiding strangers had been got down here, my tenant appeared in the character of the parson, and invited them into the house, where you tell me they were induced to make a purchase of stolen property. I do not see, I must confess, how anything could have been better designed to prevent any possibility of suspicion arising. The vicar of a parish, at home in his own vicarage! Who could imagine anything being wrong? I only hope, for the credit of my cloth, that the deception was well carried out."

"As far as I know," Trent said, "he made only one mistake. It was a small one; but the moment I heard of it I knew that he must have been a fraud. You see, he was asked about the oar you have hanging up in the hall. I didn't go to Oxford myself, but I believe when a man is given his oar it means that he rowed in an eight that did something unusually good."

A light came into the canon's spectacled eyes. "In the year I got my colours the Wadham boat went up five places on the river. It was the happiest week of my life."

"Yet you had other triumphs," Trent suggested. "For instance, didn't you get a Fellowship at All Souls, after leaving Wadham?"

"Yes, and that did please me, naturally," the canon said. "But that is a different sort of happiness, my dear sir, and, believe me, nothing like so keen. And by the way, how did you know about that?"

"I thought it might be so, because of the little mistake your tenant made. When he was asked about the oar, he said he had rowed for All Souls."

Canon Maberley burst out laughing, while Langley and the superintendent stared at him blankly.

"I think I see what happened," he said. "The rascal must have been browsing about in my library, in search of ideas for the part he was to play. I was a resident Fellow for five years, and a number of my books have a bookplate with my name and the name and arms of All Souls. His mistake was natural." And again the old gentleman laughed delightedly.

Langley exploded. "I like a joke myself," he said, "but I'll be skinned alive if I can see the point of this one."

"Why, the point is," Trent told him, "that nobody ever rowed for All Souls. There never were more than four undergraduates there at one time, all the other members being Fellows."

THE GYLSTON SLANDER

Herbert Jenkins

In 1912, Herbert Jenkins founded a publishing company that soon became highly successful. Jenkins (1876–1923) had an eye for talent and a flair for publicity; the most prominent author on his firm's list was P.G. Wodehouse, and he also published a portion of J.S. Fletcher's colossal output. The business survived Jenkins' premature death, and after a series of takeovers, it eventually became part of the Random House empire.

Jenkins was himself a writer, whose work included biography and humorous fiction. He also dabbled in detective stories, creating the private investigator Malcolm Sage, whose cases were collected in book form in 1921. This story, very much of its time, features a trope of Golden Age detective fiction, a rural community torn apart by a spate of poison pen letters.

* * * * *

"IT'S all very well for the Chief to sit in there like a five-guinea palmist," Gladys Norman cried one morning, as after interviewing the umpteenth caller that day she proceeded vigorously to powder her nose, to the obvious interest of William Johnson; "but what about me? If anyone else comes I must speak the truth. I haven't an unused lie left."

"Then you had better let Johnson have a turn," said a quiet voice behind her.

She span round, with flaming cheeks and white-flecked nose, to see the steel grey eyes of Malcolm Sage gazing on her quizzically through gold-rimmed spectacles. There was only the slightest fluttering at the corners of his mouth.

As his activities enlarged, Malcolm Sage's fame had increased, and he was overwhelmed with requests for assistance. Clients bore down upon him from all parts of the country; some even crossing the Channel, whilst from America and the Colonies came a flood of letters giving long, rambling details of mysteries, murders and disappearances, all of which he was expected to solve.

Those who wrote, however, were as nothing to those who called. They arrived in various stages of excitement and agitation, only to be met by Miss Gladys Norman with a stereotyped smile and the equally stereotyped information that Mr. Malcolm Sage saw no one except by appointment, which was never made until the nature of the would-be client's business had been stated in writing.

The Surrey cattle-maiming affair, and the consequent publicity it gave to the name of Malcolm Sage, had resulted in something like a siege of the Bureau's offices.

"I told you so," said Lady Dene gaily to her husband, and he had nodded his head in entire agreement.

Malcolm Sage's success was largely due to the very quality that had rendered him a failure as a civil servant, the elasticity of his mind.

He approached each problem entirely unprejudiced, weighed the evidence, and followed the course it indicated, prepared at any moment to retrace his steps, should they lead to a cul-de-sac.

He admitted the importance of the Roman judicial interrogation, "cui bono?" (whom benefits it?); yet he realised that there was always the danger of confusing the pathological with the criminal.

"The obvious is the correct solution of most mysteries," he had once remarked to Sir James Walton; but there is always the possibility of exception.

The Surrey cattle-maiming mystery had been a case in point. Even more so was the affair that came to be known as "The Gylston Slander." In this case Malcolm Sage arrived at the truth by a refusal to accept what, on the face of it, appeared to be the obvious solution.

It was through Robert Freynes, the eminent K.C., that he first became interested in the series of anonymous letters that had created considerable scandal in the little village of Gylston.

Tucked away in the north-west corner of Hampshire, Gylston was a village of some eight hundred inhabitants. The vicar, the Rev. John Crayne, had held the living for some twenty years. Aided by his wife and daughter, Muriel, a pretty and high-spirited girl of nineteen, he devoted himself to the parish, and in return enjoyed great popularity.

Life at the vicarage was an ideal of domestic happiness. Mr. and Mrs. Crayne were devoted to each other and to their daughter, and she to them. Muriel Crayne had grown up among the villagers, devoting herself to parish work as soon as she was old enough to do so. She seemed to find her life sufficient for her needs, and many were the comparisons drawn by other parents in Gylston between the vicar's daughter and their own restless offspring.

A year previously a new curate had arrived in the person of the Rev. Charles Blade. His frank, straightforward personality, coupled with his good looks and masculine bearing, had caused him to be greatly liked, not only by the vicar and his family, but by all the parishioners.

Suddenly and without warning the peace of the vicarage was destroyed. One morning Mr. Crayne received by post an anonymous letter, in which the names of his daughter and the curate were linked together in a way that caused him both pain and anxiety.

A man with a strong sense of honour himself, he cordially despised the anonymous letter-writer, and his first instinct had been to ignore that which he had just received. On second thoughts, however, he reasoned that the writer would be unlikely to rest content with a single letter; but would, in all probability, make the same calumnious statements to others.

After consulting with his wife, he had reluctantly questioned his daughter. At first she was inclined to treat the matter lightly; but on the grave nature of the accusations being pointed out to her, she had become greatly embarrassed and assured him that the curate had never been more than ordinarily attentive to her.

The vicar decided to allow the matter to rest there, and accordingly he made no mention of the letter to Blade.

A week later his daughter brought him a letter she had found lying in the vicarage grounds. It contained a passionate declaration of love, and ended with a threat of what might happen if the writer's passion were not reciprocated.

Although the letter was unsigned, the vicar could not disguise from himself the fact that there was a marked similarity between the handwriting of the two anonymous letters and that of his curate. He decided, therefore, to ask Blade if he could throw any light on the matter.

At first the young man had appeared bewildered; then he had pledged his word of honour, not only that he had not written the letters, but that there was no truth in the statements they contained.

With that the vicar had to rest content; but worse was to follow.

Two evenings later, one of the churchwardens called at the vicarage and, after behaving in what to the vicar seemed a very strange manner, he produced from his pocket a letter he had received that morning, in which were repeated the scandalous statements contained in the first epistle.

From then on the district was deluged with anonymous letters, all referring to the alleged passion of the curate for the vicar's daughter, and the intrigue they were carrying on together. Some of the letters were frankly indelicate in their expression and, as the whole parish seethed with the scandal, the vicar appealed to the police for aid.

One peculiarity of the letters was that all were written upon the same paper, known as "Olympic Script." This was supplied locally to a number of people in the neighbourhood, among others, the vicar, the curate, and the schoolmaster.

Soon the story began to find its way into the newspapers, and Blade's position became one full of difficulty and embarrassment. He had consulted Robert Freynes, who had been at Oxford with his father, and the K.C., convinced of the young man's innocence, had sought Malcolm Sage's aid.

"You see, Sage," Freynes had remarked, "I'm sure the boy is straight and incapable of such conduct; but it's impossible to talk to that ass Murdy. He has no more imagination than a tin-linnet."

Freynes's reference was to Chief Inspector Murdy, of Scotland Yard, who had been entrusted with the enquiry, the local police having proved unequal to the problem.

Although Malcolm Sage had promised Robert Freynes that he would undertake the enquiry into the Gylston scandal, it was not until nearly a week later that he found himself at liberty to motor down into Hampshire.

One afternoon the vicar of Gylston, on entering his church, found a stranger on his knees in the chancel. Note-book in hand, he was transcribing the inscription of a monumental brass.

As the vicar approached, he observed that the stranger was vigorously shaking a fountain-pen, from which the ink had evidently been exhausted.

At the sound of Mr. Crayne's footsteps the stranger looked up, turning towards him a pair of gold-rimmed spectacles, above which a bald conical head seemed to contradict the keenness of the eyes and the youthful lines of the face beneath.

"You are interested in monumental brasses?" enquired the vicar, as he entered the chancel, and the stranger rose to his feet. "I am the vicar," he explained. There was a look of eager interest in the pale grey eyes that looked out from a placid, scholarly face.

"I was taking the liberty of copying the inscription on this," replied Malcolm Sage, indicating the time-worn brass at his feet, "only unfortunately my fountain-pen has given out."

"There is pen and ink in the vestry," said the vicar, impressed by the fact that the stranger had chosen the finest brass in the church, one that had been saved from Cromwell's Puritans by the ingenuity of the then incumbent, who had caused it to be covered with cement. Then as an after-thought the vicar added, "I can get your pen filled at the vicarage. My daughter has some ink; she always uses a fountain-pen."

Malcolm Sage thanked him, and for the next half-hour the vicar forgot the worries of the past few weeks in listening to a man who seemed to have the whole subject of monumental brasses and Norman architecture at his finger-ends.

Subsequently Malcolm Sage was invited to the vicarage, where another half-hour was occupied in Mr. Crayne showing him his collection of books on brasses.

As Malcolm Sage made a movement to depart, the vicar suddenly remembered the matter of the ink, apologised for his remissness, and left the room, returning a few minutes later with a bottle of fountain-pen ink. Malcolm Sage drew from his pocket his pen, and proceeded to replenish the ink from the bottle. Finally he completed the transcription of the lettering of the brass from a rubbing produced by the vicar.

Reluctant to allow so interesting a visitor to depart, Mr. Crayne pressed him to take tea; but Malcolm Sage pleaded an engagement.

As they crossed the hall, a fair girl suddenly rushed out from a door on the right. She was crying hysterically. Her hair was disordered, her deep violet eyes rimmed with red, and her moist lips seemed to stand out strangely red against the alabaster paleness of her skin.

"Muriel!"

Malcolm Sage glanced swiftly at the vicar. The look of scholarly calm had vanished from his features, giving place to a set sternness that reflected the tone in which he had uttered his daughter's name.

At the sight of a stranger the girl had paused, then, as if realising her tear-stained face and disordered hair, she turned and disappeared through the door from which she had rushed.

"My daughter," murmured the vicar, a little sadly, Malcolm Sage thought. "She has always been very highly strung and emotional," he added, as if considering some explanation necessary. "We have to be very stern with her on such occasions. It is the only way to repress it."

"You find it answer?" remarked Malcolm Sage.

"She has been much better lately, although she has been sorely tried. Perhaps you have heard."

Malcolm Sage nodded absently, as he gazed intently at the thumb-nail of his right hand. A minute later he was walking down the drive, his thoughts occupied with the pretty daughter of the vicar of Gylston.

At the curate's lodgings he was told that Mr. Blade was away, and would not return until late that night.

As he turned from the gate, Malcolm Sage encountered a pale-faced, narrow-shouldered man with a dark moustache and a hard, peevish mouth.

To Malcolm Sage's question as to which was the way to the inn, he nodded in the direction from which he had come and continued on his way.

"A man who has failed in what he set out to accomplish," was Malcolm Sage's mental diagnosis of John Gray, the Gylston schoolmaster.

It was not long before Malcolm Sage realised that the village of Gylston was intensely proud of itself. It had seen in the London papers accounts of the mysterious scandal of which it was the centre. A Scotland Yard officer had been down, and had subjected many of the inhabitants to a careful cross-examination. In consequence Gylston realised that it was a village to be reckoned with.

The Tired Traveller was the centre of all rumour and gossip. Here each night in the public-bar, or in the private-parlour, according to their social status, the inhabitants would forgather and discuss the problem of the mysterious letters. Every sort of theory was advanced, and every sort of explanation offered. Whilst popular opinion tended to the view that the curate was the guilty party, there were some who darkly shook their heads and muttered, "We shall see."

It was remembered and discussed with relish that John Gray, the schoolmaster, had for some time past shown a marked admiration for the vicar's daughter. She, however, had made it clear that the cadaverous, saturnine pedagogue possessed for her no attractions.

During the half-hour that Malcolm Sage spent at The Tired Traveller, eating a hurried meal, he heard all there was to be heard about local opinion.

The landlord, a rubicund old fellow whose baldness extended to his eyelids, was bursting with information. By nature capable of making a mystery out of a sunbeam, he revelled in the scandal that hummed around him.

After a quarter of an hour's conversation, the landlord's conversation, Malcolm Sage found himself possessed of a bewildering amount of new material.

"A young gal don't have them highsterics for nothin'," mine host remarked darkly. "Has fits of 'em every now and then ever since she was a flapper, sobbin' and cryin' fit to break 'er heart, and the vicar that cross with her."

"That is considered the best way to treat hysterical people," remarked Malcolm Sage.

"Maybe," was the reply, "but she's only a gal, and a pretty one too," he added inconsequently.

"Then there's the schoolmaster," he continued, " 'ates the curate like poison, he does. Shouldn't be surprised if it was him that done it. 'E's always been a bit sweet in that quarter himself, has Mr. Gray. Got talked about a good deal one time, 'angin' about arter Miss Muriel," added the loquacious publican.

By the time Malcolm Sage had finished his meal, the landlord was well in his stride of scandalous reminiscence. It was with obvious reluctance that he allowed so admirable a listener to depart, and it was with manifest regret that he watched Malcolm Sage's car disappear round the curve in the road.

A little way beyond the vicarage, an admonitory triangle caused Tims to slow up. Just by the bend Malcolm Sage observed a youth and a girl standing in the recess of a gate giving access to a meadow. Although they were in the shadow cast by the hedge, Malcolm Sage's quick eyes recognised in the girl the vicar's daughter. The youth looked as if he might be one of the lads of the village.

In the short space of two or three seconds Malcolm Sage noticed the change in the girl. Although he could not see her face very clearly, the vivacity of her bearing and the ready laugh were suggestive of a gaiety contrasting strangely with the tragic figure he had seen in the afternoon.

Muriel Crayne was obviously of a very mercurial temperament, he decided, as the car swung round the bend.

The next morning, in response to a telephone message, Inspector Murdy called on Malcolm Sage.

"Well, Mr. Sage," he cried, as he shook hands, "going to have another try to teach us our job," and his blue eyes twinkled good-humouredly.

The inspector had already made up his mind. He was a man with many successes to his record, achieved as a result of undoubted astuteness in connection with the grosser crimes, such as train-murders, post-office hold-ups and burglaries. He was incapable, however, of realising that there existed a subtler form of law-breaking, arising from something more intimately associated with the psychic than the material plane.

"Did you see Mr. Blade?" enquired Malcolm Sage.

"Saw the whole blessed lot," was the cheery reply. "It's all as clear as milk," and he laughed.

"What did Mr. Blade say?" enquired Malcolm Sage, looking keenly across at the inspector.

"Just that he had nothing to say."

"His exact words. Can you remember them?" queried Malcolm Sage.

"Oh, yes!" replied the inspector. "He said, 'Inspector Murdy, I have nothing to say,' and then he shut up like a real Whitstable."

"He was away yesterday," remarked Malcolm Sage, who then told the inspector of his visit. "How about John Gray, the schoolmaster?" he queried.

"He practically told me to go to the devil," was the genial reply. Inspector Murdy was accustomed to rudeness; his profession invited it, and to his rough-and-ready form of reasoning, rudeness meant innocence; politeness guilt.

He handed to Malcolm Sage a copy of a list of people who purchased "Olympic Script" from Mr. Grainger, the local Whiteley, volunteering the information that the curate was the biggest consumer, as if that settled the question of his guilt.

"And yet the vicar would not hear of the arrest of Blade," murmured Malcolm Sage, turning the copper ash-tray round with his restless fingers.

The inspector shrugged his massive shoulders.

"Sheer good nature and kindliness, Mr. Sage," he said. "He's as gentle as a woman."

"I once knew a man," remarked Malcolm Sage, "who said that in the annals of crime lay the master-key to the world's mysteries, past, present and to come."

"A dreamer, Mr. Sage," smiled the inspector. "We haven't time for dreaming at the Yard," he added good-temperedly, as he rose and shook himself like a Newfoundland dog.

"I suppose it never struck you to look elsewhere than at the curate's lodgings for the writer of the letters?" enquired Malcolm Sage quietly.

"It never strikes me to look about for someone when I'm sitting on his chest," laughed Inspector Murdy.

"True," said Malcolm Sage. "By the way," he continued, without looking up, "in future can you let me see every letter as it is received? You might also keep careful record of how they are delivered."

"Certainly, Mr. Sage. Anything that will make you happy."

"Later I may get you to ask the vicar to seal up any subsequent anonymous letters that reach him without allowing anyone to see the contents. Do you think he would do that?"

"Without doubt if I ask him," said the inspector, surprise in his eyes as he looked down upon the cone of baldness beneath him, realising what a handicap it is to talk to a man who keeps his eyes averted.

"He must then put the letters in a place where no one can possibly obtain access to them. One thing more," continued Malcolm Sage, "will you ask Miss Crayne to write out the full story of the letters as far as she personally is acquainted with it?"

"Very well, Mr. Sage," said the inspector, with the air of one humouring a child. "Now I'll be going." He walked towards the door, then suddenly stopped and turned.

"I suppose you think I'm wrong about the curate?"

"I'll tell you later," was the reply.

"When you find the master-key?" laughed the inspector, as he opened the door.

"Yes, when I find the master-key," said Malcolm Sage quietly and, as the door closed behind Inspector Murdy, he continued to finger the copper ash-tray as if that were the master-key.

* * * * *

MALCOLM SAGE was seated at a small green-covered table playing solitaire. A velvet smoking-jacket and a pair of wine-coloured morocco slippers suggested that the day's work was done.

Patience, chess, and the cinema were his unfailing sources of inspiration when engaged upon a more than usually difficult case. He had once told Sir James Walton that they clarified his brain and co-ordinated his thoughts, the cinema in particular. The fact that in the surrounding darkness were hundreds of other brains, vital and active, appeared to stimulate his own imagination.

Puffing steadily at a gigantic meerschaum, he moved the cards with a deliberation which suggested that his attention rather than his thoughts was absorbed in the game.

Nearly a month had elapsed since he had agreed to take up the enquiry into the authorship of the series of anonymous letters with which Gylston and the neighbourhood had been flooded; yet still the matter remained a mystery.

A celebrated writer of detective stories had interested himself in the affair, with the result that the Press throughout the country had "stunted" Gylston as if it had been a heavy-weight championship, or a train murder.

For a fortnight Malcolm Sage had been on the Continent in connection with the theft of the Adair Diamonds. Two days previously, after having restored the famous jewels to Lady Adair, he had returned to London, to find that the Gylston affair had developed a new and dramatic phase. The curate had been arrested for an attempted assault upon Miss Crayne and, pleading "not guilty," had been committed for trial.

The incident that led up to this had taken place on the day that Malcolm Sage left London. Late that afternoon Miss Crayne had arrived at the vicarage in a state bordering on collapse. On becoming more collected, she stated that on returning from paying a call, and when half-way through a copse, known locally as "Gipsies Wood," Blade had sprung out upon her and violently protested his passion. He had gripped hold of her wrists, the mark of his fingers was to be seen on the delicate skin, and threatened to kill her and himself. She had been terrified, thinking he meant to kill her. The approach of a farm labourer had saved her, and the curate had disappeared through the copse.

This story was borne out by Joseph Higgins, the farm labourer in question. He had arrived to find Miss Crayne in a state of great alarm and agitation, and he had walked with her as far as the vicarage gate. He did not, however, actually see the curate.

On the strength of this statement the police had applied for a warrant, and had subsequently arrested the curate. Later he appeared before the magistrates, had been remanded, and finally committed for trial, bail being allowed.

Blade protested his innocence alike of the assault and the writing of the letters; but two handwriting experts had testified to the similarity of the handwriting of the anonymous letters with that of the curate. Furthermore, they were all written upon "Olympic Script," the paper that Blade used for his sermons.

Malcolm Sage had just started a new deal when the door opened, and Rogers showed in Robert Freynes. With a nod, Malcolm Sage indicated the chair opposite. His visitor dropped into it and, taking a pipe from his pocket, proceeded to fill and light it.

Placing his meerschaum on the mantelpiece, Malcolm Sage produced a well-worn briar from his pocket, which, having got into commission, he proceeded once more with the game.

"It's looking pretty ugly for Blade," remarked Freynes, recognising by the substitution of the briar for the meerschaum that Malcolm Sage was ready for conversation.

"Tell me."

"It's those damned handwriting experts," growled Freynes. "They're the greatest anomaly of our legal system. The judge always warns the jury of the danger of accepting their evidence; yet each side continues to produce them. It's an insult to intelligence and justice."

"To hang a man because his 's' resembles that of an implicating document," remarked Malcolm Sage, as he placed a red queen on a black knave, "is about as sensible as to imprison him because he has the same accent as a footpad."

"Then there's Blade's astonishing apathy," continued Freynes. "He seems quite indifferent to the gravity of his position. Refuses to say a word. Anyone might think he knew the real culprit and was trying to shield him," and he sucked moodily at his pipe.

"The handwriting expert," continued Malcolm Sage imperturbably, "is too concerned with the crossing of a 't,' the dotting of an 'i,' or the tail of a 'g,' to give time and thought to the way in which the writer uses, for instance, the compound tenses of verbs. Blade was no more capable of writing those letters than our friend Murdy is of transliterating the Rosetta Stone."

"Yes; but can we prove it?" asked Freynes gloomily, as with the blade of a penknife he loosened the tobacco in the bowl of his pipe. "Can we prove it?" he repeated and, snapping the knife to, he replaced it in his pocket.

"Blade's sermons," Malcolm Sage continued, "and such letters of his as you have been able to collect, show that he adopted a very definite and precise system of punctuation. He frequently uses the colon and the semicolon, and always in the right place. In a parenthetical clause preceded by the conjunction 'and,' he uses a comma *after* the 'and,' not before it as most people do. Before such words as 'yet' and 'but,' he without exception uses a semicolon. The word 'only,' he always puts in its correct place. In short, he is so academic as to savour somewhat of the pomposity of the eighteenth century."

"Go on," said Freynes, as Malcolm Sage paused, as if to give the other a chance of questioning his reasoning.

"Turning to the anonymous letters," continued Malcolm Sage, "it must be admitted that the handwriting is very similar; but there all likeness to Blade's sermons and correspondence ends. Murdy has shown me nearly all the anonymous letters, and in the whole series there is not one instance of the colon or the semicolon being used. The punctuation is of the vaguest, consisting largely of the dash, which after all is a literary evasion.

"In these letters the word 'but' frequently appears without any punctuation mark before it. At other times it has a comma, a dash, or a full stop."

He paused and for the next two minutes devoted himself to the game before him. Then he continued:

"Such phrases as 'If only you knew,' 'I should have loved to have been,' 'different than,' which appear in these letters, would have been absolutely impossible to a man of Blade's meticulous literary temperament.

As Malcolm Sage spoke, Robert Freynes's brain had been working rapidly. Presently he brought his hand down with a smack upon his knee.

"By heavens, Sage!" he cried, "this is a new pill for the handwriting expert. I'll put you in the box. We've got a fighting chance after all."

"The most curious factor in the whole case," continued Malcolm Sage, "is the way in which the letters were delivered. One was thrown into a fly on to Miss Crayne's lap, she tells us, when she and her father were driving home after dining at the Hall. Another was discovered in the vicarage garden. A third was thrown through Miss Crayne's bedroom window. A few of the earlier group were posted in the neighbouring town of Whitchurch, some on days that Blade was certainly not there."

"That was going to be one of my strongest points," remarked Freynes.

"The letters always imply that there is some obstacle existing between the writer and the girl he desires. What possible object could Blade have in writing letters to various people suggesting an intrigue between his vicar's daughter and himself; yet these letters were clearly written by the same hand that addressed those to the girl, her father and her mother."

Freynes nodded his head comprehendingly.

"If Blade were in love with the girl," continued Malcolm Sage, "what was there to prevent him from pressing his suit along legitimate and accepted lines. Murdy frankly acknowledges that there has been nothing in Blade's outward demeanour to suggest that Miss Crayne was to him anything more than the daughter of his vicar."

"What do you make of the story of the assault?"

"As evidence it is worthless," replied Malcolm Sage, "being without corroboration. The farm-hand did not actually see Blade."

Freynes nodded his agreement.

"Having convinced myself that Blade had nothing to do with the writing of the letters, I next tried to discover if there were anything throwing suspicion on others in the neighbourhood, who were known to use "Olympic Script" as note-paper.

"The schoolmaster, John Gray, was one. He is an admirer of Miss Crayne, according to local gossip; but it was obvious from the first that he had nothing to do with the affair. One by one I eliminated all the others, until I came back once more to Blade.

"It was clear that the letters were written with a fountain-pen, and Blade always uses one. That, however, is not evidence, as millions of people use fountain-pens. By the way, what is your line of defence?" he enquired.

"Smashing the handwriting experts," was the reply. "I was calling four myself, on the principle that God is on the side of the big battalions; but now I shall depend entirely on your evidence."

"The assault?" queried Malcolm Sage.

"There I'm done," said Freynes, "for although Miss Crayne's evidence is not proof, it will be sufficient for a jury. Besides, she's a very pretty and charming girl. I suppose," he added, "Blade must have made some sort of declaration, which she, in the light of the anonymous letters, entirely misunderstood."

"What does he say?"

"Denies it absolutely, although he admits being in the neighbourhood of the 'Gypsies Wood,' and actually catching sight of Miss Crayne in the distance; but he says he did not speak to her."

"Is he going into the witness-box?"

"Certainly," then after a pause he added, "Kelton is prosecuting, and he's as moral as a swan. He'll appeal to the jury as fathers of daughters, and brothers of sisters."

Malcolm Sage made no comment; but continued smoking mechanically, his attention apparently absorbed in the cards before him.

"If you can smash the handwriting experts," continued the K.C., "I may be able to manage the girl's testimony."

"It will not be necessary," said Malcolm Sage, carefully placing a nine of clubs upon an eight of diamonds.

"Not necessary?'

"I have asked Murdy to come round," continued Malcolm Sage, still intent upon his game. "I think that was his ring."

A minute later the door opened to admit the burly inspector, more blue-eyed and genial than ever, and obviously in the best of spirits.

"Good evening, Mr. Sage," he cried cheerfully. "Congratulations on the Adair business. Good evening, sir," he added, as he shook hands with Freynes.

He dropped heavily into a seat, and taking a cigar from the box on the table, which Malcolm Sage had indicated with a nod, he proceeded to light it. No man enjoyed a good cigar more than Inspector Murdy.

"Well, what do you think of it?" he enquired, looking from Malcolm Sage to Freynes. "It's a clear case now, I think." He slightly stressed the word "now."

"You mean it's Blade?' enquired Malcolm Sage, as he proceeded to gather up the cards.

"Who else?" enquired the inspector, through a cloud of smoke.

"That is the question which involves your being here now, Murdy," said Malcolm Sage dryly.

"We've got three handwriting experts behind us," said the inspector complacently.

"That is precisely where they should be," retorted Malcolm Sage quietly. "In the biblical sense," he added.

Freynes laughed, whilst Inspector Murdy looked from one to the other. He did not quite catch the allusion.

"You have done as I suggested?" enquired Malcolm Sage, when he had placed the cards in their box and removed the card-table.

"Here are all the letters received up to a fortnight ago," said the inspector, holding out a bulky packet. "Those received since have each been sealed up separately by the vicar, who is keeping half of them, whilst I have the other half; but really, Mr. Sage, I don't understand——"

"Thank you, Murdy," said Malcolm Sage, as he took the packet. "It is always a pleasure to work with Scotland Yard. It is so thorough."

The inspector beamed; for he knew the compliment was sincere.

Without a word Malcolm Sage left the room, taking the packet with him.

"A bit quaint at times, ain't he, sir?" remarked Inspector Murdy to Freynes; "but one of the best. I'd trust him with anything."

Freynes nodded encouragingly.

"There are some of them down at the Yard that don't like him," he continued. "They call him 'Sage and Onions'; but most of us who have worked with him swear by Mr. Sage. He's never out for the limelight himself, and he's always willing to give another fellow a leg-up. After all, it's our living," he added, a little inconsequently.

Freynes appreciated the inspector's delicacy in refraining from any mention of the Gylston case during Malcolm Sage's absence. After all, they represented respectively the prosecution and the defence. For nearly half an hour the two talked together upon unprofessional subjects. When Malcolm Sage returned, he found them discussing the prospects of Dempsey against Carpentier.

Handing back the packet of letters to Inspector Murdy, Malcolm Sage resumed his seat, and proceeded to re-light his pipe.

"Spotted the culprit, Mr. Sage?" enquired the inspector, with something that was very much like a wink in the direction of Freynes.

"I think so," was the quiet reply. "You might meet me at Gylston Vicarage to-morrow at three. I'll telegraph to Blade to be there too. You had better bring the schoolmaster also."

"You mean——" began the inspector, rising.

"Exactly," said Malcolm Sage. "It's past eleven, and we all require sleep."

* * * * *

The next afternoon the study of the vicar of Gylston presented a strange appearance.

Seated at Mr. Crayne's writing-table was Malcolm Sage, a small attaché-case at his side, whilst before him were several piles of sealed packets. Grouped about the room were Inspector Murdy, Robert Freynes, Mr. Gray, and the vicar.

All had their eyes fixed upon Malcolm Sage; but with varying expressions. Those of the schoolmaster were frankly cynical. The inspector and Freynes looked as if they expected to see produced from the attaché-case a guinea-pig or a white rabbit, pink-eyed and kicking; whilst the vicar had obviously not yet recovered from his surprise at discovering that the stranger, who had shown such a remarkable knowledge of monumental brasses and Norman architecture, was none other than the famous investigator about whom he had read so much in the newspapers.

With quiet deliberation Malcolm Sage opened the attaché-case and produced a spirit lamp, which he lighted. He then placed a metal plate upon a rest above the flame. On this he imposed a thicker plate of a similar metal that looked like steel; but it had a handle across the middle, rather resembling that of a tool used by plasterers.

He then glanced up, apparently unconscious of the almost feverish interest with which his every movement was being watched.

"I should like Miss Crayne to be present," he said.

As he spoke the door opened and the curate entered, his dark, handsome face lined and careworn. It was obvious that he had suffered. He bowed, and then looked about him, without any suggestion of embarrassment.

Malcolm Sage rose and held out his hand, Freynes followed suit.

"Ask Miss Muriel to come here," said the vicar to the maid as she was closing the door.

The curate took the seat that Malcolm Sage indicated beside him. Silently the six men waited.

A few minutes later Miss Crayne entered, pale but self-possessed. She closed the door behind her. Suddenly she caught sight of the curate. Her eyes widened, and her paleness seemed to become accentuated. A moment later it was followed by a crimson flush. She hesitated, her hands clenched at her side, then with a manifest effort she appeared to control herself and, with a slight smile and inclination of her head, took the chair the schoolmaster moved towards her. Instinctively she turned her eyes toward Malcolm Sage.

"Inspector Murdy," he said, without raising his eyes, "will you please open two of those packets." He indicated the pile upon his left. "I should explain," he continued, "that each of these contains one of the most recent of the series of letters with which we are concerned. Each was sealed up by Mr. Crayne immediately it reached him, in accordance with Inspector Murdy's request. Therefore, only the writer, the recipient and the vicar have had access to these letters."

Malcolm Sage turned his eyes interrogatingly upon Mr. Crayne, who bowed.

Meanwhile the inspector had cut open the two top envelopes, unfolded the sheets of paper they contained, and handed them to Malcolm Sage.

All eyes were fixed upon his long, shapely fingers as he smoothed out one of the sheets of paper upon the vicar's blotting-pad. Then, lifting the steel plate by the handle, he placed it upon the upturned sheet of paper.

The tension was almost unendurable. The heavy breathing of Inspector Murdy seemed like the blowing of a grampus. Mr. Gray glanced across at him irritably. The vicar coughed slightly, then looked startled that he had made so much noise.

Everyone bent forward, eagerly expecting something; yet without quite knowing what. Malcolm Sage lifted the metal plate from the letter. There in the centre of the page, in bluish-coloured letters, which had not been there when the paper was smoothed out upon the blotting-pad, appeared the words:—

Malcolm Sage,
August 12th, 1919.
No. 138.

For some moments they all gazed at the paper as if the mysterious blue letters exercised upon them some hypnotic influence.

"Secret ink!"

It was Robert Freynes who spoke. Accustomed as he was to dramatic moments, he was conscious of a strange dryness at the back of his throat, and a consequent huskiness of voice.

His remark seemed to break the spell. Instinctively everyone turned to him. The significance of the bluish-coloured characters was slowly dawning upon the inspector; but the others still seemed puzzled to account for their presence.

Immediately he had lifted the plate from the letter, Malcolm Sage had drawn a sheet of plain sermon paper from the rack before him. This he subjected to the same treatment as the letter. When a few seconds later he exposed it, there in the centre appeared the same words:—

Malcolm Sage,
August 12th, 1919.

but on this sheet the number was 203.

Then the true significance of the two sheets of paper seemed to dawn upon the onlookers.

Suddenly there was a scream, and Muriel Crayne fell forward on to the floor.

"Oh! father, father, forgive me!" she cried, and the next moment she was beating the floor with her hands in violent hysterics.

*   *   *   *   *

"From the first I suspected the truth," remarked Malcolm Sage, as he, Robert Freynes and Inspector Murdy sat smoking in the car that Tims was taking back to London at its best pace. "Eighty-five years ago a somewhat similar case occurred in France, that of Marie de Morel, when an innocent man was sentenced to ten years' imprisonment, and actually served eight before the truth was discovered."

The inspector whistled under his breath.

"This suspicion was strengthened by the lengthy account of the affair written by Miss Crayne, which Murdy obtained from her. The punctuation, the phrasing, the inaccurate use of auxiliary verbs, were identical with that of the anonymous letters.

"Another point was that the similarity of the handwriting of the anonymous letters to Blade's became more pronounced as the letters themselves multiplied. The writer was becoming more expert as an imitator."

Freynes nodded his head several times.

"The difficulty, however, was to prove it," continued Malcolm Sage. "There was only one way; to substitute secretly marked paper for that in use at the vicarage.

"I accordingly went down to Gylston, and the vicar found me keenly interested in monumental brasses, his pet subject, and Norman architecture. He invited me to the vicarage. In his absence from his study I substituted a supply of marked Olympic Script in place of that in his letter-rack, and also in the drawer of his writing-table. As a further precaution, I arranged for my fountain-pen to run out of ink. He kindly supplied me with a bottle, obviously belonging to his daughter. I replenished my pen, which was full of a chemical that would enable me, if necessary, to identify any letter in the writing of which it had been used. When I placed my pen, which is a self-filler, in the ink, I forced this liquid into the bottle."

The inspector merely stared. Words had forsaken him for the moment.

"It was then necessary to wait until the ink in Miss Crayne's pen had become exhausted, and she had to replenish her supply of paper from her father's study. After that discovery was inevitable."

"But suppose she had denied it?" questioned the inspector.

"There was the ink which she alone used, and which I could identify," was the reply.

"Why did you ask Gray to be present?" enquired Freynes.

"As his name had been associated with the scandal it seemed only fair," remarked Malcolm Sage, then turning to Inspector Murdy he said, "I shall leave it to you, Murdy, to see that a proper confession is obtained. The case has had such publicity that Mr. Blade's innocence must be made equally public."

"You may trust me, Mr. Sage," said the inspector. "But why did the curate refuse to say anything?"

"Because he is a high-minded and chivalrous gentleman," was the quiet reply.

"He knew?" cried Freynes.

"Obviously," said Malcolm Sage. "It is the only explanation of his silence. I taxed him with it after the girl had been taken

away, and he acknowledged that his suspicions amounted almost
to certainty."

"Yet he stayed behind," murmured the inspector with the air of
a man who does not understand. "I wonder why?"

"To minister to the afflicted, Murdy," said Malcolm Sage. "That
is the mission of the Church."

"I suppose you meant that French case when you referred to the
'master-key,'" remarked the inspector, as if to change the subject.

Malcolm Sage nodded.

"But how do you account for Miss Crayne writing such letters
about herself," enquired the inspector, with a puzzled expression in his eyes. "Pretty funny letters some of them for a parson's
daughter."

"I'm not a pathologist, Murdy," remarked Malcolm Sage drily,
"but when you try to suppress hysteria in a young girl by sternness,
it's about as effectual as putting ointment on a plaguespot."

"Sex-repression?" queried Freynes.

Malcolm Sage shrugged his shoulders; then after a pause, during which he lighted the pipe he had just re-filled, he added:

"When you are next in Great Russell Street, drop in at the
British Museum and look at the bust of Faustina. You will see that
her chin is similar in modelling to that of Miss Crayne. The girl
was apparently very much attracted to Blade, and proceeded to
weave what was no doubt to her a romance, later it became an
obsession. It all goes to show the necessity for pathological con-
sideration of certain crimes."

"But who was Faustina?" enquired the inspector, unable to follow the drift of the conversation.

"Faustina," remarked Malcolm Sage, "was the domestic fly in the philosophical ointment of an emperor," and Inspector Murdy laughed; for, knowing nothing of the marriage or the *Meditations* of Marcus Aurelius, it seemed to him the only thing to do.

THE LONG BARROW

H.C. BAILEY

Henry Christopher Bailey (1878–1961) was a founder member of the elitist Detection Club, founded in 1930 by Anthony Berkeley as a social network for the leading crime writers of the day. Bailey's literary career had begun with historical fiction, but after the First World War, he turned to crime. Unlike Agatha Christie, Dorothy L. Sayers, Freeman Wills Crofts, and Berkeley, all of whom started to write detective fiction at much the same time, Bailey specialised in longish short stories rather than novels.

Bailey's principal detective was Reggie Fortune, a doctor who advises Scotland Yard. As Bailey said, Reggie "has an old-fashioned mind. Insofar as this refers to morals, it means that he holds by the standard principles of conduct and responsibility, of right and wrong, of sin and punishment." Perhaps because Bailey's literary style was also rather old-fashioned, his reputation declined after the Second World War. Yet as this story illustrates, Reggie was a formidable character, and Bailey was too interesting a writer to deserve the neglect into which he has fallen.

*   *   *   *   *

MR. FORTUNE came back from the Zoo pensive. He had been called to the inquest on Zuleika the lemur—a strange, sad case.

He rang for tea, and was given a lady's card. Miss Isabel Woodall, who had no address, wished to consult Mr. Fortune: she had been waiting half an hour. Mr. Fortune sighed and went into the ante-room.

Miss Isabel Woodall stood up, a woman who had been younger, still demurely handsome. She was large and fair, but so plainly and darkly dressed that she made little of herself. "Mr. Fortune?" she said with a pleasant shy smile.

"Yes. I'm afraid you didn't know that I'm not in practice now."

"But I didn't come to see you—er—medically. I'm not a patient, Mr. Fortune. I'm not ill. At least I don't think so. I wanted to consult you about a mystery."

"Oh! I never go into a mystery except with the police, Miss Woodall."

"The police won't do anything. They laugh at us." She twisted her handkerchief in her hands. "I'm frightfully worried, Mr. Fortune. And I don't know what to do." She looked at him with large, anxious eyes. "Do you mind hearing about it?"

Reggie Fortune decided that he did not mind. She was good to look at. He opened the door of his consulting-room.

"I'm Mr. Larkin's secretary," she explained. "Mr. Joseph Larkin: do you know him?"

"The antiquary?" Reggie Fortune murmured.

"Archæologist," Miss Woodall corrected him sharply. "He's the greatest authority on the Stone Age in England, Mr. Fortune. He has a house down in Dorsetshire, just on the border of the New Forest country, Restharrow, Stoke Abbas." As she seemed to expect it Reggie made a note. "I've been working with him down there. But lately it's been horrible, Mr. Fortune." Her voice went up. "As if somebody wanted to drive me away."

"Yes. Now suppose we begin at the beginning. How long have you been Mr. Larkin's secretary?"

"Oh, more than six months now."

"And nobody was ever horrible to you before?"

She stared at him. "Of course not. Nothing ever happened to me before. What do you mean, Mr. Fortune? You don't think it's Mr. Larkin, do you?"

"I haven't begun to think," said Reggie. "Well, you lived a peaceful life till you became Mr. Larkin's secretary. And then?"

"Oh yes, and long after that. It was all quite peaceful while we were in London. But in the spring Mr. Larkin took this house at Stoke Abbas. It's a very lovely place, where the moors meet the downs. Mr. Larkin wanted to study the prehistoric remains about there. There's lots of them, ancient earthworks and burial places."

"Yes. Several long barrows on the hills."

She leaned forward clasping her hands. "That's it, Mr. Fortune," she said in a low eager voice. "Mr. Larkin has been making plans to excavate the long barrow above Stoke Abbas. Did you know about it?"

Reggie smiled. "No. No. I'm afraid Mr. Larkin hadn't attracted my attention."

She flung herself back in her chair. She gave a little cry of irritation. "Do please be serious! That's just like the stupid police down there. They only make fun of it all as if I was a nervous fool. But it's horrible, Mr. Fortune."

"Why not tell me what it is?" Reggie suggested.

"That is what is so difficult,"—she looked down at herself, arranged the blouse at her bosom. "You see, there isn't anything definite. It's as if some one was working against me: as if some one wanted to hurt me. I'm being followed, Mr. Fortune. Whenever I go out alone I'm followed."

Reggie sighed. Many people have made that complaint to patient doctors and incredulous policemen. "Who follows you?" he said wearily.

"But I don't know! Only I'm sure there is somebody. I'm being watched."

"Why should anybody watch you, Miss Woodall?"

"That's what I want to know," she cried. "But somebody does, Mr. Fortune. I've heard him. I've seen his shadow."

"Oh, you are sure it's a man," Reggie smiled.

"You don't believe me, do you?" Miss Woodall was growing angry with him. "That isn't all. When I go out alone I find dead animals."

Reggie sat up. "Do you though?"

She thought he was still satirical. "Yes, I do, Mr. Fortune. Real ones. I've found two crows and another bird—a jay, I think it was—and a weasel. Horrible." She shuddered.

"Extraordinary mortality among the animals of Stoke Abbas," Reggie murmured. "How did they die, Miss Woodall?"

"Good gracious, I don't know. They were very dead. Just on the path where I was walking."

"Yes, that's very interesting," said Reggie.

"It frightens me, Mr. Fortune. What does it mean?"

"I should rather like to know," Reggie admitted. "Yes, I'll look into it, Miss Woodall."

"You yourself? Oh, thank you so much. If you would! I do so want it cleared up." She was effusively grateful. She fumbled in her bag. "I really don't know what your fee is, Mr. Fortune."

"There isn't one, Miss Woodall." He got rid of her. He consulted a book of reference upon Mr. Joseph Larkin. "I wonder," he said, and rang again for tea.

On the next day he sat down to lunch in that one of his clubs where they understand the virtues of the herring. The chief of the Criminal Investigation Department saw him, and tripped across to his table. Both men love the simple life. They engaged upon a profound discussion whether the herring when pickled is the better for cloves. "In the delights of your conversation, Reginald," the Hon. Sidney Lomas protested at last, "I'm forgetting that I wanted to speak to you. A quaint old bird came to me this morning, one Joseph Larkin, an archæologist. He said——"

"He said," Reggie interrupted, "that he wanted to excavate a long barrow at Stoke Abbas and somebody was interferin' with the progress of science and nobody loved him, and what are the police for, anyway? Is that right, sir?"

"How do you do it, Reginald? Messages from the spirit-world, or just thought-reading?"

Reggie smiled. "Satan's Invisible World Displayed: by R. Fortune. No, Lomas, old thing. No magic. The fair Isabel told me her sorrow."

"That's Miss Woodall, the secretary? She came to you, did she? The old boy didn't tell me that."

"Well, the fair Isabel didn't tell me Joseph was going to you."

The two men looked at each other. "Curious lack of confidence about them," said Lomas.

"Yes. Several curious points. Well, what's Joseph's story? Is he followed when he goes out alone? Find dead animals in the path?"

"No carcasses for him. They're kept for Miss Woodall. He's followed. He hears strange noises at night. They come from outside the house. He's quite clear about that."

"Isabel didn't mention noises," Reggie murmured.

"No. The old boy said she hadn't heard them, and he didn't want to worry her, she was worried quite enough. That's his chief trouble. He seems rather gone on his fair secretary. What did you make of her, Reginald?"

"She's got the wind up all right. And she wasn't born yesterday. Queer case."

"Simple enough," Lomas shrugged. "The old boy goes down to this lonely place and wants to dig up an old grave and the country people don't like it and put up practical jokes to scare him off. That's what the local police think. I've been talking to them on the 'phone this morning."

"And the local police don't want to have a fuss with the local people over a couple of strangers."

"I sympathize," Lomas smiled. "Anyway, there's nothing for us."

"I wonder," Reggie said. "Why did one come to me and the other to you?"

"Oh, my dear fellow! They're both scared, and each of them wants to hide it from the other. Each of 'em thinks something horrid may happen to the other and wants protection without making the other more scared."

"Yes. All very natural. Do you know anything about 'em?"

"Joseph is a man of means. Isabel came to him six months ago. Very highly qualified, he says. Classical scholar. Woman in a thousand for his job."

Reggie smiled. "His job! My dear fellow, he hasn't got a job. He's only a crank. He's always fussing round here, there and everywhere. Why is he so mighty keen on this particular long barrow? Why is Isabel so mighty nervous about being followed? She's no chicken and no fool."

"I don't know what you're getting to, Reginald," Lomas frowned.

"Nor do I. That's what worries me. I want to go and look at Stoke Abbas. Let me have Underwood."

"But what are you thinking of?" Lomas objected.

"I think it isn't as natural as it looks," said Mr. Fortune.

In the morning his car picked up Sergeant Underwood and bore that officer away on the Southampton road. Sergeant Underwood, who looks like a nice, innocent undergraduate, lay back luxuriously enjoying the big car's purring speed. Reggie was studying an ordnance map of large scale. They were rushing the hill to Bagshot before he put it away and smiled on Underwood. "Well, my child, do you think you'll like it?"

"I like working under you, Mr. Fortune. But I don't know what I have to do."

"You have to catch butterflies. You're a promisin' young entomologist lookin' for rare species round the New Forest." He proceeded to give a lecture on English butterflies and moths. "Entomology in one lesson: by R. Fortune. Got that?"

Sergeant Underwood gasped a little. The labours of his intellect were betrayed on his comely face. "Yes, sir. Some of it. But Mr. Lomas said something about a long barrow. I don't rightly know what a long barrow is. But how does that come into butterflies?"

"It doesn't. A long barrow is the mound over an old grave. Thousands of years old." He opened the ordnance map. "This is our long barrow. Mr. Larkin and Miss Woodall—who live in that house—want to dig it up. And funny things have been happening. You're going to find a room in a nice pub somewhere near, but not too near, and watch the barrow and watch them and watch everybody—while catching butterflies."

In Southampton he bought Sergeant Underwood the complete equipment of a butterfly hunter and put him on the train to find his own way to Stoke Abbas. The car bore Mr. Fortune on through the green glades of the New Forest to the bare heath country.

It was a day of cloud, and the very air over the moors was grey, and the long waves of heather were dark as the black earth, the distant woodland had no colour, the form of the chalk hills to northward was vague and dim. Mr. Fortune stopped the car and looked about him. Some grey smoke hung in a hollow from unseen houses. As far as he could see there was no man nor any of the works of man. The moor carried no cattle. There was no sign of life but the hum of bees and the chirp of grasshoppers and the flies and butterflies in the heavy air.

"Empty, isn't it, Sam?" said Mr. Fortune, and got out of the car.

"Brighter London!" said Sam the chauffeur.

Mr. Fortune took a track across the heather. It was heavy going, rather like a ditch than a path, an old track long disused and overgrown, but its depth showed that many feet must have passed that way once. It passed by a grey hovel lurking in a dip of the moor where a shaggy donkey was tethered and some fowls of the old game-cock breed scratched in the sand. The thatch of heather was ragged, the mud walls crumbling here and there showed the wattle framework, the little windows were uncurtained.

The track led on to a bluff hill. Mr. Fortune groaned (he does not love walking) and set himself to climb. The hill-side was seared by a long scar. When he came to it he found the double ditch and bank of an old fort. He scrambled in and out and reached the flat hill-top. There rose the mound of the long barrow of Stoke Abbas.

Mr. Joseph Larkin had done no digging yet. Nor anyone else. The mound was clothed in heather and old gnarled gorse. The black sods beneath had not been turned for many a year.

Reggie looked over miles of bare moor and saw no one between him and the horizon. But on one side the hill was scooped out like a bowl, and down in the depths a rabbit scuttered to its burrow. Mr. Fortune went down that way. A man was squatting in the heather, binding bunches of it into little brooms, far too busy to look at him. "Oh, good day," said Mr. Fortune, and stopped. "What's the name of that thing up there?"

The man lifted his bent shoulders and showed a dark beardless face, wide across the cheekbones, a big head for his small size. He stared like a startled animal.

"Do you know the name of that thing up there?" Reggie said again.

"Dragon Hill, 'tis Dragon Hill," the man cried, gathered up brooms and slid away through the heather. His legs were short, he was broad in the beam, his speed was surprising.

Mr. Fortune trudged back to his car and was driven to the house of Mr. Joseph Larkin. It stood beyond the village in a shrubbery of rhododendrons, a plain red-brick box. Mr. Larkin was out. Miss Woodall was out too.

The conventional furniture of the drawing-room was dismal. It seemed to contain no book but "Paradise Lost," illustrated by Gustave Doré. Mr. Fortune shuddered and wandered drearily to and fro till he found on the writing-table the catalogue of a second-hand bookseller.

Mr. Larkin seemed to have an odd taste in books. Those which he had chosen to mark were a mixed lot—somebody's sermons, a child's picture book, Mr. Smiles on Thrift, a history of aviation, Izaak Walton. He marked them in a queer way. A line was drawn under one letter. Reggie Fortune pondered. The letters underlined were S K U T H A I: probably more farther on in the catalogue. But some one was talking outside. Reggie put the catalogue back.

A chubby old fellow came in smiling. "Mr. Reginald Fortune? I don't think I have the pleasure——"

"You called on Scotland Yard, Mr. Larkin."

"Oh, you've come from Mr. Lomas! That's very good of you, very good indeed." He smiled all over his rosy face. "Now let's just go into the study and I'll tell you all about it."

He did. He told at great length, but he did not say anything new, and in the midst of it Miss Woodall arrived in a hurry. "Mr. Fortune! You've come down yourself! But how very kind." While she took Reggie's hand she smiled on Joseph Larkin.

He needed it. He had been much disconcerted. "Oh, do you know Mr. Fortune, my dear?" he said, frowning.

"I didn't. But he is the great expert, you know. I went to him to ask his advice about this horrible business."

"But, my dear child, you didn't tell me."

"I couldn't bear you to be so worried, Mr. Larkin,"—she laid her hand on his arm.

"There, there. But you shouldn't, you know. You really shouldn't, my dear. Leave everything to me."

"You are kind," she murmured.

"I have arranged it all," Mr. Larkin chirped. "I went to the fountain head, Mr. Sidney Lomas. And here is our expert." He beamed on Reggie. "Now—now I think I've told you everything, Mr. Fortune."

"Well, not quite," Reggie murmured. "Why are you specially keen on this long barrow, Mr. Larkin?"

Mr. Larkin began to explain. It took a long time. It was something about Phœnicians. The Phœnicians, Reggie gathered, had been everywhere and done everything before the dawn of time. Mr. Larkin had given his life to prove it. He had found evidence in many prehistoric remains in many countries. When he came down to Stoke Abbas to complete his great book on "The Origins of Our World" he found this fine barrow at his very door. Miss Woodall very properly suggested to him that——

"Oh, Mr. Larkin, I'm afraid it wasn't me." Miss Woodall smiled. "I'm not expert enough to advise."

"Well, well, my dear, you're a very capable assistant. We decided that when we'd finished the book we must excavate the barrow on Dragon Hill, Mr. Fortune."

"And that's how the trouble began," Reggie murmured. "Yes. Any particular reason why you came to Stoke Abbas?"

Mr. Larkin looked at Miss Woodall. "I—I really don't know. I think this house was the most suitable of any that you saw, my dear."

"Oh, much the most suitable. Mr. Larkin must have quiet, you see, Mr. Fortune."

"And this is charmingly quiet, my dear." They purred at each other and Reggie felt embarrassed. "Charming—if only Mr. Fortune can stop this annoyance. I hope you'll stay with us, Mr. Fortune."

They went early to bed at Restharrow. About midnight Mr. Fortune, just dropping off to sleep, was roused by an odd whistling roaring noise, such a noise as a gale might make. But there was no gale. He went to the window and peered out. The moon was rising behind clouds, and he could see nothing but the dark mass of rhododendrons. There was a tap at the door and Mr. Larkin came in with a candle showing his pale face. "That's the noise, Mr. Fortune," he said. "What is it?"

"I wonder. Miss Woodall sleeps on the other side of the house?"

"Yes. I don't think she has ever heard it. It only comes and goes, you know. There! It's stopped. It'll come again. Off and on for half an hour or so. Most distressing. What can it be, Mr. Fortune?"

"I should rather like to know," Reggie murmured. They stood and listened and shivered, and when all was quiet at last he had some difficulty in getting Mr. Larkin to bed.

Reggie rose early. He saw the post come in, but Mr. Larkin and Miss Woodall were both down to take their letters. There was some mild fun about it. Mr. Larkin took the whole post by playful force and sorted it with little jokes about "censoring your correspondence, my dear." It appeared to Reggie that the old gentleman was jealous in the matter of his fair secretary. But the only thing for her was a bookseller's catalogue.

After breakfast the two shut themselves into the study to work. Mr. Fortune went walking, and upon the moor found Sergeant Underwood in pursuit of a cabbage butterfly. His style with the net was truculent. "Game and set," Mr. Fortune smiled. "Fierce fellow. Don't be brutal, my child. No wanton shedding of blood."

Sergeant Underwood retrieved his net from a bramble. "I never hit the perishing things," he said, and mopped his brow.

"Never mind. You look zealous. Keep an eye on the hut over there in the hollow. I want to know who comes out and what he does."

After lunch Mr. Larkin and Miss Woodall rested from their labours. The old gentleman withdrew to his bedroom. The lady sat in the garden. Reggie went out. To the west of the grounds of Restharrow a clump of lime and elm rose to shelter the house from the wind. Reggie went up into one of the elms and climbed till he was hidden and high. He saw Miss Woodall leave the garden alone. She turned off the road by a footpath which led across the moor. Reggie took binoculars from his pocket. She went some way, looked about her and sat down in the heather. Her back was towards him, but he could see that she bent over a paper. Ahead of her a little dark shape moved in the heather, came near the path, and turned away and was lost in the folds of the moor. Miss Woodall rose and walked on. She stopped, she drew aside, looked all about her, and went on more quickly. Reggie steadied his binoculars on the bough. She was going into the village, and among the houses he lost sight of her.

He slid to the ground and met her on her way back. "Alone, Miss Woodall? That's very brave."

"Isn't it?" She was flushed. "Do you know what I found on the path?"

"Yes. I've seen it. A dead stoat."

"Oh, horrible! What does it mean, Mr. Fortune?"

"I shouldn't worry about that," said Reggie. He went on. He saw a butterfly net waving.

"This is a rum business, sir," Sergeant Underwood protested. "A little fellow came out of that hut, kind of gipsy look, and he mooched about over the heath. Seemed to be looking at snares he had set. He found a beast over that way, and sat down there making brooms. Then a woman came down from the house, and he scuttled along and chucked the beast on to the path and cut off. Very rum game."

"Nothing in it," said Reggie sadly. "Well, we'd better deal with him. Go to your pub, my child, and have some food and a nap. I want you outside that hut after dark."

Soon after dinner that night Mr. Fortune professed himself sleepy and went to his room. He smoked a cigar there, heard the household go to bed, changed into flannels and rubber shoes, and dropped unostentatiously out of the window. Among the rhododendrons he waited. It was a calm, grey night; he could see far, he could hear the faintest sound. Yet he had seen and heard nothing when from behind the hedge which marked off the kitchen garden came that whistling roaring noise. Mr. Fortune made for it, stealthily, as it seemed to him, silently. But he had only caught sight of a little man whirling something at the end of a string when the noise ended in a whiz and the fellow ran off. Mr. Fortune followed, but running is not what he does best. The little man was leaving him from the start and soon vanished into the moor. Mr. Fortune at a sober trot made for the hovel under the hill, and as he drew near whistled.

He arrived to find Sergeant Underwood sitting on a little man who wriggled. "I'm a police officer, that's what I am," Underwood was saying. "Now don't you be nasty, or I'll have to be harsh with you."

Reggie flashed a torch in the wide, dark face of the broom-maker, and signed to Underwood to let him sit up. "You've given me a lot of trouble," he said sadly. "Why do you worry the lady? She don't like dead stoats."

"Her don't belong on the moor," said the little man sulkily. "Her should bide in her own place."

"The old gentleman, too. You've worried him with your nasty noises. It won't do."

"He should leave the land quiet. 'Tis none of hisn."

"They are quiet. Quite quiet. They've never done any harm."

"Fie, fie! That they have surely, master. They do devise to dig up old Dragon's grave. 'Tis a wicked, harmful thing."

"It don't hurt you if they see what's inside the old mound."

"Nay, it don't hurt Giles. Giles was here before they come, me and mine, ten thousand year and all. Giles will be here when they be gone their way. But 'tis evil to pry into old Dragon's grave. There's death in it, master."

"Whoever died there in your time?" Reggie said quickly.

"Nay, none to my time. But there's death in it, for sure. Bid 'em go their ways, master, and leave the moor quiet."

"They'll do you no harm, my lad. And you mustn't bother them. No more of these tricks of yours, Giles, or we'll have to put you in gaol."

The little man squeaked and took hold of his knees and stroked them. "Ah, you wouldn't be so hard. I do belong on the moor, me and mine. I don't break no laws."

"Oh yes, you do, hunting these folks. You ought to be in gaol now, my lad. You've made a lot of trouble. If there's any more of it you'll be shut up in a little close cell, not walking in the wind on the moor."

"Nay, master, you wouldn't do it to a poor man."

"You be good, then. I know all about you, you know. If the Restharrow folks have any more trouble it's gaol for Giles."

The little man breathed deep. "The old Dragon can have them for Giles."

"Don't forget. By the way, where's the thing you made the noise with?"

The little man grinned, and pulled out of his coat a bent piece of wood at the end of a cord. When he whirled it round his head it made the whistling roar of a gale.

Mr. Fortune came back to his bedroom by the window and slept the sleep of the just. He did not reach the breakfast table till Joseph and Isabel were nearly finished. "All my apologies. I had rather a busy night." Miss Woodall hoped he had not been disturbed. "No, not disturbed. Interested." Mr. Larkin visibly quivered with curiosity. He thought Mr. Fortune had gone out.

"Out on the moor at night?" Miss Woodall shuddered. "I wouldn't do that for anything."

Mr. Fortune tapped his third egg. "Why should you? But no one will meddle with you, Miss Woodall. The fellow that made the trouble won't bother you any more."

"Who was it?" she said eagerly.

"Well, I shouldn't worry. One of the local people suffering from superstition. He thought it was dangerous to dig up the old barrow. He wanted to scare you off. But I've scared him, and he's seen the evil of his ways. I think we'll give him a free pardon. He wouldn't have hurt you. You can rule him out and get on with the excavation."

"But that's magnificent, perfectly magnificent," Mr. Larkin chirped. "How quick too! You've really done wonderfully well." He twittered thanks.

"You're quite sure about it, Mr. Fortune?" said Miss Woodall.

"Nothing more to be afraid of, Miss Woodall."

"How splendid!" She smiled at him. "Oh, you don't know what a relief it is."

Mr. Larkin plunged into plans for the excavation. Old White at the Priors had promised to let him have men at any time before harvest. No time to lose. Better see the old man at once. Why not that morning? He did hope Mr. Fortune would stay and watch the excavation. Most interesting. Mr. Fortune shook his head. Perhaps he might be allowed to come down and see the result.

"That's a promise, sir. An engagement," Mr. Larkin cried. "We shall hold you to that, shan't we, my dear?"

"Of course," said Miss Woodall.

They went off together to see old White—it seemed impossible for Mr. Larkin to make any arrangements by himself. Reggie was left in the house waiting for his car. He wandered into the study. Everything had been tidied away. Everything but the books was locked up. "Careful souls," Reggie murmured, and paused by a waste-paper basket. It had some crumpled stuff in it. He smoothed out the catalogue of a draper's sale. Some articles had been marked by a line under a letter. He ran his eye over the pages. T A P H O N O I G E I N he read, and heard the horn of his car. He dropped the catalogue back in the basket and slid out of the study as the door bell rang. The maid coming to tell him his car was at the door found him in his bedroom writing a letter.

The big car purred over the heath, passed a man pursuing butterflies, slowed and stopped. The chauffeur went to examine his back tyres. The passenger leaned out and watched. When the car rolled on again there was something white by the roadside. The butterfly hunter crossed the road and picked up a letter. The passenger glanced back. "Now let her out, Sam," he said.

In the late afternoon the Hon. Sidney Lomas, making an end of his day's work in Scotland Yard, was surprised by the arrival of Mr. Fortune. "Oh, Reginald, this is so sudden," he complained. "Finished already? Has Isabel no charms?"

"Some of your weaker tea would do me no harm," said Mr. Fortune. "Isabel's a very interestin' woman, Lomas. Joseph also has points of interest. They're both happy now."

"Cleared it up, have you? What was it?"

"It was a son of the soil. Very attractive person. Bushman type. Probably a descendant of some prehistoric race. You do find 'em about in odd corners. Family lurking on that moor for centuries. He had a notion if anybody opened the old Dragon barrow death came out of it. Probably a primeval belief. So he set himself to scare off Joseph and Isabel—tokens of death for 'em—the bull-roarer at nights."

"What in wonder is a bull-roarer?"

"Oh, a bit of wood rather like a boomerang. You twirl it round on the end of a string and it makes the deuce of a row. Lots of savages use them to scare off outsiders and evil spirits. Very curious survival is Giles. Well, we caught him at it and bade him desist. He's in a holy funk of prison, and he's going to be good. And Joseph and Isabel are getting on with the excavation."

Lomas smiled. "So it was just the local rustic playing the fool. Reginald, my friend, I enjoy the rare and exquisite pleasure of saying I told you so."

"Yes." Reggie drank his tea. "Yes. Tell me some more, Lomas. Why did Joseph and Isabel go down to this place off the map and get keen on excavating its barrow? Lots of other nice barrows."

"Do you think there's something special in this one?"

"No. I think there's something special in Joseph and Isabel. I found in the house a second-hand bookseller's catalogue. Some letters in it were underlined: <u>S</u> K <u>U</u> T <u>H</u> <u>A</u> I. Probably more. I hadn't time to go on. Joseph came in, and afterwards the catalogue vanished."

"Lots of people mark catalogues," Lomas shrugged.

"Yes. But not so that the marks make a word."

"Word?"

"Lomas, my dear old thing, I thought you had a classical education. <u>S</u> K <u>U</u> T <u>H</u> <u>A</u> I is Greek for Scythians, and in Athens the policemen were Scythians."

"Oh, this is fantastic."

"Well, to-day I found a draper's catalogue in a waste-paper basket. Letters marked as before. <u>T</u> A <u>P</u> H <u>O</u> N <u>O</u> I G <u>E</u> I <u>N</u>. Probably more, again. But that's two words. Taphon oigein. To open the tomb. Either Joseph or Isabel is making very secret communications with somebody about excavating that barrow. Why?"

"You do run on," Lomas protested. "But what are you starting from? These people have been doing their damnedest to get the police to look into their affairs. If either of them was up to anything shady, that's the last thing they'd want."

"There's about a dozen answers to that," said Reggie wearily. "Have some. Suppose something suspicious happens later. Mr. Lomas will say 'Oh, nothing in it, these people must be all right, they came and asked us to look into their affairs.' Why, you're saying that already. In the second place, both of them may not be in it; perhaps one of them knew the other was going to the police and played for safety by going too. Thirdly, they were both rattled, one of them may have thought somebody knew more than was convenient and wanted to make sure. Fourthly and lastly, my brethren, whatever the job is, it has something to do with opening this barrow. They're both dead keen on that. They wanted to make sure they could do it without bother."

"Very ingenious, Reginald. And partially convincing," Lomas frowned. "If you'll tell me what they can get by excavating a barrow, I might begin to believe you."

"Nothing," said Reggie, "nothing. That's why it's interesting."

"My dear fellow! You have too much imagination."

"Oh lord, no. None. I'm the natural man. I get nerves when things aren't nice and normal. Hence my modest fame. But imaginative! Oh, Mr. Lomas, sir, how can you?"

"Well, well. Time will show," Lomas rose. "If any corpses lie out on the shining sand, I'll let you know."

"That'll be all right," said Reggie cheerfully. He did not move. "I left Underwood down there."

"The deuce you did!" Lomas stared and sat down again. "And what's he doing?"

"He's catching butterflies. He's also finding out whether Joseph or Isabel posts any catalogues and where they go to."

"Confound you, he mustn't do that on his own. If you want postal correspondence examined we must apply to the Postmaster-General. You ought to know that, Fortune."

"My dear old thing, I do. I also know country post offices. Don't be so beastly official."

"This is a serious matter."

"Yes. Yes, that's what I've been trying to indicate," Mr. Fortune smiled. "Look here. These beauties go down to a place off the map for no decent reason but that it's off the map. Joseph could write his silly books anywhere. Did Isabel take Joseph or Joseph take Isabel? Their stories don't agree. Joseph is affectionate and Isabel coy. Joseph watches her jealously and Isabel is meek. When they've been there some time they get mighty keen on digging up a barrow. Lots of barrows in lots of places, but they must have the lonely one at Stoke Abbas. Then we find them dealing in messages too secret for a letter in plain English. One message something about police, another about opening the barrow. Well, there's going to be dirty work at the cross roads, old thing."

"But it's all fanciful, Fortune. Why the deuce shouldn't they write letters? What's the use of putting a message in Greek?"

"They're all alone. Each of 'em can see all the letters the other gets, perhaps all the letters the other posts. But a catalogue wouldn't be noticed. If one of 'em don't know Greek the marked letters would be absolutely secret. SKUTHAI didn't suggest anything to the Chief of the Criminal Investigation Department."

"But what do you suppose the game is?"

"No, dear,"—Mr. Fortune smiled—"I have no imagination. You've got all the facts. Oh, not quite. I did a little distant snapshot of Joseph and Isabel." He laid a roll of film on the table. "Get the faces enlarged big. Some of your fellows might know 'em. Goodbye. I've got to dine with my young niece—the one that married a gunner. Always merry and bright. Very exhausting."

After which nothing happened for a couple of weeks. Lomas when he met Mr. Fortune in their clubs made sarcastic remarks about the Greek language and the use of the imagination. Then Joseph Larkin wrote to Mr. Fortune that the excavation was nearly complete, urging him to come and see the result. Mr. Fortune told Lomas over the telephone and Lomas made scornful noises. "I'm going," said Mr. Fortune.

"You've got a lot of time to waste," said the telephone.

But three days afterwards, while the car stood at his door to take him to Stoke Abbas, the telephone spoke again. "Hallo, Fortune. Are you up? Marvellous. Just come round here."

Lomas was in an early morning temper. "Some more crazy stuff about that Stoke Abbas case." He stared at Reggie with a bilious eye. "I put the post office people on to it, more fool me. Here's a report. A bookseller's catalogue was posted on Monday with a number of letters from Restharrow. It was addressed to Miss George, 715 Sand Street, Bournemouth. In it a number of letters were marked, a, b, four e's, g, h, two i's, l, m, n, p, r, two s's, t and u."

"As you say," Reggie groaned.

"What do you mean?"

"You said more fool you. Quite so. Why didn't you leave it to Underwood? He'd have got it all right. And I told him to give us the letters in order."

"Confound you, we can't tamper with the mail."

"My dear old thing, you're too good for this world." Reggie took pen and paper. "Say it again. A, b——" He wrote down ABEEEEGHIILMNPRSSTU, lit a cigar and pondered. "You moral men give me a lot of trouble. Here you are. PRESBUS GAMEIN THELEI. And very interesting too. That clears up several points."

"What the deuce does it mean?"

"What did you learn at school, Lomas? I've often wondered. It means 'The old man desires to marry.' Yes, I thought so. I told you you had all the facts. You remember Joseph said Isabel had had a classical education. Not like you, Lomas. She's sending the messages. She's caught Joseph. It's opening out. Now tell your priceless post office folks to report the order of the letters in future. I don't want to work cryptograms because you've got a conscience. And send somebody to look into Miss George, of 715 Sand Street, good and quick. I'm going down to Stoke Abbas. They've opened the barrow. Oh, by the way, what about the snapshots?"

"They enlarged well enough. Nobody here knows the people."

"Not known to the police? Well, well. Get a snap of Miss George. Good-bye."

That evening Mr. Fortune stood on Dragon Hill with Joseph and Isabel. Half a dozen labourers rested on their spades and grinned. The long mound of the barrow was gone. It lay in scattered heaps of grey sand around the cromlech which it had covered, three upright stones supporting one flat. Under that flat stone, as a man might lie under a table, lay a skeleton. Reggie knelt down and took up the skull. "Ah, genuine antique,"—he gave a sigh of relief.

Miss Woodall shuddered. "He looks like a monkey."

"No, I wouldn't say that," said Reggie gently, still intent on the bones.

"I am convinced he was a Phœnician," Mr. Larkin announced.

"Oh lord, no," said Reggie. He was not interested in Mr. Larkin's theory that everything old was Phœnician. He was thinking that this man of the barrow with his long head and his big cheek-bones and his short wide body must have been much like Giles of the hovel on the moor. An ancestor perhaps: five thousand years ago the family of Giles the broom-maker were kings on the sand-hills. But Mr. Larkin went on talking about Phœnicians. ... "Yes, very interesting," said Reggie wearily, and stood up.

"Poor dead man," Miss Woodall sighed. "He looks so lonely."

"My dear," said Mr. Larkin affectionately. "What pretty thoughts you have." They walked back to Restharrow, and he proved again that the skeleton was Phœnician, and it was most gratifying, and he was going to give it to the British Museum and Reggie was bored.

In that condition he remained for the duration of his visit to Restharrow. When Mr. Larkin was not talking about Phœnicians, or (worse still) reading extracts from his new book on "The Origins of Our World," he was (worst of all) being affectionate with Miss Woodall. A mawkish little man. But there was no mystery about them. The great book was published, the barrow was opened. Mr. Larkin was going to write a pamphlet about it, close it down again, marry Miss Woodall, and take her off to South Africa where he meant to find many more traces of the Phœnicians. Reggie wished them joy, and as soon as he decently could went back to London.

Two days afterwards Lomas found him having breakfast in his bedroom, a rare thing, a sure sign of depression. "My dear fellow, are you ill?"

"Yes, very ill. Go away. I don't like you. You look distressin'ly cheerful, and it's very bad for me."

"There's been another message. TUCHEAPELTHE."

"Don't gargle, spell it," said Mr. Fortune peevishly. "Yes, TUCHE APELTHE. Two words. 'Fortune has gone away.' Very kind of her to notice it."

Lomas smiled. "So Isabel wanted Miss George to know Mr. Fortune had gone away. That's interesting. And we've got something about Miss George, Reginald. She isn't a woman. Oh no. She's a middle-aged man, who calls himself George Raymond. He don't live at 715 Sand Street. That's a little shop where they take in letters to be called for. George Raymond has lodgings the other end of the town, and lives very quiet. My fellows have a notion he's American."

"Fortune has gone away," Reggie murmured. "I wonder if Fortune ought to have stayed. No. Nothing would happen with me in the house. I wonder if anything will happen."

"What, are you giving up the case?" Lomas laughed.

"No. There's a case all right. But I don't know whether we'll ever get it. Joseph and Isabel are going to marry, and be off to South Africa."

Lomas was much amused. "And that's the end of it all! My poor Reginald! What a climax! Mr. Fortune's own particular mystery. All orange blossom and wedding cake."

"Yes. With Miss George as best man. I hope your fellows are looking sharp after Miss George."

"He's giving no trouble. They won't miss him. We've got a photograph too. Nobody knows him, but we'll have it enlarged."

"Well, watch him."

"Oh, certainly: anything to oblige. Have they asked you to the wedding, Reginald? You really ought to send them a present."

Lomas says that Reggie then snarled.

Two weeks passed. Reggie received an angry letter from Mr. Larkin stating that the British Museum had refused the skeleton, and he was replacing it in the barrow and publishing the full facts to inform the public of the blind prejudice of the official world against his work. He was leaving immediately for South Africa, where he had no doubt of obtaining conclusive proof of the theory of the Phœnician origin of all civilization. Mrs. Larkin sent Mr. Fortune kind thoughts and best wishes.

Mr. Fortune moved uneasily in his chair. "And they lived happily ever after," said Mr. Fortune. "Kind thoughts and best wishes. Dear Isabel." He rang up Lomas to ask how Miss George was getting on.

"Many thanks for kind inquiries," said the voice of Lomas. "Nothing doing. Not by George. He lives the life of a maiden lady. What did you say?"

"I said damn," said Mr. Fortune.

That evening came a letter from Sergeant Underwood. He was plaintive. He thought Mr. Fortune ought to know there seemed nothing more to do at Stoke Abbas. The barrow was being covered up. The servants were leaving Restharrow. Mr. Larkin and Miss Woodall were going to be married at the registry office to-morrow, and the next day sailing from Southampton. Mr. Fortune spent a restless night.

He was fretting in the library of his dreariest club next morning when the telephone called him to Scotland Yard. Lomas was in conference with Superintendent Bell. Lomas was brisk and brusque. "They've lost George Raymond, Fortune. He left Bournemouth this morning with a suit-case. He went to Southampton, put it in the cloakroom, went into one of the big shops and hasn't been seen since. When they found they'd lost him they went back to the station. His suit-case was gone."

"Well, well," said Mr. Fortune. "You have been and gone and done it, Lomas." But he smiled.

"What do you want us to do now?"

"Oh, you might watch the Cape boat. Make sure G. Raymond isn't on the Cape boat when she sails. If you can."

"I've arranged for all that. Anything else?"

"You might give me a time-table," said Mr. Fortune. "I'm going down to the long barrow."

"Good Gad!" said Lomas.

As darkness fell on the moors that night, Mr. Fortune and Superintendent Bell stopped a hired car a mile away from Stoke Abbas and walked on through the shadows. When they came near the shrubberies of Restharrow a voice spoke softly from behind a clump of gorse. "Got your wire, sir. All clear here. They were married this morning. Both in the house now. Servants all gone. No one else been here."

Reggie sat down beside Sergeant Underwood. "Seen anyone strange about?"

"I did fancy I saw some one going up towards the barrow a while ago."

"Work up that way quietly. Don't show yourself."

Sergeant Underwood vanished into the night. Bell and Reggie sat waiting while the stars grew dim in a black sky. The door of Restharrow opened; and a bar of light shot out. They heard voices.

"A beautiful night," said Mr. Larkin. "The most beautiful night that ever happened," said Mrs. Larkin. They came out. "Let us go up to the dear old barrow," she said. "I shall always love it, you know. It brought us together, my dearest."

"My dear child," Mr. Larkin chirped. "You are full of pretty thoughts."

They walked on arm in arm.

A long way behind, Reggie and Superintendent Bell followed.

When they came to the crest of the hill, where the turned sand was white in the gloom, "Dear place," said Mrs. Larkin. "How sweet it is here. I think that old Phœnician was lucky, don't you, Joseph dearest?"

A man rose up behind Joseph dearest and grasped his head. There was no struggle, no noise, a little swaying, a little scuffle of feet in the sand and Joseph was laid on his back and Isabel knelt beside him. The other man turned aside. There was the sound of a spade. Then Sergeant Underwood arrived on his back. They went down together. Bell charged up the hill to catch Mrs. Larkin as she rushed to help. But Underwood already had his man handcuffed and jerked him on to his feet.

Reggie came at his leisure and took a pad of cottonwool from Mr. Larkin's face. "Who is your friend with the chloroform, Mrs. Larkin?" he said gently.

"You devil," she panted. "Don't say a word, George."

"Oh, yes, I know he's George," said Reggie, and flashed a torch on the man.

Sergeant Underwood gasped. Sergeant Underwood stared from the man in handcuffs to the man on the ground. "Good Lord!

Which have I got, sir?" For the man who stood was of the same small plump size as Mr. Larkin, grey-haired, clean-shaven too, dressed in the like dark clothes.

"Yes, a good make up. That was necessary, wasn't it, Mrs. Larkin? Well, we'd better get the real Mr. Larkin to hospital." He whistled across the night and flashed his torch and the hired car surged up to the foot of the hill. Mr. Larkin was carried to it, it bore him and Reggie away and behind them Mrs. Larkin and George, handcuffed wrist to wrist, tramped long miles to a police station.

A little man lying in the heather on the hill watched them go. "Old Dragon hath taken her," he chuckled. "Giles knew he would have her," and he capered home to his hut on the moor.

Superintendent Bell coming into the coffee-room of an inn at Wimborne next morning saw Mr. Fortune dealing heartily with grilled salmon. "You had a bad night, sir," he said with sympathy.

"Yes. Poor Joseph was very upset. Spiritually and physically. Can you wonder? It's disheartening to a husband when his wife attempts murder on the wedding night. Destroys confidence."

"Confidence! They're a pair of beauties, the woman and this chap George. I suppose they were going to bury poor Larkin alive."

"Yes. Yes. He wouldn't have been very lively, of course."

"I should say not. What do you think that fellow had on him, sir?"

"Well, chloroform, of course. A pistol, I suppose. Probably some vitriol."

"That's it." Superintendent Bell gazed at him with reverent admiration. "It's wonderful how you know men, Mr. Fortune."

Mr. Fortune smiled and passed Bell his plate of nectarines. "I knew they'd think of everything. That's their weakness. Just a little too careful. But it's a beautiful plan. Grave all ready, nice light soil, spades handy, chloroform the old man, pour vitriol over him, bury him. Not likely anyone would open that barrow again in a century. If they did, only an unknown corpse inside. Nobody missing. No chance anybody would think the corpse was Mr. Larkin who sailed for South Africa alive and kicking. And George and Isabel are Mr. and Mrs. Larkin and live happy ever after on the Larkin fortune. If only she hadn't taken such pains about a grave, if only she hadn't bothered about Giles, if only they hadn't been so clever with their secret messages, they'd have brought it off. Poor old Joseph, though. He's very cut up. He fears Isabel never really loved him. But he don't want to give evidence against her, poor old thing."

"I don't wonder," said Bell. "He'll look a proper fool in the witness-box."

"Yes. Yes. Not a wise old boy. But human, Bell, quite human."

There was a sprightly noise without. Lomas came tripping in and on the heels of Lomas a solid man with the face of a Roman emperor. "Reginald, my dear fellow, all my congratulations," Lomas chuckled. "You told me so. You really did. Splendid case. This is Mr. Bingham Jackson of the American service."

"I want to know you, sir," said Mr. Bingham Jackson magisterially. "This is right good work. We wanted those two and we wanted 'em bad."

"When Mr. Jackson saw your photographs of George and Isabel he called for champagne," Lomas chuckled.

"Yes. I thought somebody ought to know them," said Mr. Fortune. "I thought they weren't new to the business."

"No, sir." Mr. Jackson nodded impressively. "Not new. Isabel and George Stultz are American citizens of some reputation. We shall be right glad to have them back. They eliminated Mrs. Stanton Johnson of Philadelphia and got off with her collection of antique jewels. They used morphia and a cellar then. One of our best crimes."

"This is going to hush up Joseph's trouble," said Mr. Fortune with satisfaction. "You'll claim their extradition for murder?"

"Sure thing. We didn't get in on our case early like you. They brought the murder off our side. You always had 'em on a string. But I want to say, Mr. Fortune, I do admire your work. You have flair."

"Not nice people, you know," said Reggie dreamily. "I get nerves when people aren't nice and ordinary."

"Some nerves," said Mr. Jackson.

THE NATURALIST AT LAW

R. AUSTIN FREEMAN

Richard Austin Freeman (1862–1943) was a doctor who turned to writing detective fiction to supplement his income after ill health affected his career; he had contracted blackwater fever while working for the Colonial Service in west Africa. At first he collaborated with the medical officer at Holloway Prison, J.J. Pitcairn, but he found fame after branching out on his own, and creating Dr John Thorndyke.

Thorndyke, a specialist in medico-legal jurisprudence, with chambers at King's Bench Walk, first appeared in *The Red Thumb Mark* (1907), and his popularity was such that Freeman continued to write about him to the end of his life. The Thorndyke mysteries derive their strength from Freeman's scientific knowledge. He researched his plots meticulously, and this cleverly crafted story is one of his finest.

* * * * *

A HUSH had fallen on the court as the coroner concluded his brief introductory statement and the first witness took up his position by the long table. The usual preliminary questions elicited that Simon Moffet, the witness aforesaid, was fifty-eight years of age, that he followed the calling of a shepherd and that he was engaged in supervising the flocks that fed upon the low-lying meadows adjoining the little town of Bantree in Buckinghamshire.

"Tell us how you came to discover the body," said the coroner.

" 'Twas on Wednesday morning, about half-past five," Moffet began. "I was getting the sheep through the gate into the big meadow by Reed's farm, when I happened to look down the dyke, and then I noticed a boot sticking up out of the water. Seemed to me as if there was a foot in it by the way it stuck up, so as soon as all the sheep was in, I shut the gate and walked down the dyke to have a look at un. When I got close I see the toe of another boot just alongside. Looks a bit queer, I thinks, but I couldn't see anything more, 'cause the duck-weed is that thick as it looks as if you could walk on it. Howsever, I clears away the weed with my stick, and then I see 'twas a dead man. Give me a rare turn, it did. He was a-layin' at the bottom of the ditch with his head near the middle and his feet up close to the bank. Just then young Harry Walker comes along the cart-track on his way to work, so I shows him the body and sends him back to the town for to give notice at the police station."

"And is that all you know about the affair?"

"Ay. Later on I see the sergeant come along with a man wheelin' the stretcher, and I showed him where the body was and helped to pull it out and load it on the stretcher. And that's all I know about it."

On this the witness was dismissed and his place taken by a shrewd-looking, business-like police sergeant, who deposed as follows:

"Last Wednesday, the 8th of May, at 6.15 a.m., I received information from Henry Walker that a dead body was lying in the ditch by the cart-track leading from Ponder's Road to Reed's farm. I proceeded there forthwith, accompanied by Police-Constable

Ketchum, and taking with us a wheeled stretcher. On the track I was met by the last witness, who conducted me to the place where the body was lying and where I found it in the position that he has described; but we had to clear away the duck-weed before we could see it distinctly. I examined the bank carefully, but could see no trace of footprints, as the grass grows thickly right down to the water's edge. There were no signs of a struggle or any disturbance on the bank. With the aid of Moffet and Ketchum, I drew the body out and placed it on the stretcher. I could not see any injuries or marks of violence on the body or anything unusual about it. I conveyed it to the mortuary, and with Constable Ketchum's assistance removed the clothing and emptied the pockets, putting the contents of each pocket in a separate envelope and writing the description on each. In a letter-case from the coat pocket were some visiting cards bearing the name and address of Mr. Cyrus Pedley, of 21 Hawtrey Mansions, Kensington, and a letter signed Wilfred Pedley, apparently from deceased's brother. Acting on instructions, I communicated with him and served a summons to attend this inquest."

"With regard to the ditch in which you found the body," said the coroner, "can you tell us how deep it is?"

"Yes; I measured it with Moffet's crook and a tape measure. In the deepest part, where the body was lying, it is four feet two inches deep. From there it slopes up pretty sharply to the bank."

"So far as you can judge, if a grown man fell into the ditch by accident, would he have any difficulty in getting out?"

"None at all, I should say, if he were sober and in ordinary health. A man of medium height, standing in the middle at the deepest part, would have his head and shoulders out of water; and the sides are not too steep to climb up easily, especially with the grass and rushes on the bank to lay hold of."

"You say there were no signs of disturbance on the bank. Were there any in the ditch itself?"

"None that I could see. But, of course, signs of disturbance soon disappear in water. The duck-weed drifts about as the wind drives it, and there are creatures moving about on the bottom. I noticed that deceased had some weed grasped in one hand."

This concluded the sergeant's evidence, and as he retired, the name of Dr. Albert Parton was called. The new witness was a young man of grave and professional aspect, who gave his evidence with an extreme regard for clearness and accuracy.

"I have made an examination of the body of the deceased," he began, after the usual preliminaries. "It is that of a healthy man of about forty-five. I first saw it about two hours after it was found. It had then been dead from twelve to fifteen hours. Later I made a complete examination. I found no injuries, marks of violence or any definite bruises, and no signs of disease."

"Did you ascertain the cause of death?" the coroner asked.

"Yes. The cause of death was drowning."

"You are quite sure of that?"

"Quite sure. The lungs contained a quantity of water and duck-weed, and there was more than a quart of water mixed with duck-weed and water-weed in the stomach. That is a clear proof of death by drowning. The water in the lungs was the immediate cause of death, by making breathing impossible, and as the water and weed in the stomach must have been swallowed, they furnish conclusive evidence that deceased was alive when he fell into the water."

"The water and weed could not have got into the stomach after death?"

"No, that is quite impossible. They must have been swallowed when the head of the deceased was just below the surface; and the water must have been drawn into the lungs by spasmodic efforts to breathe when the mouth was under water."

"Did you find any signs indicating that deceased might have been intoxicated?"

"No. I examined the water from the stomach very carefully with that question in view, but there was no trace of alcohol—or, indeed, of anything else. It was simple ditch-water. As the point is important I have preserved it, and——" here the witness produced a paper parcel which he unfastened, revealing a large glass jar containing about a quart of water plentifully sprinkled with duck-weed. This he presented to the coroner, who waved it away hastily and indicated the jury; to whom it was then offered and summarily rejected with emphatic head-shakes. Finally it came to rest on the table by the place where I was sitting with my colleague, Dr. Thorndyke, and our client, Mr. Wilfred Pedley. I glanced at it with faint interest, noting how the duck-weed plants had risen to the surface and floated, each with its tassel of roots hanging down into the water, and how a couple of tiny, flat shells, like miniature ammonites, had sunk and lay on the bottom of the jar. Thorndyke also glanced at it; indeed, he did more than glance, for he drew the jar towards him and examined its contents in the systematic way in which it was his habit to examine everything. Meanwhile the coroner asked:

"Did you find anything abnormal or unusual, or anything that could throw light on how deceased came to be in the water?"

"Nothing whatever," was the reply. "I found simply that deceased met his death by drowning."

Here, as the witness seemed to have finished his evidence, Thorndyke interposed.

"The witness states, sir, there were no definite bruises. Does he mean that there were any marks that might have been bruises?"

The coroner glanced at Dr. Parton, who replied:

"There was a faint mark on the outside of the right arm, just above the elbow, which had somewhat the appearance of a bruise, as if the deceased had been struck with a stick. But it was very indistinct. I shouldn't like to swear that it was a bruise at all."

This concluded the doctor's evidence, and when he had retired, the name of our client, Wilfred Pedley, was called. He rose, and having taken the oath and given his name and address, deposed:

"I have viewed the body of deceased. It is that of my brother, Cyrus Pedley, who is forty-three years of age. The last time I saw deceased alive was on Tuesday morning, the day before the body was found."

"Did you notice anything unusual in his manner or state of mind?"

The witness hesitated but at length replied:

"Yes. He seemed anxious and depressed. He had been in low spirits for some time past, but on this occasion he seemed more so than usual."

"Had you any reason to suspect that he might contemplate taking his life?"

"No," the witness replied, emphatically, "and I do not believe that he would, under any circumstances, have contemplated suicide."

"Have you any special reason for that belief?"

"Yes. Deceased was a highly conscientious man and he was in my debt. He had occasion to borrow two thousand pounds from me, and the debt was secured by an insurance on his life. If he had committed suicide that insurance would be invalidated and the debt would remain unpaid. From my knowledge of him, I feel certain that he would not have done such a thing."

The coroner nodded gravely, and then asked:

"What was deceased's occupation?"

"He was employed in some way by the Foreign Office, I don't know in what capacity. I know very little about his affairs."

"Do you know if he had any money worries or any troubles or embarrassments of any kind?"

"I have never heard of any; but deceased was a very reticent man. He lived alone in his flat, taking his meals at his club, and no one knew—at least, I did not—how he spent his time or what was the state of his finances. He was not married, and I am his only near relative."

"And as to deceased's habits. Was he ever addicted to taking more stimulants than was good for him?"

"Never," the witness replied emphatically. "He was a most temperate and abstemious man."

"Was he subject to fits of any kind, or fainting attacks?"

"I have never heard that he was."

"Can you account for his being in this solitary place at this time—apparently about eight o'clock at night?"

"I cannot. It is a complete mystery to me. I know of no one with whom either of us was acquainted in this district. I had never heard of the place until I got the summons to the inquest."

This was the sum of our client's evidence, and, so far, things did not look very favourable from our point of view—we were retained on the insurance question, to rebut, if possible, the suggestion of suicide. However, the coroner was a discreet man, and having regard to the obscurity of the case—and perhaps to the interests involved—summed up in favour of an open verdict; and the jury, taking a similar view, found that deceased met his death by drowning, but under what circumstances there was no evidence to show.

"Well," I said, as the court rose, "that leaves it to the insurance people to make out a case of suicide if they can. I think you are fairly safe, Mr. Pedley. There is no positive evidence."

"No," our client replied. "But it isn't only the money I am thinking of. It would be some consolation to me for the loss of my poor brother if I had some idea how he met with his death, and could feel sure that it was an unavoidable misadventure. And for my own satisfaction—leaving the insurance out of the question—I should like to have definite proof that it was not suicide."

He looked half-questioningly at Thorndyke, who nodded gravely.

"Yes," the latter agreed, "the suggestion of suicide ought to be disposed of if possible, both for legal and sentimental reasons. How far away is the mortuary?"

"A couple of minutes' walk," replied Mr. Pedley. "Did you wish to inspect the body?"

"If it is permissible," replied Thorndyke; "and then I propose to have a look at the place where the body was found."

"In that case," our client said, "I will go down to the Station Hotel and wait for you. We may as well travel up to town together, and you can then tell me if you have seen any further light on the mystery."

As soon as he was gone, Dr. Parton advanced, tying the string of the parcel which once more enclosed the jar of ditch-water.

"I heard you say, sir, that you would like to inspect the body," said he. "If you like, I will show you the way to the mortuary. The sergeant will let us in, won't you, sergeant? This gentleman is a doctor as well as a lawyer."

"Bless you, sir," said the sergeant, "I know who Dr. Thorndyke is, and I shall feel it an honour to show him anything he wishes to see."

Accordingly we set forth together, Dr. Parton and Thorndyke leading the way.

"The coroner and the jury didn't seem to appreciate my exhibit," the former remarked with a faint grin, tapping the parcel as he spoke.

"No," Thorndyke agreed; "and it is hardly reasonable to expect a layman to share our own matter-of-fact outlook. But you were quite right to produce the specimen. That ditch-water furnishes conclusive evidence on a vitally material question. Further, I would advise you to preserve that jar for the present, well covered and under lock and key."

Parton looked surprised.

"Why?" he asked. "The inquest is over and the verdict pronounced."

"Yes, but it was an open verdict, and an open verdict leaves the case in the air. The inquest has thrown no light on the question as to how Cyrus Pedley came by his death."

"There doesn't seem to me much mystery about it," said the doctor. "Here is a man found drowned in a shallow ditch which he could easily have got out of if he had fallen in by accident. He was not drunk. Apparently he was not in a fit of any kind. There are no marks of violence and no signs of a struggle, and the man is known to have been in an extremely depressed state of mind. It looks like a clear case of suicide, though I admit that the jury were quite right, in the absence of direct evidence."

"Well," said Thorndyke, "it will be my duty to contest that view if the insurance company dispute the claim on those grounds."

"I can't think what you will have to offer in answer to the suggestion of suicide," said Parton.

"Neither can I, at present," replied Thorndyke. "But the case doesn't look to me quite so simple as it does to you."

"You think it possible that an analysis of the contents of this jar may be called for?"

"That is a possibility," replied Thorndyke. "But I mean that the case is obscure, and that some further inquiry into the circumstances of this man's death is by no means unlikely."

"Then," said Parton, "I will certainly follow your advice and lock up this precious jar. But here we are at the mortuary. Is there anything in particular that you want to see?"

"I want to see all that there is to see," Thorndyke replied. "The evidence has been vague enough so far. Shall we begin with that bruise or mark that you mentioned?"

Dr. Parton advanced to the grim, shrouded figure that lay on the slate-topped table, like some solemn effigy on an altar tomb, and drew back the sheet that covered it. We all approached, stepping softly, and stood beside the table, looking down with a certain awesome curiosity at the still, waxen figure that, but a few hours since, had been a living man like ourselves. The body was that of a good-looking, middle-aged man with a refined, intelligent face—slightly disfigured by a scar on the cheek—now set in the calm, reposeful expression that one so usually finds on the faces of the drowned; with drowsy, half-closed eyes and slightly parted lips that revealed a considerable gap in the upper front teeth.

Thorndyke stood awhile looking down on the dead man with a curious questioning expression. Then his eye travelled over the body, from the placid face to the marble-like torso and the hand which, though now relaxed, still lightly grasped a tuft of waterweed. The latter Thorndyke gently disengaged from the limp hand, and, after a glance at the dark green, feathery fronds, laid it down and stooped to examine the right arm at the spot above the elbow that Parton had spoken of.

"Yes," he said, "I think I should call it a bruise, though it is very faint. As you say, it might have been produced by a blow with a stick or rod. I notice that there are some teeth missing. Presumably he wore a plate?"

"Yes," replied Parton; "a smallish gold plate with four teeth on it—at least, so his brother told me. Of course, it fell out when he was in the water, but it hasn't been found; in fact, it hasn't been looked for."

Thorndyke nodded and then turned to the sergeant.

"Could I see what you found in the pockets?" he asked.

The sergeant complied readily, and my colleague watched his orderly procedure with evident approval. The collection of envelopes was produced from an attaché-case and conveyed to a side table, where the sergeant emptied out the contents of each into a little heap, opposite which he placed the appropriate envelope with its written description. Thorndyke ran his eye over the collection—which was commonplace enough—until he came to the tobacco pouch, from which protruded the corner of a scrap of crumpled paper. This he drew forth and smoothed out the creases, when it was seen to be a railway receipt for an excess fare.

"Seems to have lost his ticket or travelled without one," the sergeant remarked. "But not on this line."

"No," agreed Thorndyke. "It is the Tilbury and Southend line. But you notice the date. It is the 18th; and the body was found on the morning of Wednesday, the 19th. So it would appear that he must have come into this neighbourhood in the evening; and that he must have come either by way of London or by a very complicated cross-country route. I wonder what brought him here."

He produced his notebook and was beginning to copy the receipt when the sergeant said:

"You had better take the paper, sir. It is of no use to us now, and it isn't very easy to make out."

Thorndyke thanked the officer, and, handing me the paper, asked:

"What do you make of it, Jervis?"

I scrutinised the little crumpled scrap and deciphered with difficulty the hurried scrawl, scribbled with a hard, ill-sharpened pencil.

"It seems to read Ldn to 'C.B. or S.B., Hit'—that is some 'Halt,' I presume. But the amount, 4/9, is clear enough, and that will give us a clue if we want one." I returned the paper to Thorndyke, who bestowed it in his pocket-book and then remarked:

"I don't see any keys."

"No, sir," replied the sergeant, "there aren't any. Rather queer, that, for he must have had at least a latchkey. They must have fallen out into the water."

"That is possible," said Thorndyke, "but it would be worth while to make sure. Is there anyone who could show us the place where the body was found?"

"I will walk up there with you myself, sir, with pleasure," said the sergeant, hastily repacking the envelopes. "It is only a quarter of an hour's walk from here."

"That is very good of you, sergeant," my colleague responded; "and as we seem to have seen everything here, I propose that we start at once. You are not coming with us, Parton?"

"No," the doctor replied. "I have finished with the case and I have got my work to do." He shook hands with us heartily and watched us—with some curiosity, I think—as we set forth in company with the sergeant.

His curiosity did not seem to me to be unjustified. In fact, I shared it. The presence of the police officer precluded discussion, but as we took our way out of the town I found myself speculating curiously on my colleague's proceedings. To me, suicide was written plainly on every detail of the case. Of course, we did not wish to take that view, but what other was possible? Had Thorndyke some alternative theory? Or was he merely, according to his invariable custom, making an impartial survey of everything, no matter how apparently trivial, in the hope of lighting on some new and informative fact?

The temporary absence of the sergeant, who had stopped to speak to a constable on duty, enabled me to put the question:

"Is this expedition intended to clear up anything in particular?"

"No," he replied, "excepting the keys, which ought to be found. But you must see for yourself that this is not a straightforward case. That man did not come all this way merely to drown himself in a ditch. I am quite in the dark at present, so there is nothing for it but to examine everything with our own eyes and see if there is anything that has been overlooked that may throw some light on either the motive or the circumstances. It is always desirable to examine the scene of a crime or a tragedy."

Here the return of the sergeant put a stop to the discussion and we proceeded on our way in silence. Already we had passed out of the town, and we now turned out of the main road into a lane or by-road, bordered by meadows and orchards and enclosed by rather high hedgerows.

"This is Ponder's Road," said the sergeant. "It leads to Renham, a couple of miles farther on, where it joins the Aylesbury Road. The cart track is on the left a little way along."

A few minutes later we came to our turning, a narrow and rather muddy lane, the entrance to which was shaded by a grove of tall elms. Passing through this shady avenue, we came out on a grass-covered track, broken by deep wagon-ruts and bordered on each side by a ditch, beyond which was a wide expanse of marshy meadows.

"This is the place," said the sergeant, halting by the side of the right-hand ditch and indicating a spot where the rushes had been flattened down. "It was just as you see it now, only the feet were just visible sticking out of the duck-weed, which had drifted back after Moffet had disturbed it."

We stood awhile looking at the ditch, with its thick mantle of bright green, spotted with innumerable small dark objects and showing here and there a faint track where a water-vole had swum across.

"Those little dark objects are water-snails, I suppose," said I, by way of making some kind of remark.

"Yes," replied Thorndyke; "the common Amber shell, I think—*Succinea putris.*" He reached out his stick and fished up a sample of the duck-weed, on which one or two of the snails were crawling. "Yes," he repeated. "*Succinea putris* it is; a queer little left-handed shell, with the spire, as you see, all lop-sided. They have a habit of swarming in this extraordinary way. You notice that the ditch is covered with them."

I had already observed this, but it hardly seemed to be worth commenting on under the present circumstances—which was apparently the sergeant's view also, for he looked at Thorndyke with some surprise, which developed into impatience when my colleague proceeded further to expand on the subject of natural history.

"These water-weeds," he observed, "are very remarkable plants in their various ways. Look at this duck-weed, for instance. Just a little green oval disc with a single root hanging down into the water, like a tiny umbrella with a long handle; and yet it is a complete plant, and a flowering plant, too." He picked a specimen off the end of his stick and held it up by its root to exhibit its umbrella-like form; and as he did so, he looked in my face with an expression that I felt to be somehow significant; but of which I could not extract the meaning. But there was no difficulty in interpreting the expression on the sergeant's face. He had come here on business and he wanted to "cut the cackle and get to the hosses."

"Well, sergeant," said Thorndyke, "there isn't much to see, but I think we ought to have a look for those keys. He must have had keys of some kind, if only a latchkey; and they must be in this ditch."

The sergeant was not enthusiastic. "I've no doubt you are right, sir," said he; "but I don't see that we should be much forrader if we found them. However, we may as well have a look, only I can't stay more than a few minutes. I've got my work to do at the station."

"Then," said Thorndyke, "let us get to work at once. We had better hook out the weed and look it over; and if the keys are not in that, we must try to expose the bottom where the body was lying. You must tell us if we are working in the right place."

With this he began, with the crooked handle of his stick, to rake up the tangle of weed that covered the bottom of the ditch and drag the detached masses ashore, piling them on the bank and carefully looking them through to see if the keys should chance to be entangled in their meshes. In this work I took my part under the sergeant's direction, raking in load after load of the delicate, stringy weed, on the pale green ribbon-like leaves of which multitudes of the water-snails were creeping; and sorting over each batch in hopeless and fruitless search for the missing keys. In about ten minutes we had removed the entire weedy covering from the bottom of the ditch over an area of from eight to nine feet—the place which, according to the sergeant, the body had occupied; and as the duck-weed had been caught by the tangled masses of waterweed that we had dragged ashore, we now had an uninterrupted view of the cleared space save for the clouds of mud that we had stirred up.

"We must give the mud a few minutes to settle," said Thorndyke.

"Yes," the sergeant agreed, "it will take some time; and as it doesn't really concern me now that the inquest is over, I think I will get back to the station if you will excuse me."

Thorndyke excused him very willingly, I think, though politely and with many thanks for his help. When he had gone I remarked:

"I am inclined to agree with the sergeant. If we find the keys we shan't be much forrader."

"We shall know that he had them with him," he replied. "Though, of course, if we don't find them, that will not prove that they are not here. Still, I think we should try to settle the question."

His answer left me quite unconvinced; but the care with which he searched the ditch and sorted out the weed left me in no doubt that, to him, the matter seemed to be of some importance. However, nothing came of the search. If the keys were there they were buried in the mud, and eventually we had to give up the search and make our way back towards the station.

As we passed out of the lane into Ponder's Road, Thorndyke stopped at the entrance, under the trees, by a little triangle of turf which marked the beginning of the lane, and looked down at the muddy ground.

"Here is quite an interesting thing, Jervis," he remarked, "which shows us how standardised objects tend to develop an individual character. These are the tracks of a car, or more probably a tradesman's van, which was fitted with Barlow tyres. Now there must be thousands of vans fitted with these tyres; they are the favourite type for light covered vans, and when new they are all alike and indistinguishable. Yet this tyre—of the off hind-wheel—has acquired a character which would enable one to pick it out with certainty from ten thousand others. First, you see, there is a deep cut in the tyre at an angle of forty-five, then a kidney-shaped 'Blakey' has stuck in the outer tyre without puncturing the inner; and finally some adhesive object—perhaps a lump of pitch from a newly-mended road—has become fixed on just behind the 'Blakey.' Now, if we make a rough sketch of those three marks and indicate their distance apart, thus"—here he made a rapid sketch in his notebook, and wrote in the intervals in inches—"we have the means of swearing to the identity of a vehicle which we have never seen."

"And which," I added, "had for some reason swerved over to the wrong side of the road. Yes, I should say that tyre is certainly unique. But surely most tyres are identifiable when they have been in use for some time."

"Exactly," he replied. "That was my point. The standardised thing is devoid of character only when it is new."

It was not a very subtle point, and as it was fairly obvious I made no comment, but presently reverted to the case of Pedley deceased.

"I don't quite see why you are taking all this trouble. The insurance claim is not likely to be contested. No one can prove that it was a case of suicide, though I should think no one will feel any doubt that it was, at least that is my own feeling."

Thorndyke looked at me with an expression of reproach.

"I am afraid that my learned friend has not been making very good use of his eyes," said he. "He has allowed his attention to be distracted by superficial appearances."

"You don't think that it was suicide, then?" I asked, considerably taken aback.

"It isn't a question of thinking," he replied. "It was certainly not suicide. There are the plainest indications of homicide; and, of course, in the particular circumstances, homicide means murder."

I was thunderstruck. In my own mind I had dismissed the case somewhat contemptuously as a mere commonplace suicide. As my friend had truly said, I had accepted the obvious appearances and let them mislead me, whereas Thorndyke had followed his golden rule of accepting nothing and observing everything. But what was it that he had observed? I knew that it was useless to ask, but still I ventured on a tentative question.

"When did you come to the conclusion that it was a case of homicide?"

"As soon as I had had a good look at the place where the body was found," he replied promptly.

This did not help me much, for I had given very little attention to anything but the search for the keys. The absence of those keys was, of course, a suspicious fact, if it was a fact. But we had not proved their absence; we had only failed to find them.

"What do you propose to do next?" I asked.

"Evidently," he answered, "there are two things to be done. One is to test the murder theory—to look for more evidence for or against it; the other is to identify the murderer, if possible. But really the two problems are one, since they involve the questions, Who had a motive for killing Cyrus Pedley? and Who had the opportunity and the means?"

Our discussion brought us to the station, where, outside the hotel, we found Mr. Pedley waiting for us.

"I am glad you have come," said he. "I was beginning to fear that we should lose this train. I suppose there is no new light on this mysterious affair?"

"No," Thorndyke replied. "Rather there is a new problem. No keys were found in your brother's pockets, and we have failed to find them in the ditch; though, of course, they may be there."

"They must be," said Pedley. "They must have fallen out of his pocket and got buried in the mud, unless he lost them previously, which is most unlikely. It is a pity, though. We shall have to break open his cabinets and drawers, which he would have hated. He was very fastidious about his furniture."

"You will have to break into his flat, too," said I.

"No," he replied, "I shan't have to do that. I have a duplicate of his latchkey. He had a spare bedroom which he let me use if I wanted to stay in town." As he spoke, he produced his key-bunch and exhibited a small Chubb latchkey. "I wish we had the others, though," he added.

Here the up-train was heard approaching and we hurried on to the platform, selecting an empty first-class compartment as it drew up. As soon as the train had started, Thorndyke began his inquiries, to which I listened attentively.

"You said that your brother had been anxious and depressed lately. Was there anything more than this? Any nervousness or foreboding?"

"Well, yes," replied Pedley. "Looking back, I seem to see that the possibility of death was in his mind. A week or two ago he brought his will to me to see if it was quite satisfactory to me as the principal beneficiary; and he handed to me his last receipt for the insurance premium. That looks a little suggestive."

"It does," Thorndyke agreed. "And as to his occupation and his associates, what do you know about them?"

"His private friends are mostly my own, but of his official associates I know nothing. He was connected with the Foreign Office; but in what capacity I don't know at all. He was extremely reticent on the subject. I only know that he travelled about a good deal, presumably on official business."

This was not very illuminating, but it was all our client had to tell; and the conversation languished somewhat until the train drew up at Marylebone, when Thorndyke said, as if by an after-thought:

"You have your brother's latchkey. How would it be if we just took a glance at the flat? Have you time now?"

"I will make time," was the reply, "if you want to see the flat. I don't see what you could learn from inspecting it; but that is your affair. I am in your hands."

"I should like to look round the rooms," Thorndyke answered; and as our client assented, we approached a taxi-cab and entered while Pedley gave the driver the necessary directions. A quarter of an hour later we drew up opposite a tall block of buildings, and Mr. Pedley, having paid off the cab, led the way to the lift.

The dead man's flat was on the third floor, and, like the others, was distinguished only by the number on the door. Mr. Pedley inserted the key into the latch, and having opened the door, preceded us across the small lobby into the sitting-room.

"Ha!" he exclaimed, as he entered, "this solves your problem." As he spoke, he pointed to the table, on which lay a small bunch of keys, including a latchkey similar to the one that he had shown us.

"But," he continued, "it is rather extraordinary. It just shows what a very disturbed state his mind must have been in."

"Yes," Thorndyke agreed, looking critically about the room; "and as the latchkey is there, it raises the question whether the keys may have been out of his possession. Do you know what the various locked receptacles contain?"

"I know pretty well what is in the bureau; but as to the cupboard above it, I have never seen it open and don't know what he kept in it. I always assumed that he reserved it for his official papers. I will just see if anything seems to have been disturbed."

He unlocked and opened the flap of the old-fashioned bureau and pulled out the small drawers one after the other, examining the contents of each. Then he opened each of the larger drawers and turned over the various articles in them. As he closed the last one, he reported: "Everything seems to be in order—cheque-book, insurance policy, a few share certificates, and so on. Nothing seems to have been touched. Now we will try the cupboard, though I don't suppose its contents would be of much interest to anyone but himself. I wonder which is the key."

He looked at the keyhole and made a selection from the bunch, but it was evidently the wrong key. He tried another and yet another with a like result, until he had exhausted the resources of the bunch.

"It is very remarkable," he said. "None of these keys seems to fit. I wonder if he kept this particular key locked up or hidden. It wasn't in the bureau. Will you try what you can do?"

He handed the bunch to Thorndyke, who tried all the keys in succession with the same result. None of them was the key belonging to the lock. At length, having tried them all, he inserted one and turned it as far as it would go. Then he gave a sharp pull; and immediately the door came open.

"Why, it was unlocked after all!" exclaimed Mr. Pedley. "And there is nothing in it. That is why there was no key on the bunch. Apparently he didn't use the cupboard."

Thorndyke looked critically at the single vacant shelf, drawing his finger along it in two places and inspecting his finger-tips. Then he turned his attention to the lock, which was of the kind that is screwed on the inside of the door, leaving the bolt partly exposed. He took the bolt in his fingers and pushed it out and then in again; and by the way it moved I could see that the spring was broken. On this he made no comment, but remarked:

"The cupboard has been in use pretty lately. You can see the trace of a largish volume—possibly a boxfile—on the shelf. There is hardly any dust there, whereas the rest of the shelf is fairly thickly coated. However, that does not carry us very far; and the appearance of the rooms is otherwise quite normal."

"Quite," agreed Pedley. "But why shouldn't it be? You didn't suspect——"

"I was merely testing the suggestion offered by the absence of the keys," said Thorndyke. "By the way, have you communicated with the Foreign Office?"

"No," was the reply, "but I suppose I ought to. What had I better say to them?"

"I should merely state the facts in the first instance. But you can, if you like, say that I definitely reject the idea of suicide."

"I am glad to hear you say that," said Pedley. "Can I give any reasons for your opinion?"

"Not in the first place," replied Thorndyke. "I will consider the case and let you have a reasoned report in a day or two, which you can show to the Foreign Office and also to the insurance company."

Mr. Pedley looked as if he would have liked to ask some further questions, but as Thorndyke now made his way to the door, he followed in silence, pocketing the keys as we went out. He accompanied us down to the entry and there we left him, setting forth in the direction of South Kensington Station.

"It looked to me," said I, as soon as we were out of ear-shot, "as if that lock had been forced. What do you think?"

"Well," he answered, "locks get broken in ordinary use, but taking all the facts together, I think you are right. There are too many coincidences for reasonable probability. First, this man leaves his keys, including his latchkey, on the table, which is an extraordinary thing to do. On that very occasion, he is found dead under inexplicable circumstances. Then, of all the locks in his rooms, the one which happens to be broken is the one of which the key is not on the bunch. That is a very suspicious group of facts."

"It is," I agreed. "And if there is, as you say—though I can't imagine on what grounds—evidence of foul play, that makes it still more suspicious. But what is the next move? Have you anything in view?"

"The next move," he replied, "is to clear up the mystery of the dead man's movements on the day of his death. The railway receipt shows that on that day he travelled down somewhere into Essex. From that place, he took a long, cross-country journey of which the destination was a ditch by a lonely meadow in Buckinghamshire. The questions that we have to answer are, What was he doing in Essex? Why did he make that strange journey? Did he make it alone? and, if not, Who accompanied him?

"Now, obviously, the first thing to do is to locate that place in Essex; and when we have done that, to go down there and see if we can pick up any traces of the dead man."

"That sounds like a pretty vague quest," said I; "but if we fail, the police may be able to find out something. By the way, we want a new *Bradshaw*."

"An excellent suggestion, Jervis," said he. "I will get one as we go into the station."

A few minutes later, as we sat on a bench waiting for our train, he passed to me the open copy of *Bradshaw*, with the crumpled railway receipt.

"You see," said he, "it was apparently 'G.B.Hlt.,' and the fare from London was four and ninepence. Here is Great Buntingfield Halt, the fare to which is four and ninepence. That must be the place. At any rate, we will give it a trial. May I take it that you are coming to lend a hand? I shall start in good time tomorrow morning."

I assented emphatically. Never had I been more completely in the dark than I was in this case, and seldom had I known Thorndyke to be more positive and confident. Obviously, he had something up his sleeve; and I was racked with curiosity as to what that something was.

On the following morning we made a fairly early start, and half-past ten found us seated in the train, looking out across a dreary waste of marshes, with the estuary of the Thames a mile or so distant. For the first time in my recollection Thorndyke had come unprovided with his inevitable "research case," but I noted that he had furnished himself with a botanist's vasculum—or tin collecting-case—and that his pocket bulged as if he had some other appliances concealed about his person. Also that he carried a walking-stick that was strange to me.

"This will be our destination, I think," he said, as the train slowed down; and sure enough it presently came to rest beside a little makeshift platform on which was displayed the name "Great Buntingfield Halt." We were the only passengers to alight, and the guard, having noted the fact, blew his whistle and dismissed the little station with a contemptuous wave of his flag.

Thorndyke lingered on the platform after the train had gone, taking a general survey of the country. Half a mile away to the north a small village was visible; while to the south the marshes stretched away to the river, their bare expanse unbroken save by a solitary building whose unredeemed hideousness proclaimed it a factory of some kind. Presently the station-master approached deferentially, and as we proffered our tickets, Thorndyke remarked:

"You don't seem overburdened with traffic here."

"No, sir. You're right," was the emphatic reply. "'Tis a dead-alive place. Excepting the people at the Golomite Works and one now and then from the village, no one uses the halt. You're the first strangers I've seen for more than a month."

"Indeed," said Thorndyke. "But I think you are forgetting one. An acquaintance of mine came here last Tuesday—and by the same token, he hadn't got a ticket and had to pay his fare."

"Oh, I remember," the station-master replied. "You mean a gentleman with a scar on his cheek. But I don't count him as a stranger. He has been here before; I think he is connected with the works, as he always goes up their road."

"Do you happen to remember what time he came back?" Thorndyke asked.

"He didn't come back at all," was the reply. "I am sure of that, because I work the halt and level crossing by myself. I remember thinking it queer that he didn't come back, because the ticket that he had lost was a return. He must have gone back in the van belonging to the works—that one that you see coming towards the crossing."

As he spoke, he pointed to a van that was approaching down the factory road—a small covered van with the name "Golomite Works" painted, not on the cover, but on a board that was attached to it. The station-master walked towards the crossing to open the gates, and we followed; and when the van had passed, Thorndyke wished our friend "Good morning," and led the way along the road, looking about him with lively interest and rather with the air of one looking for something in particular.

We had covered about two-thirds of the distance to the factory when the road approached a wide ditch; and from the attention with which my friend regarded it, I suspected that this was the something for which he had been looking. It was, however, quite unapproachable, for it was bordered by a wide expanse of soft mud thickly covered with rushes and trodden deeply by cattle. Nevertheless, Thorndyke followed its margin, still looking about him keenly, until, about a couple of hundred yards from the factory, I observed a small decayed wooden staging or quay, apparently the remains of a vanished footbridge. Here Thorndyke halted, and unbuttoning his coat, began to empty out his pockets, producing first the vasculum, then a small case containing three wide-mouthed bottles—both of which he deposited on the ground—and finally a sort of miniature landing-net, which he proceeded to screw on to the ferrule of his stick.

"I take it," said I, "that these proceedings are a blind to cover some sort of observations."

"Not at all," he replied. "We are engaged in the study of pond and ditch natural history, and a most fascinating and instructive study it is. The variety of forms is endless. This ditch, you observe, like the one at Bantree, is covered with a dense growth of duck-weed: but whereas that ditch was swarming with succineæ, here there is not a single succinea to be seen."

I grunted a sulky assent, and watched suspiciously as he filled the bottles with water from the ditch and then made a preliminary sweep with his net.

"Here is a trial sample," said he, holding the loaded net towards me. "Duck-weed, horn-weed, Planorbis nautileus, but no succineæ. What do you think of it, Jervis?"

I looked distastefully at the repulsive mess, but yet with attention, for I realised that there was a meaning in his question. And then, suddenly, my attention sharpened. I picked out of the net a strand of dark green, plumy weed and examined it.

"So this is horn-weed," I said. "Then it was a piece of horn-weed that Cyrus Pedley held grasped in his hand; and now I come to think of it, I don't remember seeing any horn-weed in the ditch at Bantree."

He nodded approvingly. "There wasn't any," said he.

"And these little ammonite-like shells are just like those that I noticed at the bottom of Dr. Parton's jar. But I don't remember seeing any in the Bantree ditch."

"There were none there," said he. "And the duck-weed?"

"Oh, well," I replied, "duck-weed is duck-weed, and there's an end of it."

He chuckled aloud at my answer, and quoting:

> "A primrose by the river's brim
> A yellow primrose was to him,"

bestowed a part of the catch in the vasculum, then turned once more to the ditch and began to ply his net vigorously, emptying out each netful on the grass, looking it over quickly and then making a fresh sweep, dragging the net each time through the mud at the bottom. I watched him now with a new and very lively interest; for enlightenment was dawning, mingled with some self-contempt and much speculation as to how Thorndyke had got his start in this case.

But I was not the only interested watcher. At one of the windows of the factory I presently observed a man who seemed to be looking our way. After a few seconds' inspection he disappeared, to reappear almost immediately with a pair of field-glasses, through which he took a long look at us. Then he disappeared again, but in less than a minute I saw him emerge from a side door and advance hurriedly towards us.

"We are going to have a notice of ejectment served on us, I fancy," said I.

Thorndyke glanced quickly at the approaching stranger but continued to ply his net, working, as I noticed, methodically from left to right. When the man came within fifty yards he hailed us with a brusque inquiry as to what our business was. I went forward to meet him and, if possible, to detain him in conversation; but this plan failed, for he ignored me and bore straight down on Thorndyke.

"Now, then," said he, "what's the game? What are you doing here?"

Thorndyke was in the act of raising his net from the water, but he now suddenly let it fall to the bottom of the ditch while he turned to confront the stranger.

"I take it that you have some reason for asking," said he.

"Yes, I have," the other replied angrily and with a slight foreign accent that agreed with his appearance—he looked like a Slav of some sort. "This is private land. It belongs to the factory. I am the manager."

"The land is not enclosed," Thorndyke remarked.

"I tell you the land is private land," the fellow retorted excitedly. "You have no business here. I want to know what you are doing."

"My good sir," said Thorndyke, "there is no need to excite yourself. My friend and I are just collecting botanical and other specimens."

"How do I know that?" the manager demanded. He looked round suspiciously and his eye lighted on the vasculum. "What have you got in that thing?" he asked.

"Let him see what is in it," said Thorndyke, with a significant look at me.

Interpreting this as an instruction to occupy the man's attention for a few moments, I picked up the vasculum and placed myself so that he must turn his back to Thorndyke to look into it. I fumbled awhile with the catch, but at length opened the case and began to pick out the weed strand by strand. As soon as the stranger's back was turned Thorndyke raised his net and quickly picked out of it something which he slipped into his pocket. Then he advanced towards us, sorting out the contents of his net as he came.

"Well," he said, "you see we are just harmless naturalists. By the way, what did you think we were looking for?"

"Never mind what I thought," the other replied fiercely. "This is private land. You have no business here, and you have got to clear out."

"Very well," said Thorndyke. "As you please. There are plenty of other ditches." He took the vasculum and the case of bottles, and having put them in his pocket, unscrewed his net, wished the stranger "Good-morning," and turned back towards the station. The man stood watching us until we were near the level crossing, when he, too, turned back and retired to the factory.

"I saw you take something out of the net," said I. "What was it?"

He glanced back to make sure that the manager was out of sight. Then he put his hand in his pocket, drew it out closed, and suddenly opened it. In his palm lay a small gold dental plate with four teeth on it.

"My word!" I exclaimed; "this clenches the matter with a vengeance. That is certainly Cyrus Pedley's plate. It corresponds exactly to the description."

"Yes," he replied, "it is practically a certainty. Of course, it will have to be identified by the dentist who made it. But it is a foregone conclusion."

I reflected as we walked towards the station on the singular sureness with which Thorndyke had followed what was to me an invisible trail. Presently I said:

"What is puzzling me is how you got your start in this case. What gave you the first hint that it was homicide and not suicide or misadventure?"

"It was the old story, Jervis," he replied; "just a matter of observing and remembering apparently trivial details. Here, by the way, is a case in point."

He stopped and looked down at a set of tracks in the soft, earth road—apparently those of the van which we had seen cross the line. I followed the direction of his glance and saw the clear impression of a Blakey's protector, preceded by that of a gash in the tyre and followed by that of a projecting lump.

"But this is astounding!" I exclaimed. "It is almost certainly the same track that we saw in Ponder's Road."

"Yes," he agreed. "I noticed it as we came along." He brought out his spring-tape and notebook, and handing the latter to me, stooped and measured the distances between the three impressions. I wrote them down as he called them out, and then we compared them with the note made in Ponder's Road. The measurements were identical, as were the relative positions of the impressions.

"This is an important piece of evidence," said he. "I wish we were able to take casts, but the notes will be pretty conclusive. And now," he continued as we resumed our progress towards the station, "to return to your question. Parton's evidence at the inquest proved that Cyrus Pedley was drowned in water which contained duck-weed. He produced a specimen and we both saw it. We saw the duck-weed in it and also two Planorbis shells. The presence of those two shells proved that the water in which he was drowned must have swarmed with them. We saw the body, and observed that one hand grasped a wisp of horn-weed. Then we went to view the ditch and we examined it. That was when I got, not a mere hint, but a crucial and conclusive fact. The ditch was covered with duck-weed, as we expected. *But it was the wrong duck-weed.*"

"The wrong duck-weed!" I exclaimed. "Why, how many kinds of duck-weed are there?"

"There are four British species," he replied. "The Greater Duck-weed, the Lesser Duck-weed, the Thick Duck-weed, and the Ivy-leaved Duck-weed. Now the specimens in Parton's jar I noticed were the Greater Duck-weed, which is easily distinguished by its roots, which are multiple and form a sort of tassel. But the duck-weed on the Bantree ditch was the Lesser Duck-weed, which is smaller than the other, but is especially distinguished by having only a single root. It is impossible to mistake one for the other.

"Here, then, was practically conclusive evidence of murder. Cyrus Pedley had been drowned in a pond or ditch. But not in the ditch in which his body was found. Therefore his dead body had been conveyed from some other place and put into this ditch. Such a proceeding furnishes *prima facie* evidence of murder. But as soon as the question was raised, there was an abundance of confirmatory evidence. There was no horn-weed or Planorbis shells in the ditch, but there were swarms of succineæ, some of which would inevitably have been swallowed with the water. There was an obscure linear pressure mark on the arm of the dead man, just above the elbow: such a mark as might be made by a cord if a man were pinioned to render him helpless. Then the body would have had to be conveyed to this place in some kind of vehicle; and we found the traces of what appeared to be a motor-van, which had approached the cart-track on the wrong side of the road, as if to pull up there. It was a very conclusive mass of evidence; but it would have been useless but for the extraordinarily lucky chance that poor Pedley had lost his railway ticket and preserved the receipt; by which we were able to ascertain where he was on the day of his death and in what local-ity the murder was probably committed. But that is not the only way in which Fortune has favoured us. The station-master's infor-mation was, and will be, invaluable. Then it was most fortunate for us that there was only one ditch on the factory land; and that that ditch was accessible at only one point, which must have been the place where Pedley was drowned."

"The duck-weed in this ditch is, of course, the Greater Duck-weed?"

"Yes. I have taken some specimens as well as the horn-weed and shells."

He opened the vasculum and picked out one of the tiny plants, exhibiting the characteristic tassel of roots.

"I shall write to Parton and tell him to preserve the jar and the horn-weed if it has not been thrown away. But the duck-weed alone, produced in evidence, would be proof enough that Pedley was not drowned in the Bantree ditch; and the dental plate will show where he was drowned."

"Are you going to pursue the case any farther?" I asked.

"No," he replied. "I shall call at Scotland Yard on my way home and report what I have learned and what I can prove in court.

Then I shall have finished with the case. The rest is for the police, and I imagine they won't have much difficulty. The circumstances seem to tell their own story. Pedley was employed by the Foreign Office, probably on some kind of secret service. I imagine that he discovered the existence of a gang of evil-doers—probably foreign revolutionaries, of whom we may assume that our friend the manager of the factory is one; that he contrived to associate himself with them and to visit the factory occasionally to ascertain what was made there besides Golomite—if Golomite is not itself an illicit product. Then I assume that he was discovered to be a spy, that he was lured down here; that he was pinioned and drowned some time on Tuesday night and his body put into the van and conveyed to a place miles away from the scene of his death, where it was deposited in a ditch apparently identical in character with that in which he was drowned. It was an extremely ingenious and well-thought-out plan. It seemed to have provided for every kind of inquiry, and it very narrowly missed being successful."

"Yes," I agreed. "But it didn't provide for Dr. John Thorndyke."

"It didn't provide for a searching examination of all the details," he replied; "and no criminal plan that I have ever met has done so. The completeness of the scheme is limited by the knowledge of the schemers, and, in practice, there is always something overlooked. In this case, the criminals were unlearned in the natural history of ditches."

Thorndyke's theory of the crime turned out to be substantially correct. The Golomite Works proved to be a factory where high explosives were made by a gang of cosmopolitan revolutionaries who were all known to the police. But the work of the latter was simplified by a detailed report which the dead man had deposited at his bank and which was discovered in time to enable the police to raid the factory and secure the whole gang. When once they were under lock and key, further information was forthcoming; for a charge of murder against them jointly soon produced King's Evidence sufficient to procure a conviction of the three actual perpetrators of the murder.

A PROPER MYSTERY

Margery Allingham

Margery Allingham (1904–1966) was the daughter of two writers. Her mother wrote short fiction for women's magazines, while her father edited the *Christian Globe*, and also ran the *London Journal,* before abandoning journalism to become a freelance writer of magazine fiction. Allingham's first novel, *Blackerchief Dick*, was written and published while she was still in her teens. In her mid-twenties, she created her most famous character, Albert Campion, who made his first appearance in *The Crime at Black Dudley* (1929).

Allingham's most famous novel, *The Tiger in the Smoke* (1952), makes excellent use of its setting in London, but she lived in and loved the Essex countryside, and was equally adept when it came to writing rural mysteries. Her non-fiction book *The Oaken Heart* (1941) is a notable account of life in the countryside during wartime. "A Proper Mystery" was first published just a year later. It originally appeared in *The Lights of Essex* magazine in May 1942, and was republished in the *Essex Countryside* magazine in October 1986.

*   *   *   *   *

'Har, that's a highly remarkable thing, no mistake about it, yes, yes', said Lefty, quacking away in his high flat voice like a whole pond full of ducks. (Lefty Bowers that was, not Lefty

Sheldrake, who married Mrs Wild's daughter. He was mouthy, but no harm in him.)

'Highly re-markable', agreed old Harry, putting his whole face in his mug again. No one really heard him, and anyway the observation was just an affirmative noise. He was a kind of an echo. Sitting there at the corner of the table under the picture of the trotting horse, his blue serge cap with the button on the point where all the seams fell flat on his bald head, he looked so familiar he might have been part of the Dog's tap furniture.

'A mystery', bellowed Lefty meaningly, and looking at Mr Light who had long been in there and was standing wonderfully quiet as well he might.

'I don't think much to 'ut, I don't', said old Bill Fish from his corner, and everybody looked at him sharply. As every Essex man knows, the phrase is a very strong one. People 'don't think much to a thing' when their feelings are pretty near to explosion point, and no one wanted anything seriously unpleasant to happen now that the damage had been done. After all, there was no point in anyone getting wholly riled when the Flower Show was over a fortnight ago, and the judging of the plots in the Garden Field a thing of the past. No peccatory on earth would bring back those succulent lettuces, no hollering in creation restore those trodden onions, no back talk in a year return the ruined splendour of those feathery carrots and sizable marrows.

The disaster itself was not complicated. Rather, it was one of those occurrences which possess all the simple awfulness of Greek Tragedy.

Briefly, Mr Light, acting against all advice, as was his nature (but also his undeniable right in a free England), had put his young beasts into the Narrow Meadow on Midsummer Eve. It was his own meadow, and he had satisfied himself that the hedge which divided it from the Garden Field was sound. However, just as everybody had predicted, when the moon was full and the air was fresh off the sea, the animals had got out, and by morning all the little plots which had been awaiting the Show judges were despoiled, wasted, as though a cloud of heavy-footed locusts had passed that way. The destruction on this occasion was ruthless and final, and fourteen out of the twenty keen competitors in the most important contest of the year had been eliminated in one gigantic bovine holiday. It was a catastrophe. That was about the size of it.

All the prime favourites were down at one stroke, and Bill Fish, the best gardener and carrot king not only of the village but of the county (and, in that case, who knew, but possibly of the world?), had fallen with the rest.

After a blow like that the whole Flower Show had lost interest; the fire had gone out of it. The Major had taken The Herbaceous, as usual. Miss McTavish had swept off the Table Decorations, Buttonhole and Posy in her normal form, and what excitement there was lay in the Bottled Fruit exhibits and the scandal of the same old jar of cherries getting the first prize yet again. The all-important Cottage Plot entry was scarcely worth discussing. There was nothing of any real standard left to go in. Pitcher Cater, of all people, got the first, and they had to give Willie Brooke the second for his little mound behind his hen'us, while the third prize was just not given at all. It was a disgrace, that was all, just an ordinary disgrace.

Not only that either, but the destruction of the garden plots was so complete that the Basket of Mixed Vegetables class was a mockery too. Old Harry got away with the first prize there, simply because of his two great cucumbers. They were the only things he could get to grow really well, for he had a single great frame covering pretty well the same area as the shack in which he lived. For the rest, he had but a spadeful of garden, although what there was of it was good enough soil, it being on the verge which bordered the precious field itself. No one begrudged the poor old chap his little triumph. In a way it was almost a fair thing, because in the ordinary way he could only be certain of winning the cucumber prize, which was a mere one and six, whereas the mixed vegetables brought in ten bob, if one pulled it off. Still, taken by and large, and allowing for small mercies, it was a regular maddening thing to have happened, and Mr Light was unpopular, and aware of it.

In the pause which followed Bill Fish's strong words, Grecian, the shoemaker came in, and smelling the subject under discussion (which was not difficult, since none other had come up in the 'Dog and Duck' for the past three weeks), he went off like a little old alarm clock, as one would expect of him.

'I said it, I said it, I said it! I always hev said it. It were always so. Always. Always. In my father's time, in my eldest brother's time, when I were a little old boy. Whenever beasts were put in the Narrow Meadow on Midsummer's Eve they got out into the Garden Field. I told you. I give you the warning'. Nothing on earth would keep him quiet. He was fairly dancing, glistening with excitement and ancient. 'Always!, always!' he repeated with apparent delight. 'Never was a time when that didn't happen. Beasts get out of the Narrow Meadow on Midsummer's Eve. I told you. I told you in time. You can't say I didn't'.

Mr Light is a quick-tempered man. Not bad tempered, you understand, but hot and quick to fly: so there was a quiet time while everybody stood awaiting. Mr Light grew wonderfully rosy. Presently he opened his mouth, and several words which no one expected to hear under a roof came out of his mouth.

'Now, now. Har, Mr Light, I'm took aback!' said Miss Evelina, the hostess, in her closing-time voice, and there was silence until she'd retired to the passage where she was technically out of ear-shot. Grecian (who got his name from a mule he'd had a lot to do with in the Army, and who, in turn, had got its name from a race horse called Grecian Hero, which it did not resemble) took the temporary quiet for a victory, which was rather the sort of mistake he did make at times. Deathly, as you might say.

'Always hes!' he repeated. 'Always hes. I said so, and no one but an ignorant person would have gone against it'.

Mr Light never spoke much, but he did now.

'I see you', he said, breathing very hard and saying each word as if he was seeking after it and finding it only just in time to save his meaning from bursting from his head in gas. 'I see you, Grecian, in a kind of haze!'

Well, it was a terrible thing to see two men getting on in life a-rolling on the floor hammering at one another as if they were little old boys. Miss Evelina shrieked like a train. Bill Fish was wiped clean off his chair, which made him more spiteful than ever, and lay leaning against the walls, laughing as if they were gates creaking in the wind. Pitchy was doubled up with the stitch and looked as if he were to come in half. Old Harry was protected by the angle of the table in the corner, poor old chap. He stayed where he was, looking right terrified. The policeman was in the big clubroom across the passage, and when he heard Miss Evelina shrieking he came in at once and pulled the two apart.

He was a wonderfully sensible kind of man for a policeman, but he was born in the county and had been in the village nearly three years. His uniform produced silence, as the Law does. All the same the whole thing was remarkably funny, and some of the young ones guggled in their throats. Old Grecian was sitting on the floor looking completely staggered, regular astounded, same as if one of those bombs had hit him, while Mr Light, properly ashamed of himself, but not going to admit it, not if he died, began to say things he had not ought before anybody, let alone the policeman. Everyone took it very nicely of the policeman. He didn't get flustered or take out his book or do anything awkward. He just waited until Mr Light gave up, exhausted, and then he said very quietly and with dignity:

'You're not quite the thing are you, Mr Light?'

That did it, you know. People were crying with laughter already. Pitchy just shook till the tears ran down his face and then began to heave with his weak stomach and had to be hurried outside. After that, which was the final straw, the only sound in the taproom was a sort of sobbing. Everyone writhed in ecstasy, except old Harry, who looked really terrified, poor old chap, and, of course, the three in the centre.

'That'll do', said the policeman, when he reckoned they'd had their laugh. 'What about is all this here exactly?' Of course, he knew as well as any body, having had a plot in the Garden Field trodden down himself. So the question was largely rhetorical, but it gave him a chance to say something he'd evidently been thinking about for a long time.

'There's a bit of a mystery here', he said. 'Some people might say a considerable mystery. I've been a-looking at that hedge of yours, Mr Light, and in my opinion as a gardener and not as a policeman, for I can't commit myself in my official capacity understand, I have an idea that one of they little old quick bushes in it has been took up and put back at some time not so long ago. Very likely at night'.

This was a pretty staggering statement even for a policeman in the capacity of a gardener, and it electrified the whole room. As you might say if you were Essex born: 'That lit it up'. Men looked at each another and understood. The mystery was not a magical one any more.

Immediately there was a tremendous quacking. You could hear it as far as the school. Bill Fish just got up and rushed away on his bicycle without a word. He was going to look and see. It was so simple when you had it given out to you. It doesn't take long to drive a few head of cattle through a gap, does it?

Grecian forgot his injuries in his excitement.

'At's it!' he said, scrambling to his feet. 'At's it! At's it! Now you've hit it. There's someone done 'at deliberate. At's it! And I'll tell you something else. It's not the first time. Little old bushes always were a-dying along that hedge. If you take 'em up they do die after. Seen it scores of times. In my father's time, in my brother's time. Always hev seen it'. He shut off then, because Mr Light and the policeman (as well as most other people in the room) were looking at him sort of earnest and peculiar, and it was as though they had become kind of allies, if you follow me.

'Highly re-markable!' said Lefty again, but he said it soft this time, and wonderingly.

'Now', said the policeman, putting in a warning, 'we don't none of us want to run away with any silly ideas, because there's no proof of nothing. If there hadda been I should have found it in these last few weeks while I've been investigating, but sometimes a man will do a wonderfully silly thing to make hisself look right, even when it's a blessed silly tale of Midsummer's Eve being special or magical or something that he's been letting off his mouth about. This ain't no official opinion – consider I'm astanding here without my uniform – but I do say, as a gardener, that it would be a very sensible thing if some people didn't say so much and talk so loud that they hev to spite all their neighbour's hard work for a twelve month to get theirselves believed. Nobody', he added with sudden heat, 'nobody but a particular old fule would do it either. It's rep-rehensible, there's no other word for it – and I don't mind using it in uniform or out – it's rep-rehensible'.

Grecian began to talk nineteen to the dozen, but it was as though nobody had heard him. He cursed. He swore. He kicked the table, splashing old Harry's beer. He protested. He made a regular exhibition of himself, but nobody sort of even saw him. He said he'd go to Maldon and see somebody Big. He said he'd go to Chelmsford, but nobody so much as even looked at him or the place whereon he stood.

By and by, people began to go to work. Mr Light and the policeman went off together talking about Foot and Mouth as happy and friendly as if not a word out of place had been spoken in each other's hearing. Grecian tried everyone, even Lefty, but he wasn't in the right kind of mood for chatting, he said. He said he'd do that on Midsummer's Eve, he reckoned. Presently Grecian himself had to go, and he went down the road to his little old shop very nearly crying. He's called Midsummer Grecian to this very day, and always will be.

No one was left but poor old Harry, who had been saving a little drop in the bottom of his mug to drink in quiet, as he always did. He took it at last, and sighed at the pleasure it gave him, then wiped his mouth and stood up, looking like a very thin old leathery terrier dog stretching his stomach.

Presently, when he was sure he was alone and Miss Evelina was out at the back, he took a very crumpled blue first prize ticket out of his inside pocket and looked at it. When he put it back he allowed a wicked smile to creep over his face. Sly, it was, and you would not have thought it could come out of him if you had not known his grandfather and his great grandfather before that. Regularly evil, old Harry's smile was.

'Har', he said, with deep satisfaction. 'Highly remarkable'. And he went off laughing to himself all the way back to the field where he was working.

When Miss Evelina came in later she saw he had not paid her for his pint again, but she was a good old girl, and he was a poor little old chap, so she put it on the slate and wiped it off again. 'There's not much for them when they're that age', she said to her sister, who protested. 'What's he got to live for, save those old cowcumbers he grows? And besides, he had a bit of a shock this morning, those two carrying on so disgraceful'.

DIRECT EVIDENCE

ANTHONY BERKELEY

Anthony Berkeley was one of the pseudonyms used by Anthony Berkeley Cox (1893–1971), founder of the legendary Detection Club, and one of the most gifted authors of Golden Age detective fiction. He was an enigmatic man who shunned personal publicity, and whose abrupt abandonment of crime writing, shortly after the outbreak of the Second World War, left the genre poorer.

Berkeley was fascinated by the idea that a mystery puzzle might have a variety of possible solutions, and he also loved to keep tinkering with plot ideas. After his death, two intriguing typescripts of short stories were found among his papers. "Double Bluff" and "Direct Evidence" were in essence the same story, but told differently, and with different outcomes. The former story is to be found in *The Avenging Chance,* a collection edited by Tony Medawar and Arthur Robinson for the American press Crippen & Landru. Until now, "Direct Evidence" has only appeared in *The Roger Sheringham Case-Book*, compiled by Ayresome Johns (a pseudonym for the rare book dealer George Locke), a collector's item of which only ninety-five copies were printed.

*　*　*　*　*

"A GRAIN of circumstantial evidence," said Roger Sheringham oracularly, "is worth a ton of direct evidence, almost every time. Almost every time, Alec," he repeated with emphasis.

Alec Grierson's eyes, which had wandered to the open book on his knee, jerked themselves back, with an evident effort, to the face of his host. "A ton," he repeated dutifully. "Is it really?"

"Well, say a couple of pounds," Roger amended, with the air of one making a concession. "It's the fashion, of course, to sneer at circumstantial evidence – the fashion, that is, among counsel for the defence and detective novelists. It makes their jobs so much easier. The only evidence really worth having, they say, is direct evidence. A saw B putting C's pearls in his trouser-pocket. Then we know where we are."

"Seems reasonable," agreed his audience, with a wistful glance at his book.

"It seems, yes," Roger pursued with energy. He was shaping out the lines of an article for the *Daily Courier* and clarifying his ideas by putting them into words, but his audience did not know that. "But how does theory tally with practice? As usual, the human factor has been overlooked. And when it comes to the human factor – well, how many women positively identified Adolf Beck as the man who had defrauded them?"

"Haven't the foggiest," said Alec. "How many?"

"That's beside the point," quickly returned Roger, who had no idea either. "What matters is that they were all wrong. How many other wrongful identifications could one remember, just on the spur of the moment? Hundreds. But circumstantial evidence eliminates the human factor. Circumstantial evidence is the only evidence by which a case can really be *proved*, logically and irrefutably. If the circumstantial evidence is strong enough – "He broke off, at a gentle knock on the door. "Come in," he said, not without irritation.

His man hovered correctly in the doorway. "There is a young lady inquiring for you, sir. She did not wish to give her name. Will you see her?" He expressed in some subtle way, by the tones of his voice and the lines of his shoulders, his opinion that the young lady might, on the whole, be seen.

"Show her in here, Barker," Roger replied.

Alec rose. "Shall I clear out?" he asked, with a gratuitously offensive grin.

"Don't be obvious, Alec. But if in a few minutes you have a feeling that you may be a little *de trop*, well … Though I can't imagine who it can be," he added, less humorously. "Refused to give her name, too." He crossed to the window and glanced out. "Alec, this sounds rather pleasingly mysterious. I wonder –"

His speculation was cut short by the appearance of the young lady in question. He looked at her with interest as she walked quickly past Barker into the room. She was wearing a blue knitted suit, with a small blue leather hat and brogue shoes, and her tall, lithe figure gave an impression of youthful health and energy. She was not so much pretty as good-looking, with very dark hair and a firm mouth, the lips of which were as red as nature had made them and no more so. "Mr Sheringham?" she asked tentatively, but with no trace of diffidence in her manner.

Roger stepped forward. "Good afternoon. Did you have a good run up from Dorset?"

The girl stared at him. "How did you know I had come up from Dorset?"

"I was doing the Sherlock Holmes stuff," Roger explained, not without pride. "I'll do some more of it if you like. You run a

Morris Oxford saloon; your hobby is tennis; and you live within easy reach of the sea. How's that?"

The girl's astonishment was all that Roger could have desired, and even Alec look surprised. "But I've never seen you before in my life," she exclaimed. "How on earth do you know all this?"

"Sherlock Holmes never liked explaining," Roger said regretfully. "I can feel with him. I recognised you, Miss Meadows. I watched you win the final of the Ladies' Singles in the Torquay tournament last July. I was with the Andersons, who told me all about you. And I saw your car in the street outside. That's all. I'm sorry."

But the girl did not return his smile. "You know the Andersons? Oh, well, that's some sort of an introduction then. Or an excuse, shall we say? Because of course you'll have realised why I'm here."

Roger looked a trifle nonplussed. "That," he admitted, "has so far escaped me."

"Why, because of Jimmy," cried the girl.

A great light broke on Roger. "Good heavens! You're James Meadows' sister?"

"Yes. Mr Sheringham, you will help me, won't you? It's awful cheek of me to ask you of course, but I know what you did in that Wychford business and I feel you're the only person who can find out the truth. You see, I know James didn't do it. He couldn't. It's out of the question. So I've come up to ask you to – to look into it on our behalf."

For so self-possessed a young woman, the girl was clearly on the verge of collapse. Roger pushed a chair forward and spoke in deliberately light tones as she sank gratefully into it. "Have a cigarette, won't you? Yes, of course I saw about the affair, but I didn't realise that it was your brother who was involved. And after the first day or two, the papers haven't said very much about it." He did not add that this was owing to the complete obviousness of James Meadows' guilt, which was so glaring as largely to rob the case of interest. "But I don't know all the facts, and if you feel up to running quickly through them – oh, by the way, you needn't mind Grierson here. He's my Watson. He was at Wychford with me." He introduced the two and busied himself with arranging chairs and lighting cigarettes in order to give the girl time to compose herself.

"There's really very little to tell you," she began, when they were ready. "Jimmy and this woman –"

"No, right from the beginning, Miss Meadows, please," Roger interrupted gently. "As if we knew nothing at all. I want not only the facts, you see, but your angle of looking at them."

"Oh. Very well; I'll try. Jimmy and I are orphans, then, and I'm four years older than him; he's twenty-three and I'm twenty-seven. Our mother died when I was nine, and father about three years ago. We're quite comfortably off and we live at a little place called Monckton Regis in Dorset, not far from Bridport. Jimmy went down from Oxford this summer.

"I don't know if the Andersons pointed Jimmy out to you at Torquay, but if they didn't I must tell you that he's not a bit like me. Except that we've both got dark hair, we hardly have anything in common at all. I'm fond of games, Jimmy's fond of books; I hate using my brains, Jimmy does nothing else (he took a double-first at Oxford, by the way; Honour Mods and History); I'm physically as sound as a bell, Jimmy's health isn't any too good; I've got eyes like a hawk's, Jimmy has to wear glasses; I'm noisy, Jimmy's quiet. And so on. So if you can sum me up and then take the exact opposite, you'll get a pretty fair idea of Jimmy. Which, if you take what people say about marriage, may be the reason why we're so fond of each other." She looked a little defiantly at Roger, as if defending this reference to sentiment. He nodded.

"Well, about two years ago Jimmy showed signs of being distinctly attracted towards a woman called Mrs Greyling. She and her husband live in our neighbourhood and I suppose she was all right, but she wasn't my type; she was small and fluffy and appealing, with big blue eyes and tiny little hands and all the rest of it. She must have been at least eight years older than Jimmy. Well, he fell pretty badly. Of course I saw it all happening; I knew the woman was a scalphunter, and she just wanted Jimmy's scalp to hang with all the others at her belt. I did what I could to warn him, but of course Jimmy wouldn't hear a word against her. In fact we had one or two quite large-sized rows over the woman, which is a thing we never, never do in the ordinary way.

"I don't want you to think there was anything wrong. If I knew Mona Greyling, she was the kind that will take anything and give nothing. Not that Jimmy would have taken anything she had to give; he'd put her on a pedestal and used to talk about his ideals to me till I was nearly sick. I mean, Mr Sheringham – well, when you know someone's a little rotter, and – well, it was rather awkward."

Roger nodded again, sympathetically. "And it's no use saying anything either, of course. Yes?"

"Well, to add to the trouble, Mr Greyling was horribly jealous of his wife – as well he might have been! I don't think he trusted her further than he could see her; which I should think was very wise of him. Anyhow, about three weeks ago, so Jimmy told me, he forbade her to have anything more to do with Jimmy at all. They'd been in the habit of going motoring together and all that sort of thing, and naturally people were beginning to talk. Well, that was to stop and they were to meet in future only in public. I was thankful to hear it, but I was rather worried by the way Jimmy told me. He didn't seem to care a bit; he was more amused than anything. And curiously excited, too. I didn't take much notice at the time, but I've realised since that the reason was because they'd agreed to meet secretly, and that must have been much more exciting for a boy of twenty-three – meeting a married woman secretly after her husband had forbidden it, and all that sort of thing."

"It would have been a compliment to him too," Roger put in. "It meant that the husband was taking him seriously."

"Yes, of course. The place they'd agreed on for their meetings," the girl went on, in the same direct, straight-forward way, "was a little dell in some woods, called Tommy Deaton's Hole. They met there a few times for a fortnight or so, and they'd arranged to meet there last Tuesday afternoon. It's very secluded, I should say; right off the main roads and down a little lane where nobody goes from one year's end to another. In fact, so far as being seen went, they couldn't have hit on a better place. And that was just the trouble, because nobody saw Jimmy waiting there the whole of Tuesday afternoon for the woman, who didn't turn up."

"He did wait there?" Roger put in impassively.

"He did, Mr Sheringham," the girl replied, with a dignity which Roger found impressive. "He told me so." She eyed him for a moment as if to challenge him to question her brother's word, and then resumed. "While he was waiting there, Mrs Greyling was murdered, in full view of nearly a dozen people – shot through the head on the main road just outside the village. And every one of those dozen people swears it was Jimmy who did it!" She paused and swallowed. "He came up in the car, they say, and –"

"Yes, I know the rest of the details," Roger interrupted, anxious to spare her. "And of course the police are satisfied it was your brother. Naturally. They couldn't be anything else. It's a deuced awkward situation, Miss Meadows."

"Don't I realise it?" said the girl pluckily. "But I'm going to fight it for all that. Now, Mr Sheringham, I don't know whether you ever undertake private work of this kind, but I've come to London to appeal to you to find the real murderer." She flushed in obvious embarrassment. "As I said, we're quite comfortably off, and whatever your – your fee might be, I – we – should be only too willing to –"

"Fee?" ejaculated Roger, both pained and indignant. "My dear girl, if there's any question of fee it's the one I owe you for inviting my help. And what you've told me throws a new light on the affair; I feel there's quite a chance for your brother now, after all. When will you be ready to start back for Dorset? In half an hour? I'll ring for tea to be got ready while we're packing."

The girl, who had risen to her feet, stammered inarticulate thanks, evidently almost overcome again by this successful end of her mission. Roger, who had a dread of scenes, hastily bundled himself and Alec out of the room.

It took him less than five minutes to throw what things he would need into a bag. Then he sought out Alec, who was a slower packer.

"This is a bad business, Alec," he remarked, throwing himself into a chair.

Alec paused in the act of putting his hair brushes tidily into their case. "Oh? I thought you sounded quite hopeful just now."

"I had to keep that poor girl's spirits up; but so far as I can see there isn't the faintest doubt that her brother shot the woman. As she said, there were about a dozen witnesses to it. How on earth can one get round that?"

"Direct evidence, eh?" observed Alec. "And I thought you were saying not long ago that direct evidence isn't worth anything?"

"If I was saying that, then there must be something in it. I wonder –" He jumped up and ran out of the room.

A minute later he was back, a newspaper in his hand. "Here's the report of it, in yesterday's paper. I'll just go through it again." He ran his eye rapidly over the column. "Yes, it doesn't appear to leave young Meadows much of a loop hole. Apparently he was driving in his car along the road to the village and met Mrs Greyling not more than a hundred yards from the last house in it. There were a couple of labourers in a field, a woman in the garden of the nearest house, another woman at the window of the next house, and two or three people in the village street. All of them saw the whole thing and their reports agree exactly. Young Meadows stopped his car and began to upbraid the woman quite loudly, leaning out of the window of the car. There were the beginnings of a very pretty quarrel, of which the onlookers could not distinguish more than an unimportant word or two.

"Just as things were working up, a car came round a bend of the road behind them, about two hundred yards away. Meadows glanced round at it and then whipped out a revolver, shot the woman through the head, slipped in his clutch and drove off as hard as he could straight on through the village, leaving her lying in the middle of the road. Not only did all the onlookers recognise him, but the two occupants of the oncoming car, strangers to the neighbourhood, seeing that something was happening, took a note of Meadows car number. And lastly both he and the car were recognised in the village street, where he nearly ran over a child as he tore through it. Do you see any loop hole there, Alec?"

"I do not," said Alec firmly.

"Nor do I," confessed Roger. "Not the very faintest glimmering of one. I'm much afraid we're off on a wild goose chase, Alec."

He was careful, however, to give no inkling of this foreboding to the distracted girl when they joined her in the other room. During their hasty tea he let her talk as much as she would about the case, both because he realised that it was a safety valve for her over-charged emotions and because he hoped that some new fact would come out to help him. But of this there was no sign. Claire Meadows knew her brother was innocent because he could not possibly be anything else; but of solid evidence to support this contention there was not a jot. Roger's feeling of hopelessness increased rather than diminished.

They got into the car and set off.

The girl was a good driver, and the mental strain upon her seemed to be lessened while the wheel was in her hands. Roger knew that she was tired already and by the time they reached their destination would be almost played out, but he thought that this would be no bad thing for her; she would sleep the sleep of exhaustion that night at any rate.

The drive was rather a silent one. Before they reached Basingstoke it had been settled that Roger and Alec were to stay at Manor Regis, the Meadows' home, Roger's feeble protestations about the proprieties being swept scornfully aside. Alec, who was feeling somewhat out of place, suggested that they should drop him at Winchester and let him make his way to his own home by train, but Roger expressed such an urgent desire for his help that he allowed himself to be persuaded, by no means unwillingly.

They stopped an hour for dinner in Winchester, and then pushed hurriedly on again, but it was not till nearly eleven o'clock that the car swept at last through that same broad street of Monckton Regis where the tragedy had occurred, and drew up, five minutes later, before the solid Georgian front of Manor Regis.

Obviously there was nothing to be done that night, and Roger expressed a tactful desire to go to bed at once so that he could begin operations as early as possible the next morning. The butler showed them to their rooms, which were adjoining, and Roger, having waited till the coast was clear, stole into Alec's and sat there, smoking cigarettes and discussing the case interminably, till the small hours. But though he and Alec each succeeded in producing several quite fantastic theories to account for young Meadows' innocence, not a single line of profitable research had suggested itself to either of them when Roger retired to his own room just before two.

At breakfast the next morning, from which their hostess had sent a message excusing herself, Roger was no nearer a method of approach. "All I can do," he told Alec in despair, "is to go ahead blindly and trust to something turning up. And as the first thing, obviously, is to hear what young Meadows has to say about it, I shall borrow the car and go into Bridport."

"Will they let you see him?" Alec queried doubtfully. Alec's sympathies were engaged perhaps more closely than ever before. Claire Meadows! Dash it all, he'd often heard of her. Seen her play once or twice, too, for that matter. And a very sound ball she hit. Quite unthinkable that the brother of a girl who could play tennis like that should have committed a murder!

"I'm dam' well going to see him," said Roger grimly. "And I'll take a pair of scissors with me to cut their red tape."

In the end, however, the scissors were not needed. Roger explained himself and the semi-official connection he had had from time to time with the police, and offered to ring up Chief Inspector Moresby of Scotland Yard if the superintendent was not satisfied. But the superintendent was satisfied. He had heard all about Roger and was interested to meet him, and he did not worry about red tape. Within a surprisingly short time Roger found himself in the prisoner's cell, confronting a white-faced boy with a shock of black hair and frightened eyes peering through tortoiseshell-rimmed spectacles.

Roger explained his mission and a ray of hope illuminated the pale scholarly face, but of help Roger could get none. All the boy could do was to reiterate over and over again that he had been the whole time in Tommy Deaton's Hole and knew nothing about anything.

"With your car?" Roger asked desperately.

"With my car," affirmed the other.

Roger stayed half an hour, but got nothing more.

"Went berserk, or whatever they call it, I suppose," said the superintendent, not unkindly, as he saw him off the premises. "Ran amuck. If I can't have her, then no one else will. That sort of thing. Pity. Nice young fellow. But highly strung, Mr Sheringham, sir. That's his trouble. Not a shadow of doubt he did it, of course, if that's what you were hoping."

"And yet, do you know, Superintendent, I don't know that he did," said Roger.

The other stared at him. "Oh, come now, Mr Sheringham. How in the world can you make that out?"

"I can't," said Roger mournfully. "That's the trouble."

But he repeated his opinion still more forcibly to Alec.

"Alec, he's telling the truth! I'm sure he is. I feel it in every bone I've got. And he's not the sort that commits murder, not in his wildest moments; and a cold-blooded affair like that – no, that girl's perfectly right: he simply couldn't have done it."

"Well, if he didn't it's up to you to prove it," said Alec, and added, with rare encouragement: "And I bet you will, in the end. Where to now?"

"Tommy Deaton's Hole, I suppose," Roger replied gloomily. "We may as well have a look at the place. It's out Charmouth way; I marked it on the map last night."

Alec bowled the Morris Oxford out of the town. "He sticks to it that he was there all the time?"

"Yes, and I believe him. But there doesn't seem a chance of proving it. Nobody saw him, and it's too late now for obvious things like fresh cigarette ends."

Roger was right. When at last they did discover the place, he searched it as closely as it could be searched. There were plenty of indications of human visitation at some indefinite time, and car tracks as well, but not a single thing to show that Jimmy Meadows had sat for two crucial hours on a log that Tuesday afternoon, within sight of the very car that was sworn by a dozen witnesses to have been ten miles away.

"Hell!" said Roger morosely, as they turned back for lunch.

The car was stopped for a few minutes at the scene of the crime, but the latter had nothing to offer them, beyond a slight increase of their perplexities. "For why," as Roger pointed out, "was she shot here, within full view of anybody who cared to take a look? Why didn't the murderer get her aboard the car and take her somewhere less conspicuous? It looks as if he simply lost his head and really didn't know what he was doing."

"Who did?" Alec asked acutely. "Young Meadows?"

"Upon my soul," Roger had to admit, "I'm beginning to wonder. Even the victim recognised him, you see. The superintendent told me. The men in the field didn't hear much, but they did hear her call out 'Jimmy!' as he stopped the car. How on earth can one get over that? And yet I'd have staked my life that that boy was speaking the truth this morning."

"I suppose," Alec said diffidently, "he couldn't have done it and then had a sort of brain storm and forgotten all about it? Really believed he was somewhere else all the time?"

"Amnesia of some kind?" Roger nodded. "Yes, I'd thought of that myself. And I'm getting more and more sure that it's the real explanation. But if that's the case, we're going to have the very deuce of a job to save him from the gallows."

And with no more comforting news than this for their hostess, they went back to lunch.

After the meal Roger disappeared. He had a few routine enquiries to make, he said, and thought he could get on with them better alone. Alec was left with the embarrassing task of fending off Claire Meadows' very pertinent enquiries as to their progress on the case.

Roger did not get back till Alec was dressing for dinner, but looked into the latter's room for a moment to report, though he had little enough to tell.

"I've ferreted out all the witnesses to the shooting, except the two in the other car, and they all tell exactly the same story. They all knew Meadows by sight, too, and I couldn't shake a single one of them on the question of identification; they're all positive."

"It *was* Meadows," Alec said helplessly. "There doesn't seem any doubt of it. We were right: it was Meadows, out of his mind."

"He certainly must have been out of his mind," Roger remarked, turning to the door. "He behaved like a lunatic. Not only did he shoot the woman under the eyes of all those people, but before doing so he appears to have raved at her in the most insane way, just meaningless shouts of mad rage. At least, that's how it struck the witnesses."

"It's a rotten business," Alec opined.

Dinner was not a cheerful meal, and an uninspired evening was spent. Claire Meadows must have guessed at the growing hopelessness felt by her guests, but refrained from asking too many questions.

The next morning Roger took Alec aside after breakfast. "We're going into Dorchester, and I'm going to take that girl with us. If she doesn't do something active soon, she'll break down."

"What are we going to do?" Alec asked.

"Well, I'd thought of buying a camera and taking pictures of the scene of the crime, and Tommy Deaton's Hole, and any other fauna or flora connected with the case. It can't do any harm, and it ought to keep her spirits up a bit longer."

"I say, you don't think there's the faintest chance for him?"

Roger shrugged his shoulders. "If they can prove insanity at the trial...."

Claire Meadows accepted the invitation into Dorchester with alacrity, and the camera was duly bought, with a roll of films inside it. As they were coming out of the shop, the girl caught Roger by the arm and jerked him back into the doorway. She indicated a tall, spare man of about forty-five, walking alone on the opposite pavement.

"I'm sorry, but that's Mr Greyling – that tall, fair-haired man without a hat over there. I don't want to meet him just now."

"Of course," Roger murmured, watching the rather bowed form of the bereaved husband as the sun glinted on his ash-blond hair. "Pure Nordic, eh?"

"Nordic?" said the girl doubtfully.

"A racial type. Fair hair, blue eyes, clear skin, and all that. Is he cutting up rough, by the way?"

The girl flushed. "Very. He's cutting me too now, dead." She sighed. "I suppose it's natural. He was devoted to his wife, and –" She laughed in a forced way. "Well, the impression he gives me is that the only joy he's got left is to hear that Jimmy's been hanged. He was positively hounding the police after him, on that dreadful Tuesday. Oh, well; it's natural enough, if he thinks Jimmy did it. Well, Mr Sheringham, what are you going to photograph first?"

"Mr Greyling," Roger answered, on a sudden impulse. "After all, he's a very important part of the case, isn't he?" Without waiting for an answer he ran across the road ahead of Greyling, strolled down towards him, planted himself exactly in the other's path, and said suddenly in a loud voice: "Excuse me, sir." Greyling stopped dead, and Roger whisked the camera from behind his back and snapped the shutter.

For an instant Greyling stood motionless, while his features contorted with anger. Then he lifted his walking stick and aimed a smashing blow at the camera. Roger jumped nimbly aside, murmured: "Sorry. Press photographer," and hurried back to join the others.

"Rotten thing to do," he said swiftly as he approached them. "He didn't like it. I'm not surprised. Stand still, Miss Meadows;

I'm going to pretend to take one of you, to soften his wrath." The girl stood on the pavement, and Roger ostentatiously snapped her. "Stand by, Alec, and look big," he muttered. Out of the corner of his eye he had caught sight of Greyling approaching them.

Greyling did not mince his words. "You'll excuse me, Miss Meadows," he said stiffly, "but I'm sure you have no more desire than I have for publicity in the rag this fellow is touting for. If you publish either of those snapshots," he added to Roger, after a glance at Alec who was looking as big as he could, "I'll bring an action against you and your editor. Now clear out." He turned on his heel and strode away.

"Well, well," said Roger mildly, and led the way to the car.

For the rest of the morning they took photographs assiduously. Roger arranged a little tableau on the scene of the murder, with Alec enacting the part of the murderer and leaning out of the car window with a pipe levelled at Claire Meadows, and took careful photographs of it from the point of view of each witness. The village street was snapped, and several pictures secured of Tommy Deaton's Hole. To Miss Meadows' questions regarding his object in all this, and they were many, Roger preserved a mysterious silence and hinted at surprising theories; but he had his reward in the colour he could see creeping back into the girl's cheeks and the vanishing of the haunted look from her eyes.

When they got back to the house, Roger had a word or two with Alec as they went upstairs to wash. "Take her out for a walk this afternoon, Alec, and leave the car to me. That business this morning has given me an idea after all."

"You're on the track of something?" Alec asked eagerly.

"I can see a bare possibility," Roger replied, not too hopefully. "It'll probably come to nothing, but I want to explore it."

At lunch he asked if there was a dark room on the premises, and seemed disappointed at hearing there was not.

The other two did not see him again till late that night. Then he returned in a state of jubilation bordering on delirium and carrying a long thin package under his arm wrapped in brown paper. He marched into the drawing room, where the other two were trying to sustain a disjointed conversation, and beamed on them.

"I'm going to clear your brother, Claire. You don't mind me calling you Claire, by the way, do you? I think I've earned it. Here's the first piece of evidence – the faked number-plates used by the murderer." He unwrapped the package and displayed two plates, bearing the same number as that of Meadows' car, handling them gingerly by the edges. "Don't touch them. I'm praying there are fingerprints."

"Good for you, Roger!" almost shouted Alec.

Miss Meadows' comment was less coherent but no less enthusiastic.

"Found 'em just where I expected, near Tommy Deaton's Hole," Roger explained proudly. "It took me four hours of hard searching, but I've never spent four hours to better purpose."

"But why did you expect them there?" asked Claire.

"Well, I reasoned that the murderer would want to get them off his own premises at the earliest possible moment. They're damning evidence, you see. And where could he hide them better, till he had time to destroy them at leisure, than in a secluded spot like Tommy Deaton's Hole, far enough away from it so that the chances were a million to one against their ever being found by chance, but near enough to it so that if the millionth chance did turn up the finder would assume that it was your brother who had put them there." He had been examining them from all angles, and now put them back in their paper with a sigh. "No, as I'd feared. Not a sign of a fingerprint. He's a cunning devil, this man."

"But – but who is he?" Claire asked breathlessly.

Roger shook his head. "That, I'm afraid, I'm not yet in a position to say. But I've another line on him, which will take me up to London tomorrow, perhaps for a few days. And now, have you got such a thing as a hunk of bread in the house, and even a drop of coffee? The reaction has set in, and I feel human again. Extremely human, in fact."

But Claire, prudent housewife, had given orders that supper was to be left ready in the dining room. Roger fell to with zest, and while he ate questioned Claire closely about her brother's friends. Had he, so far as she knew, any enemies? Had he, particularly, any enemies with black hair, who could be mistaken at a short distance for himself? So far as Claire knew, Jimmy had no enemies. Then did she know whether Mrs Greyling had any enemies? Or had she any quondam friends who might now be enemies? Had Claire ever seen her about with a young man who might be mistaken for Jimmy? Had she even seen such a young man in the neighbourhood at all?

It was very late before they got to bed, and by that time Claire had not been able to produce a single young man with black hair, or anything else of the least help. But Roger did not seem depressed at her failure. "I've got a feeling that I'm on the right track," he told her as they parted for the night. "And I've got another feeling that the truth lies not here at all, but in London. Anyhow, that's where I'm going up tomorrow to look for it."

Claire ran them into Dorchester the next morning, and Roger promised to wire her immediately he discovered anything definite, following up his wire if possible with a report in person. It was a very much less distracted girl who drove back along to Monckton Regis than had left it for London two days before.

So far as Monckton Regis was concerned, Roger and Alec ceased to exist for forty-eight hours.

Then came a telegram.

"Case ended have identified man arriving Dorchester tomorrow twelve twenty. Sheringham."

Trembling with excitement, Claire met the train. A large grin, closely followed by Roger, descended from a first class carriage. He took her hands and pump-handled them with enthusiasm. "It's all right," he beamed at her. "I've reported the whole thing to Scotland Yard, and given them the evidence. Here, Moresby!"

A large man in a blue suit and a bowler hat, who had followed Roger out of the carriage, joined paternally in the general beaming.

"Chief Inspector Moresby, of the C.I.D.," Roger explained. "He's come down, as a personal favour to me, to put things to the local police here. Quite unofficially, of course, because Scotland Yard hasn't been called in."

"That's right," agreed Chief Inspector Moresby. "It's most irregular, but we don't seem to be able to resist Mr Sheringham at the Yard whenever he's set his heart on anything, Miss Meadows."

"And Jimmy?" breathed the excited girl. "My brother?"

"He'll be at liberty this afternoon. Just a few formalities to go through first. Well, I must be getting along. See you later, Mr Sheringham, at the station? Good-bye, Miss Meadows." He disappeared into the dwindling crowd at the barrier.

"Who *was* the man, Mr Sheringham?" demanded Claire.

Roger looked at his watch. "I'm not allowed to tell you that for exactly two hours and twenty-three minutes."

"Mr Sheringham! Why ever not?"

"Because at that time he'll be under arrest, or in the act of being arrested. So in the meantime, are you going to lunch here with me in Dorchester, or am I going to lunch with you at Manor Regis?"

It was decided that they should run over to Manor Regis to lunch, because Claire had so many things to ask.

But ask as she might, Roger refused with the utmost resolution to answer a single one of them. It was not until lunch was finished and they were sitting in the drawing room over their coffee that he would say anything about the case at all, and then at last he gave her the story she had been demanding.

"Frankly, at first," said Roger, "I was absolutely at a loss."

He explained how he had been convinced that Jimmy Meadows was speaking the truth, and yet how impossible it had seemed to overcome such positive evidence on the part of so many witnesses, touching upon the theory of amnesia to which at one time he had been driven.

"And then," he went on, "I tried to look at it this way: direct evidence is notoriously open to danger; these witnesses undoubtedly believed they were speaking the truth, but was there any way in which they might have made an honest mistake? So I went through all that business of photographing you and Grierson at the scene of the murder in order to try and look at the thing with their eyes instead of my own; and I soon realised that every one of them was near enough to be able to detect a general resemblance, but nobody was near enough to be able to pick out any minute points of difference.

"That was a step in the right direction, and the next thing I did was to ask myself: was there anything peculiar about the murder itself? Well, of course there was. Several things. The first one was the scene of it. Why shoot Mrs Greyling under the noses of all those witnesses? It could not have been necessary, and to lose one's head to that extent was to verge on sheer insanity. But the murderer had not lost his head; not, that is, unless he carried a revolver as part of the tool-kit of his car. The presence of that revolver argued to me not a crime on the spur of the moment but a premeditated one.

"But the most curious thing of all was the way the murderer shouted. Not content with shooting the woman under all those eyes which happened to be looking, he shouted at the top of his voice, with the inevitable result of drawing any other eyes which might not have been on him already. And he did not shout words: he just shouted incoherently. Indeed he was deliberately doing all those very things which a man about to commit a premeditated murder would be most anxious to avoid. He even delayed shooting her till a car came round the corner behind him and the occupants could see him do it. Unless he was a sheer lunatic, then, he was doing all this with a purpose. What purpose? Obviously to call very particular attention to the crime. With what object?

So that there would be a dozen witnesses to swear that Mr James Meadows, sitting in his own car, with the correct number-plates, had deliberately murdered Mrs Greyling."

"You mean – somebody was impersonating Jimmy?"

"Exactly. Now consider. Your car is a blue Morris Oxford saloon. There are hundreds of blue Morris Oxford saloons, thousands. To all intents and purposes, one blue Morris Oxford saloon can be distinguished from another only by the number. What could be easier than to hire a blue Morris Oxford saloon, mount it with faked number-plates, and carry on?

"Then consider your brother. What are his most obvious characteristics? A shock of untidy black hair, a thin, white face, and horn-rimmed spectacles. A black wig, a little French chalk, another pair of horn-rimmed spectacles – why, the thing was child's-play. So I went up to London to identify a man who had bought a black wig at a fairly recent date. And if I didn't find him in London, I was prepared to go all over the country looking for him; it was only a question of time before I found him."

"And you did find him?"

"I did. I already knew whom I was looking for, you see. Because I had already had the luck (or if you call it the wit, I won't dispute it) to identify a man who had hired a blue Morris Oxford saloon on that Tuesday, at a garage not twenty miles from here. They recognised him at once from his photograph, and –"

"Oh, you'd got hold of a photograph of him? It was someone you suspected, then?"

"Yes, I'd got hold of a photograph of him; though as a matter of fact I didn't begin to suspect him till after I'd got it."

"Oh, Mr Sheringham, what was his name?"

"Baker," Roger grinned. "Mr Edward Baker."

"Edward Baker?" echoed the girl, in mystified tones. "Who on earth –?"

"Well, that's what they knew him as at the garage. And they knew him quite well too. He'd often dropped in to hire a Morris Oxford saloon. He preferred a Morris Oxford saloon to any other kind of car. He'd told them so, frequently."

"But I don't understand. What does it mean?"

"Why," Roger explained, "this man who called himself Baker had been preparing the ground very carefully in advance; that's what it means. But he hadn't prepared it quite carefully enough."

"But who is he? Oh, do tell me, Mr Sheringham?"

Roger glanced at his watch. "Yes, they'll be arresting him just about now. Why, Claire, haven't you already guessed? Think! You said your brother had no enemies, but he had; one. Who was known to be of a madly jealous disposition? Who was so terribly anxious not to have his photograph published in the paper, in case it might be recognised as the photograph of somebody with a totally different name? Who found out that your brother was safely tucked away from observation at Tommy Deaton's Hole and was in a position to ensure Mrs Greyling's presence, on some pretext or other, on that particular piece of road at that particular time? Who was trying to kill, very literally, two birds with one stone – an unfaithful wife, as he supposed, and her lover? A quick, merciful death for one, and a long-drawn-out agony for the other? Who, in short –"

"Mr Greyling!"

"Exactly," Roger agreed gravely. "Mr Greyling." He glanced at his watch again. "And now, what about running back into Dorchester? We should be just in time to catch your brother on the threshold of his cell, so to speak."

INQUEST

LEONORA WODEHOUSE

Leonora Wodehouse was the step-daughter of P.G. Wodehouse, who in 1914 married her mother, the twice-widowed actress and dancer Ethel Rowley. Wodehouse adopted Leonora, who was ten years old at the time of the wedding, and called her by the nickname "Snorky". She later became his "confidential secretary and adviser", before marrying the racehorse trainer Peter Cazalet in 1932, and having two children. Her sudden death in May 1944 left the novelist distraught.

P.G. Wodehouse loved detective fiction, and was friendly with Agatha Christie, Dorothy L. Sayers, and Anthony Berkeley. Leonora seems to have shared his enthusiasm for the genre, and contributed this story (which he described as "marvellous") to the *Strand Magazine*, under the pen-name "Loel Yeo" in 1932. Its quality is such that it is a pity her untimely death put paid to any chance that she might develop her literary career.

*   *   *   *   *

MEMORY is an odd thing. I can always remember to perfection a mass of unimportant details. So many men stretched end on end would encircle the earth; the exact number is 23,549,115. Thirty and a quarter square yards equal one square rod, pole, or perch. These things and many more I never forget. Yet on the occasional days I can snatch to go up to London (and I being a country doctor they are rare enough), I never fail to leave my shopping list behind. It is only as the train pulls out of London that I remember the instruments I meant to buy.

I overtook the Stanton express as it was grumbling out of the station, and flung myself on to somebody's lap. My apologies were accepted. He was elderly and inconspicuous and neat, and I knew I had seen him before, but though I still knew rice, sago, and pepper to be the chief exports of North Borneo, I couldn't remember where we had met.

People who live the same sort of lives grow to look alike. Thirty years of the same office, the same suburb, the same daily papers, and they end with the same face. Thin and a little anaemic. Eyes the faded blue of much-washed laundry. In summer and winter always a raincoat and an evening paper.

It was a chilly, foggy evening, the typical raw January day which the inconsequence of the English climate always produces in the middle of October; the window-panes were steaming with the heat of the compartment, and I lay back recovering my breath, wondering where I had seen the man opposite me before. A high white collar held his chin erect. He sat upright on the edge of the seat.

Suddenly he coughed. It was more of a mannerism than a cough, you felt it did his throat no good at all. And I remembered that we had last met on the afternoon of the coroner's inquest two years ago at Langley Abbey.

As one noticed little things in the midst of great excitement during the occasional silences in the dining-room on that day, I remember watching the shadow of the elms stretch themselves across the lawn, hearing the cawing of the rooks, and in the room the creaking of the constable's boots and the dry little cough of the solicitor's clerk who gave his unimportant but necessary evidence clearly and concisely.

The only thing about Langley that suggests an Abbey is the stained-glass window of the bathroom, otherwise it is just one of those solid square Georgian houses. Its gardens and park are lovely. I was practically brought up there with the Neville boys, so I know the place backwards. When they were both killed in 1917 old Sir Guy Neville sold it as it stood to John Hentish.

It's funny how the character of a place changes with its owner. Under the Nevilles, Langley had been a friendly house. The park gates stood open and so did the doors and windows of the house itself, muslin curtains swinging gaily in the breeze. There were village fêtes in the park, and the Abbey was part of the life and conversation of all the villages round.

With John Hentish there came a change. Sir Guy was asked to inform the county that the future tenants disliked society, and hoped people would not give themselves the trouble of calling. The park gates were shut and stayed shut. The windows were tightly closed and the muslin curtains hung straight and lifeless behind them. The house developed a thin-lipped, austere look. The only people who gave themselves the trouble of calling were the post-man and the tradesmen. And gradually Langley Abbey dropped out of the annals and conversation of the county.

As for me, the house that had been so much a part of my life having shut me out, for ten years as I drove over to Maddenly to prescribe for Miss Taunton's varicose veins or dose Master Willie

Twinger, I averted my eyes from the park gates as one would passing a friendly dog whose temper had become changed and uncertain. And then one afternoon four years ago I found a message in my consulting room asking me to go up to the Abbey at once.

After that I went there regularly, at least three times a week. Practically the whole house, I found, presumably through lack of interest, had been left exactly as it was bought from the Nevilles. The hall was large and ran the width of the house, that is French windows opening on to the lawn faced the front door. The floor had a higher polish than I remembered, and there were fewer lights. The furniture was ugly but solid, mostly Victorian. Two long tables, an oak chest, some stiff chairs, and a Burmese gong. There were several pairs of antlers on the walls, some lithographs of the early Christian martyrs, Saint Sebastien looking extraordinarily fit and cheerful with about forty arrows through his body, a twenty-pound trout Sir Guy had caught in Scotland, and one fairly good tapestry.

Old Hentish had converted what had been Lady Neville's morning-room into a bedroom and bathroom. Off the bedroom, what we had known as the drawing-room had been made into a very beautiful library. Both rooms were large, with high ceilings, and had French windows opening on to the lawn. He lived almost entirely in this suite and seldom left it.

Hentish, though he had faith in me as a doctor, disliked me as he consistently disliked everyone. He was, without exception, the most unpleasant, disagreeable old swine I have ever met. Practically the only pleasure I ever received in his company was derived from jabbing the needle into his arm. He soon exhausted the supply of

London nurses, and finally I persuaded Miss Mavey from Maddenly village to take the post, she having nursed an invalid mother for fifteen years who could have given even old Hentish points for unpleasantness. No man, of course, could live long in John Hentish's condition, for, besides heart-trouble, he had advanced cirrhosis of the liver, but because death frightened him he listened to me, and so with electrical treatments, diet, and drugs, his general health improved.

Some women are eerie. Miss Taunton has been bedridden for years, yet she's one of those women whose cousin always knew the murdered man's aunt. This time her sister-in-law's maid's niece had married the son of the overseer of the Hentish Paper Mills in Ontario. Like all women, Miss Taunton had a profound contempt for detailed accuracy, but fundamentally her facts are always correct. Hentish, apparently, during the first forty years of his life had spent seven separate fortunes; the figures are Miss Taunton's. He had been the most dissolute man in London, also in Buenos Aires, where the standard is higher and competition keener. He was hard, grasping, and avid for power; there wasn't a man in his paper mills or his gold mine that wouldn't be glad to see him boiled in oil. 'And that,' said Miss Taunton, impressively, 'I got more or less straight from the lips of his own overseer.'

Miss Taunton's attitude to God is rather that of a proud aunt; she sees all the motives so clearly and is often a jump ahead of the game. When John Hentish's health failed, her attitude was that of one whose advice had been taken, for she was a firm believer in the wages of sin. Her own varicose veins she knew had been sent to test her—take the well-known case of Job—she took them rather as a compliment than otherwise, applauded God's attempt at impartiality, and forgave him frequently.

I never knew whether old Hentish had any affection for his nephew or not. William was his heir and they quarrelled, of course—over money, among other things—but I think more than disapproval he enjoyed the sense of power it gave him to see his nephew flush as he threatened to stop his allowance, which was a generous one. William's specialities were women and horses. I suppose he was good-looking in a dark, sinister sort of way; he had inherited all his uncle's unpleasantness and developed it with some ideas of his own. He used to motor down to Langley occasionally for two or three days at a time.

So life drifted on placidly and uneventfully. Sometimes after I had seen old Hentish I used to wander down to the boathouse, for the lawn sloped down to a lake fringed with red willow, and I would sit there thinking out beautiful unappetizing diets for the old man. Then one afternoon my telephone rang. It was Miss Mavey.

'Dr Mellan? Oh, Dr Mellan, will you please come down at once. Mr Hentish is dead!'

John Hentish had died from an overdose of morphia taken in a glass of sal volatile. The inquest was held that same evening in the Abbey dining-room. Mr Duffy, the coroner, sat with Police-constable Perker at the table, the rest of the household at the end of the room. Mr Duffy blew his nose, and the Vapex on his handkerchief mingled with the smell of leather and pickles. He turned a watery eye on Croucher, the butler.

'Is everybody here?'

'Everyone with the exception of Mr William Hentish, sir. He has not yet returned home.'

'Thank you. Call Dr Mellan.'

My testimony did not take long. History of John Hentish's illness, cause of death, etc. Miss Mavey was called next, and under the impression that she was on trial for her life, opened with a magnificent defence, giving seven distinct alibis for the afternoon.

'You say,' the coroner asked her, 'that the morphia with which you sometimes had occasion to inject the deceased in order to relieve intense pain was kept on the top shelf of a medicine cupboard, clearly labelled "morphia"?'

'I do,' said Miss Mavey, looking like the Trial of Mary Dugan. 'Anyone else will say the same.'

'The cupboard has a glass door, I understand. The sal volatile and a glass were placed on a small table beneath the cupboard containing the morphia. Is that correct, Miss Mavey?'

Miss Mavey paled, knowing that all she said would be used in evidence against her.

'In a sense, yes.'

'In a sense?'

'A spoon was also kept on the table,' said Miss Mavey, determined to conceal nothing.

'This medicine, this sal volatile, did the deceased take it at regular hours?'

Miss Mavey turned this over. A trap?

'No, sir, only to relieve the pain if it came on sudden,' she said, guardedly.

'When Dr Mellan gave his opinion that death was not due to natural causes, but to an overdose of morphia, you looked in the bathroom. You found the phial, which when you went off duty was in the cupboard and had contained twenty grains of morphia, lying empty on the table beside the sal volatile. Is that correct?'

'Dr Mellan asked me to look when he saw that the morphia had been put in the glass of sal volatile. I touched nothing, I swear it before Almighty God.'

'Was Mr Hentish in the habit of helping himself to this sal volatile?'

'Yes, sir, if there was no one in the room to get it for him.'

'Miss Mavey, are you of the same opinion as Dr Mellan that the morphia could not have been taken accidentally?'

'No.'

'No! Then you think it could have been taken accidentally?'

'Yes. I mean yes I'm of the opinion that no it couldn't have been taken accidentally.'

'That is all. Thank you.'

Miss Mavey, still under the shadow of the scaffold, gave a shuddering sigh, and borrowing the coroner's Vapex, sank on to a chair, inhaling deeply.

Croucher, the butler, was questioned next.

'You say,' said the coroner, 'that on receipt of the telegram this morning, Mr Hentish showed signs of anger?'

'Distinctly, sir.'

'What then?'

'He asked if Mr William was in.'

'Was he?'

'No, sir, he had left in his car at 9.30.'

'What then?'

'He told me to go to hell, sir, and take his blasted nephew with me, sir, but before I went to get Troubridge and Hay on the telephone.'

'His solicitors?'

'Exactly, sir.'

'Then what?'

'He rang and gave me instructions for the car to meet the 1.45 train. His solicitors were sending down a member of the firm.'

'On arrival he was shown straight into the library, I understand?'

'Yes, sir.'

'What then?'

'After about fifteen minutes the library bell rang and Mr Hentish asked me to witness his signature to a new will.'

'After you had signed the will, anything else?'

'The usual instructions to go to hell, sir.'

'Then I understand the house was quiet until 4.30?'

'Yes, sir. The solicitor's gentleman left the library a few moments after I did. There were standing instructions never to disturb Mr Hentish until Miss Mavey woke him at 4.30. Today the bell pealed violently, and on my entering the library Miss Mavey informed me that Mr Hentish was dead. I remained in the room until the doctor's arrival.'

The solicitor's clerk was called.

'Your firm had instructions from Mr Hentish by telephone this morning, I understand, to draft out a new will?'

'Yes, sir.'

'You were shown into the library on your arrival. What happened?'

'I read Mr Hentish the new draft, which he approved with one alteration. He rang for the butler and we both witnessed the signature.'

'Did it strike you there was anything in Mr Hentish's manner to suggest he contemplated suicide?'

'Difficult to say, sir.'

'And after you had signed the will?'

'I remained with Mr Hentish ten minutes or so. He wished to discuss a matter of income tax. I then left the library and went and sat in the garden until train time, as is my custom.'

'You've been here before then? On the same errand?'

'Usually, sir.'

'Mr Hentish was in the habit of changing his will?'

'Yes, sir.'

'Often?'

'Seven times in the last ten years, sir.'

There was a silence. The butler was called again.

'I find a memorandum on Mr Hentish's desk, Twiller and Dwight, Thursday at 12. Can you explain this?'

'His tailors, sir. He told me to telephone and have a fitter sent down tomorrow at twelve.'

'When did he give this order?'

'At breakfast, sir.'

'Then as late as the breakfast hour he was obviously not contemplating suicide. Was he in a bad or good mood?'

'Mr Hentish was never exactly sunny-tempered, sir, but he seemed average.'

'It was only after he received the telegram that his mood changed for the worse?'

'Yes, sir.'

'Mr William came down from London last night, you say?'

'Yes, sir.'

'Did he appear on good terms with his uncle?'

'He seemed slightly nervous at dinner, if I may say so, but trying to be pleasant, I thought, sir.'

'You say he hasn't been in all day?'

'Oh yes, sir. He returned this afternoon but went out again.'

'This afternoon! At what time?'

'Well, sir, I noticed his car in the drive when I passed through the hall to witness the signature, sir. That would be about 2.30, and it was still there when Miss Mavey rang, but when I opened the front door to the doctor about fifteen minutes later it had gone.'

In the silence the smell of pickles became sharper. All our chairs creaked. The same idea had suddenly occurred to everybody.

'Did Mr William know of the arrival of the telegram?'

'No, sir, he had already left when it came.'

There was another silence.

'Then he didn't know that Mr Hentish intended changing his will or that Mr—Mr—that his solicitor was sending down a representative?'

'No, sir.'

People are funny; they can see a man every day for twenty years, know his face, mannerisms, idiosyncrasies, but they've only to hear that his wife has left him, that he's shot his mother, and they'll stand for hours waiting for a glimpse of him.

Practically all of us at the inquest had seen Mr William Hentish frequently during the last two years, some longer; and none of us had ever been particularly elated at the sight, yet when the front door banged as Croucher stopped speaking, and footsteps echoed on the polished floor of the hall, all the eyes in the room turned and became fixed on the handle of the mahogany door. There were people in that room to my certain knowledge, notably the butler and myself, whose day ordinarily could be made simply by not seeing Mr William Hentish, yet as his footsteps echoed nearer, the drone of a solitary bluebottle in the room seemed like the roar of an aeroplane in the silence. Our chairs creaked as each of us leant forward and became still.

The footsteps stopped, the handle turned, and our chairs creaked sharply once again.

I don't know exactly what change we all expected to see in William Hentish, but I remember a feeling of vague disappointment as he stood in the doorway looking just the same as when I had last seen him. When he was told of his uncle's death, and the manner of it, he seemed surprised.

I've often wondered why magistrates and coroners ask the questions they do. Mr Duffy knew William Hentish as well as I did, he'd been splashed often enough with mud from his car in the winter in our narrow village street, yet the next fifteen minutes was entirely taken up with proving his identity.

The questions seemed to go on endlessly. William Hentish wore his customary look of not caring much for the smell of those immediately about him, but he gave his answers quietly and without emotion. He said that he had returned soon after lunch, gone straight through the hall on to the lawn to the boathouse. He sat there until the stable clock struck 4.30, then returned to the house, intending to go in and see his uncle, who, he knew, would be awake by then. He didn't go in because when he reached the hall the library door was ajar.

Police-constable Perker, the official recorder at the inquest, was taking down notes in longhand. A hollow moan was his signal that the pace was too much for him and the questions would cease until he caught up. Presently the coroner continued:

'Through the open door you say you heard Miss Mavey telephone Dr Mellan? But why should this stop you from seeing your uncle?'

'I thought he had probably had another attack and wouldn't want to see me just then.'

'I understand you were not here when the telegram arrived.'

'Telegram?'

The coroner turned to Perker. 'Constable, please read out the telegram.'

Police-constable Perker first got his notes up to date, then there was a roll of drums as he cleared his throat.

'Telegram to John Hentish, Langley Abbey, Langley, Norfolk. Subject secretly married to Miriel Demar yesterday two p.m. Duke Street register office. Awaiting instructions. Signed Ross.'

All our eyes were on William Hentish. I think be became a little more rigid and a pulse throbbed in his temple. The cruet-stand on the table rattled like an express train as Constable Perker settled down to his notes again.

'Is this information correct, Mr Hentish?'

'Yes.'

'You were not aware that your uncle had your movements watched?'

'No.'

'You were married secretly, I presume, because you felt Miss Demar would not have been your uncle's choice of a wife for you?'

William Hentish flushed. 'My uncle was a difficult man. He disapproved of whatever he hadn't arranged himself. My wife was a chorus girl. In time he would have come round, he always did.'

'And in the meantime?'

'He would have forbidden me the house for a month or two, I suppose.'

'And cut you off in his will?'

'Probably.'

'Supposing he had died before reinstating you in the will?'

William Hentish smiled.

'That is a remote contingency now.'

There was an angry moan from Constable Perker, who spelt by ear and preferred words that he had heard before.

'You haven't seen this gentleman before, then?'

Mr Duffy pointed out the solicitor's clerk, who coughed discreetly. William Hentish looked at him, then turned back to the coroner.

'Not consciously. Who is he?'

'He was sent down on your uncle's instructions from Troubridge and Hay with the draft of a new will.'

William Hentish turned quickly to the clerk.

'Did my uncle sign it?'

'Yes, sir.'

'May I ask the contents of the new will, the existing one?'

The clerk managed to clear his throat in the form of a question to the coroner, who nodded back an answer.

'Mr Hentish left his entire fortune to cancer research.'

'And the former will? The one he revoked?' the coroner asked.

'Everything to his nephew, William Hentish.'

While the clerk was speaking William Hentish sat silent, except that a pulse hammered again in his temple. By chance he caught the cook's eye. I saw him start. She was so obviously a woman who hadn't murdered her uncle looking at a man who had murdered him. And I think it was only then that he realized the danger of the case building up against him.

He had known his uncle would disapprove of a marriage which could probably not remain secret long. He had known his uncle's precarious state of health, had often prepared John Hentish's sal volatile for him, and knew about the morphia. He had only to walk into the library from the garden. He would know from experience that his uncle's rage at being disturbed in the middle of the afternoon would be enough to bring on an attack; and as he had often done before, he would get old Hentish some sal volatile from the bathroom, this time with a generous helping of morphia. Perhaps he had stood with curiosity watching his uncle gulp it down, had seen the purple settle under the eyes, then picking up his book, had walked quietly back to the boathouse. Perhaps he had even sat there reading until the stable clock chimed.

The coroner spoke.

'You say, Mr Hentish, that you didn't leave the garden until you heard the clock strike?'

Until then William Hentish had answered the questions put to him abruptly and with an appearance of indifference. Now his answers became more hesitant, and he paused before he spoke. He was already on the defensive. Our chairs creaked as we leant forward for his answer.

'No.'

'You didn't go near the library the whole afternoon?'

'No.'

'But you could have. Without being observed. Isn't that so, Mr Hentish?'

'Yes, I suppose so. But I repeat that I didn't.'

The cook's sniff re-echoed round the room, which had become nearly dark. Our faces were now only a blurred outline, and a cold breeze rustled Constable Perker's notes. The stable clock clanged eight.

'Then we have only your word for it that you sat in the boathouse all afternoon, Mr Hentish?'

'I'm afraid so.'

There was a silence. Suddenly the solicitor's clerk cleared his throat and spoke.

'It is quite true what Mr Hentish says with regard to his move-ments. I can substantiate that. Directly I left Mr Hentish I went and sat under the cedar tree whilst waiting my train time. I noticed young Mr Hentish sitting in the boathouse smoking. I don't think he saw me, but his statement is correct. He never left there until the stable clock struck.'

Human nature is weird. Instead of a deep sense of thankful-ness that a fellow-creature's hands were not stained with the blood of another fellow-creature, I think that everyone in that room, with perhaps the exception of the coroner, who saw a chance of getting home to a hot mustard bath after all, felt aggrieved that William Hentish's hands were not stained with blood. Prob-ably it was because anyone with an eye for drama could see that William Hentish was perfect for the role of villain, an aggressive manner, tall, with a black moustache and large white teeth. His hands *should* have been stained with his uncle's blood, he looked better that way, it suited him. Speaking for myself, preferring, as I do, like the rest of mankind, to believe the worst of my fellow-men, I felt that if he had not murdered his uncle, it was simply because he didn't happen to think of it.

After we had recovered from our natural disappointment, Croucher lit the gas brackets, and the questions, innumerable and interminable, began again. The clerk could add nothing, he could only say that he had seen Mr Hentish sitting as he had said in the boathouse the whole afternoon. The butler was called again, so were Miss Mavey, still at bay, and I. The question of the morphia arose.

'Might not Mr Hentish's insistence,' Mr Duffy asked the room in general, 'on the presence of morphia easily accessible, be attributed, apart from its properties in the alleviation of pain, to his possible contemplation of self-destruction?'

Constable Perker put down his pencil.

'That's coming it too hot for me, sir. Can I put it in my own words? You mean, did he pop himself off, sir?'

The questions and answers continued, but the evidence of a completely disinterested witness was too overwhelming, and on a statement from Miss Mavey that the old man had often spoken wholeheartedly in favour of self-slaughter (actually, I think, he was advocating it for her and not for himself), the coroner, as the stable clock clanged nine, brought in a verdict of suicide while of an unsound mind.

I didn't see whether William Hentish spoke to the little clerk in the dining-room or not, but he walked, frowning, across the hall as if it were empty, through the huddled group of servants, past the rest of us without a sign or word; the front door slammed, his motor roared and whined, and he was gone.

The presence of death does strange things to a place. As we stood in a group near the front door, making arrangements for the following day, the hall seemed lifeless and cold, our footsteps and voices had a hollow sound; somehow the windows reminded me of staring, dead black eyes, for the curtains had not been drawn. The gas jet droned and made the shadows of the stag's head and horns flicker and leap jerkily across the ceiling. A steady draught from an open door edged behind the tapestry, bellying it out till a naked old satyr leaned amorously towards Miss Mavey. She stood gazing after William Hentish.

'Think of losing a fortune, all that money wasted on charity!'

She sighed and sneezed. The solicitor's clerk put down his satchel and helped her on with her coat.

'It won't be wasted,' he said, gently.

A car drew up to the door, the coroner looked at his watch and turned to the clerk. 'That will be the car to take you to the station, I think. Thank you for your evidence. We shall need you again, I'm afraid. I'll communicate with you in a day or so.'

The clerk picked up his satchel and coat and hat.

'I shall be at your convenience, sir. Goodnight, gentlemen.'

The screech of the engine's whistle jerked me awake. I must have dozed for about two hours, because the train was already rattling over the points approaching Cranham Junction. My back was numb from lying so long in one position, huddled in my overcoat. I stretched myself. The clerk was still opposite, sitting stiffly erect, his worn gloves neatly buttoned over his wrists, his satchel by his side. I leant forward.

'You don't remember me?'

'Indeed, yes, sir. It is Dr Mellan. I had the pleasure at the inquest at Langley Abbey.' He coughed. 'The Abbey is still for sale, I understand.'

'Yes. Quite deserted. I often wander over there; I've known the place all my life, you know.'

I yawned.

'So the Hentish fortune went to charity after all. I wonder young William didn't contest the will. He would have had a case—uncertain temper of the old man, suicide while of unsound mind, etc.'

'I suppose he was afraid he might be reaccused of murder, sir. There was only my word for it that he didn't leave the boathouse. My word between him and a certain accusation of murder with strong motives for it.'

'He's gone abroad, they say.'

'To South America, sir. His mother left him a piece of property in the Argentine. He is doing well, I understand, sir. Mr Troubridge, head of my firm, sir, says it has been the making of him.'

'He'd have only gambled the money away if he'd had it. He promised to be as hard and selfish as his uncle was. It's funny— though he altered his will so often, I always thought old Hentish meant his nephew to have the money in the end. I thought he just enjoyed frightening William by disinheriting him.'

'A sense of power, sir?'

'Yes, the idea of doing good always seemed to sicken him. Odd, he loathed humanity, yet he will be remembered as one of its great benefactors. All that money to cancer research…'

I leant forward.

'It's curious,' I said, 'that no one has ever noticed that you can't see the boathouse from the cedar tree. The willows screen it from view. I've often wondered if you planned it or whether it was on an impulse.'

The lights flickered as the train rattled through a tunnel. The little clerk coughed.

'Purely impulse, sir. In a small way I am a student of literature, and it has always struck me as curious that it is generally considered the unhappy ending if charity gets the money instead of the dissolute young heir. An alternative to be averted at all costs. The book I am reading now, sir, deals with a missing will. The hero is at the moment lying handcuffed and gagged on a deserted wharf.'

'And the tide is rising?'

'Swiftly, sir. He has three hours till midnight, in which to find a certain paper, otherwise his aunt's fortune reverts to charity.'

'And he finds it in time?'

'Yes, sir.'

'You'd have ended it differently?'

'Yes, sir.'

There was a silence.

'I've always wanted to know when the idea occurred to you,' I said.

He coughed.

'Mr Hentish's days were obviously numbered, sir. When he was signing the will I thought what a fine thing it would be if he should die before a change of heart. Otherwise, I knew I should soon be down at the Abbey to alter the will again in young Mr Hentish's favour, and I knew him too well to hope that anyone but himself and the bookmakers would benefit by the money. Too like his uncle, sir.'

'I suppose old Hentish started talking about William and got into a rage at having been deceived over the wedding. That would bring on one of his attacks.'

'Yes, sir. His face got purple and his lips went white. I stood watching him, hoping it might be fatal. He told me to go and pour him out a glass of medicine from the bottle on the table in the bathroom. The directions were on the bottle, he said. I'm a little short-sighted, sir; it took me a little while to get my bearings. When I got my reading glasses on the first thing that caught my eye was the phial labelled morphia, and while he was yelling at me from the library I opened the cupboard door, took out the morphia, and poured it into the glass of medicine. He took the glass from me. "You damn fool," he said, and drank it down.'

'Swallowed it too quickly to suspect anything, I suppose.'

'He just drew a deep breath, closed his eyes, and leaned back in the chair. I went into the bathroom and wiped my fingerprints off everything, which I understand is the correct procedure in murder. Then I returned to the library, collected my papers and replaced them in my brief case. Mr Hentish sat perfectly still. I don't know whether he was breathing or not. When everything was in order I went out into the hall, closing the library door quietly behind me. I rang the bell for Mr Croucher, and told him I should remain in the garden till my train time. "Is the old screw quiet?" he asked me, and I said he was.'

'Did it occur to you that William Hentish might be accused?'

'No, sir; the fact that the will was not in his favour seemed to preclude that. I didn't know he was unaware of my presence at the Abbey, or the reason for it.'

'I suppose you saw him across the lawn to the boathouse?'

'No, sir, I didn't. I must have been dozing at the time. I took a chance on corroborating his story. It was the least I could do, I thought, sir.'

'Do you never feel a twinge of remorse about it?'

He looked surprised.

'Remorse! The money went to cancer research, sir. Have you read their last report? They've made great strides forward. Remorse! Oh no, sir. I've too great a regard for human life for that.'

The train quivered as the brakes checked the engine's speed, and the clerk peered out of the window. 'This will be my station, I think.' He gathered up the evening paper and his brief case. As the train groaned to a standstill a porter flung the door open and the fog bellied into the carriage.

'Cranham Junction. All change for Kedam, Stukely, Rye, and Wyming. All change,' he chanted. 'Any baggage, sir?'

'No thank you.' He turned to me. 'I've enjoyed our conversation very much, sir. I wish you good night.'

There is no silence more complete than the silence which follows the cessation of machinery. It intensifies all other sounds, the hiss of escaping steam, the clank and rattle of milk cans and the muffled chant of the porter. 'All ch-aa-nn-ge.' Suddenly the engine throbs, there is a jerk and a scraping as the wheels turn. Green lights, red lights, porters, old women, solicitors' clerks, loom large in the mist for a second through the moisture on the window-panes; the scraping of the wheels becomes more rhythmic, takes on a deeper whine; and the train rolls you on beyond them all.

THE SCARECROW

Ethel Lina White

Ethel Lina White (1876–1944) was, like Anthony Berkeley, another Golden Age writer who valued her privacy. Born in Abergavenny, Monmouthshire, she wrote the books on which the classic suspense movies *The Lady Vanishes* and *The Spiral Staircase* were based, but little is known about her life. The most informative biographical account has been written by the rare book dealer Mark Sutcliffe, who discovered that she was known by her relatives and contemporaries as "Dell", and was one of a family of twelve raised by Welsh nursemaids. In a letter to her publisher, she recalled the lurid stories told her by the nursemaids – "probably excellent training for a future thrill-writer!"

White threw up a safe but boring job with the Ministry of Pensions "on the strength of a ten-pound offer for a short story" and "scratched a living on short stuff for quite a time before my first novel was published". Her favourite form of relaxation was watching films ("I used to go to the Pictures before it was general") and this may account for the involving narrative style of her mysteries, and the fact that they are well suited to film and TV adaptation. This story is characteristically vivid.

* * * * *

"THIS is death!" thought Kay.

It had come so suddenly that she felt no fear. The first pang of horror had not yet stirred within her brain. She was numb with sheer surprise.

A moment ago, she had been laughing into the eyes of a man whom she believed to be her friend. They were dull eyes, dark in colour.

Suddenly, they had grown dense as mud, and then burst into a green flame. Even as she stared, hypnotised by the change, his fingers shot out and gripped her throat.

The supper-room was of discreet arrangement. Other couples were whispering on the other side of the screen. The orchestra jerked out jazz in a deafening blare.

Kay had one moment of stark realisation. Rescue seemed hopeless. The fingers around her neck were clamped like an iron vice. Already everything was beginning to swim.

"The end!" she thought.

Then it grew dark.

THAT was over three years ago. Today, Kay was, apparently, not a penny the worse for her experience. She carried no scar on her throat, and only the least bruise on her nerves.

A waiter—who had miraculously chanced to glance round the screen—had been her salvation. Afterwards, she had a conversation with the head doctor of the mental hospital where Waring was confined.

"It was such a shock," she said, "when he suddenly turned on me, because I always thought he liked me—quite."

"May I ask the exact nature of your relations?" inquired the doctor.

"He'd asked me to marry him," answered Kay frankly, "and I had refused him. But we went on being friends. I had not the slightest idea that he harboured any grudge."

Dr. Perry smiled down at her, for he liked her type; a healthy bobbed-haired girl with resolute brown eyes.

"I hope you will try to forget all this bad business," he said. "Remember, you've now nothing to fear."

And now, for the first time in three years, Kay was afraid.

It was all William's fault.

William was the man to whom she was engaged. He was a doctor in the nearest town, and he rang her up whenever he had a chance. The wire was their blessed line of communication, and Kay rushed to the telephone the instant she heard the preliminary tinkle.

She was about to broadcast a kiss, when she was arrested by his words.

"Look here, Kay. I've news. But—don't be alarmed! There's nothing in the world to be frightened about."

And then, of course, she began to feel afraid.

"What's the matter?" she asked.

"Well—Waring's escaped."

Involuntarily, Kay glanced out of the window. In front of her was an expanse of bare fields, with low hedges, running to meet the white skyline. It looked windswept and very empty.

She laughed, to show William Tree that she was not afraid.

"Well, if he comes here, I shall be in the soup."

William hastened to reassure her.

"I'll be over with you as soon as my old stinkpot will bring me. Don't worry about Waring! I'll fix everything all right."

Smiling, Kay hung up the receiver. It was a definite comfort to know that she would soon be seeing William. As he resembled an ardent pugilist rather than a soothing young physician, the mere sight of him would be bracing.

She lit a cigarette and sat down to think. But her thoughts were curded with memories of the old hectic life, when she had been an art student at Chelsea, and the harmless flirtations, which had culminated in the tragedy of Waring.

Again she saw the tawdry restaurant revolving around her in mad circles of light and colour, as the fingers tightened round her throat.

She shuddered. It was unpleasant to reflect that, at this moment, Waring was in her neighbourhood—hiding behind outhouse or hayrick—picking up her trail. He might be twenty miles away—or he might be near.

Unpleasant, too, to dwell on her isolation. She and her mother were alone on the chicken-farm, for they could afford no outside labour. And her mother—called by maternal request 'Milly'— was, at this juncture, hopeless.

In other respects, however, she was the mainstay of their spec- ulation, for, while Kay did the rough land-work, she tended the incubators, with excellent results. The worst thing about her was her appearance; a featherweight of a woman with hollow rouged cheeks, she looked ridiculous in the trousers which were her idea of a smart country outfit.

Kay shook her head in decision.

"Milly mustn't know."

She walked to the window and looked out over the checker- board of fields. The nearest bungalow was more than a quarter of a mile away. She could see the telegraph wires which bordered the main road, and also her own solitary line, shaking in the wind.

But, with the bareness, came a sense of security. She was grateful for the absence of undergrowth with its sinister suggestion of concealment.

Suddenly, as her eyes wandered on, her heart gave a sharp double-knock and then seemed to stop.

Standing amid the young trees of the cherry orchard, was a man.

THE next moment she burst into a peal of laughter.

Her man was a scarecrow.

She had made him the preceding evening—shamelessly neglecting her chores and her proper share of work, in the thrill of a new job. Her artistic training had assisted in his manufacture, so that he was a padded masterpiece of reality.

To help the illusion, the scarecrow was not dressed in the usual rags. In the absence of these—and reflecting that weather could not spoil it, during the short time that the cherries were ripening—Kay had clothed her dummy in a weatherproof left behind him at the bungalow by her brother, who was on a ship.

Its collar was turned up to meet nearly the broad-brimmed slouch hat. Big boots, with padded leggings and stuffed gloves completed the outfit.

IT was almost dark when her task was completed. This was the first time she had seen the scarecrow by daylight.

It had given her a distinct shock. Her nerves were still quivering, as she stood gazing out of the window. The scarecrow was so grotesquely lifelike. In the distance, he seemed to assume a real personality. His movements appeared to be independent of the wind. As she watched it, she almost expected to see it walk from the orchard.

She began to grow nervous.

"I'm sure I never made *that*," she murmured. "It looks alive."

There was no time for idling, for she had yet to visit the egg-house. But, even as she took out the key, she knew that work was impossible, unless she first satisfied herself about the scarecrow.

She was surprised at her own distaste. As she swung open the gate leading into the orchard, she recoiled instinctively at the sight of the figure lurking amid the dwarf trees.

It seemed to be *waiting* for her. At any moment—she expected it to spring.

"Absurd!" she said aloud.

Screwing up her will-power, she ran towards it, like a young war-charger. And, as she came nearer, it lost its lifelike outlines, and became—quite definitely—a stuffed dummy.

"Thank Heaven!"

In that half-sob of relief, Kay learnt the measure of her fear.

Then, at the sound of a familiar hoot from the lane, she dropped the key of the egg-house on the grass, and rushed back to the bungalow. She reached it, just as the dilapidated car chugged to the door.

Although not given to demonstration, they hugged each other.

"I'm still here," laughed Kay, releasing herself. "You'll never get rid of me, and you'd better give up hoping."

Then Milly appeared, and before Kay could warn him, William had blurted out the situation.

"You've both of you got to clear out this instant, and come back with me into the town," he commanded. "It's only a question of hours. Dr. Perry and his staff are out, combing the district."

Kay—a big bonny girl in breeches though she appeared—was ready enough to go. The opposition came from an unexpected quarter—the fragile Milly.

"The idea!" she exclaimed. "Do you expect me to leave my chicks and incubators, at this critical stage? It's monstrous."

William and Kay beat themselves, in vain, against the wall of her resolution. She refused to hear argument.

"All I know is," she declared, "that every penny I possess is wrapped up in this farm. And as for Waring, I'm not frightened of him. I always found him most quiet and unassuming. In fact, quite impossible. Besides, I had some experience in that Chelsea riot of Kay's."

As William groaned, Kay's face suddenly lit up.

"Milly's right," she asserted. "We're safer here. To begin with, we don't know that he will want to attack me again. And if he does, how can he possibly find us here?"

William smoked in silence for a time.

"That's true," he said presently. "Presuming it is a case of *l'idée fixe*, he can't know where you are. The only way he can find out is through me."

"You?" cried Kay.

"Yes. He connects us. He was jealous of me before he went off his rocker. He'll probably make a bee-line for Chelsea. Do the people at your old studio know your address?"

Kay shook her head.

"There have been relays of tenants since then. The tide has long ago washed away all traces of poor undistinguished me."

"Good. Well, he'll do a bit of lurking there—and then he'll stalk *me*."

Kay promptly clapped his cap upon his head.

"Then back you go, my lad, before you give the show away."

Even as she spoke, a shadow chased away her smile.

"You don't think he's already followed you here?" she asked.

"Not he," said William. "He's not had time to get back from his Chelsea lurk. I believe if I do a bit of lurking myself, he'll step into my trap, and then you'll be safe again."

KAY held his arm rather tightly as they walked towards his car; and William's kiss, too, was lingering—and his voice slightly husky.

"Bless you and keep you safe! I—I don't like the idea of leaving you two women alone, without a man."

Kay began to laugh.

"But we have got a protector. One of the best. He scared me, and he'd scare off anyone."

Still laughing, she ran him round to the orchard-gate, and pointed to the scarecrow.

"Look! There's our man."

TOWARDS evening, the wind rose yet higher, driving before it sheets of torrential rain. In spite of her common sense, Kay dreaded the hours of darkness. Their ugly matchbox bungalow seemed no protection against the perils of the night. She heard footsteps in every gust of wind—voices in every howl. Sleep was out of the question, and she made no attempt to go to bed.

"If I have to die, I'll die in my boots," she resolved.

Rather to her surprise, the valiant Milly shared her vigil, although she asserted that her anxiety was on the score of the roofs of the chicken houses. Together, the two women sat in the lamplit sitting-room, listening to the rattle of corrugated iron, the slash of the rain against the windows, and the shrieking of the wind.

And, as Kay waited, those tense moments of ordeal at the Chelsea restaurant took deferred payment of her nerves. The menace of Waring overshadowed his reality. He seemed always to be just the other side of the wall, outside the window, outside the door; watching, waiting, listening—gloating over her distress.

As the hours passed slowly and the uproar increased, she felt that she would almost welcome his actual presence—as something she could get at grips with—rather than this long drawn-out torture of suspense.

Presently, a sigh from Milly distracted her attention, and she saw that her mother had fallen asleep—one rouged cheek pressed against the tablecloth.

She stirred the fire, and, having glanced at the clock, nerved herself to unbolt the window.

To her relief, the night was over. Vivid white gashes striped the torn sky.

"The dawn!" she cried joyfully.

She thought vaguely of making fresh tea; but—overpowered with sudden weariness—she sank into the nearest chair and dropped into a deep sleep.

Dr. William Tree also spent a bad night. On his homeward way, his ancient boneshaker struck permanently, so that he had to accept a tow back to the town.

His first action had been to ring up the sanatorium. Dr. Perry, who was obviously distraught with worry, had no news beyond the fact that it was believed that Waring had been recognised on the London express.

"Chelsea," murmured William.

He went to bed feeling annoyed and worried, and lay listening to the buffets of the wind. Several times, he thought that someone was making a forcible entry through his window; and it struck him that his own jerry-built villa, on the fringe of the town, must be a fortress in comparison with the lonely bungalow, exposed to the full fury of the storm.

About seven o'clock, he felt he could ring up Kay, without shortening her sleep, and he dashed to the telephone.

After waiting impatiently for several minutes, the operator spoke down the wire.

"Sorry, but the line's out of order."

William's heart grew leaden with apprehension.

"Why?" he snapped. "What's wrong?"

"It's the gale," explained the operator. "There are lines down all over the country."

William accepted the explanation, but he did not like it.

His young practice was still in the flopping stage and his case-book was awkwardly spaced. It would be impossible to get out to the bungalow until the late afternoon; but he decided to express a letter which would reach Kay that morning, to cheer her with news of his intended visit.

He dashed off his note, meaning to cycle with it to the post office, before breakfast. Just as he was on the point of leaving the surgery, however, his ears caught the exaggerated sound of laurel-bushes scraping against the thin outside wall of the villa.

In a flash, he concealed himself behind the door and waited.

The lower sash of the open window was lifted still higher, and a man slipped into the room. William had a vision of a furtive figure and an unshaven blur of face, as the intruder tiptoed to the mantelshelf and pounced on the letter addressed to Kay.

It made William sick to listen to his exultant pants and chuckles, as he gloated over his prize. He felt his own muscle, and thanked his Maker for endowing him with supernormal strength.

TEN minutes later, Dr. Perry was listening to his breathless but triumphant message.

"Dr. Tree speaking. I'm holding your man here. How soon can you lift him?"

"Immediately," was the prompt answer. "I can just catch the express. That'll be quicker than car, and bring me in at nine-thirty. Hold him, whatever you do. He's cunning and slippery as an eel."

William rang off, and then called up a colleague to take his morning round. Deciding to postpone his meal, since it was doubtful whether the brain-specialist had yet breakfasted, he sank into a chair, to wait, in lethargic relief, after his strain.

Presently, he glanced at the clock. It was twenty minutes past nine. His responsibility was nearly over. He decided to walk to the gate, in five minutes' time, in order to greet Dr. Perry.

He drew a deep breath at the thought. Heaven alone knew what it would mean for his peace of mind, when he knew that Waring was safe back in the sanatorium.

He looked up, with a start of surprise, as his housekeeper opened the door and Dr. Perry hurried into the dining-room.

"Got him safe?" he asked.

"Boxed and barred."

"Good."

The specialist wiped his brow and accepted a cup of coffee.

"A couple of my men are coming along directly," he explained. "I hadn't time to wait for them. The instant I got your message I dropped everything and came. He'll take some shifting."

"He's a bit of a man-eater," admitted William. "I'm very sorry I didn't meet you, Doctor. I fully intended to."

As he spoke, he glanced at the clock. It was still twenty minutes past nine.

"Hullo!" he exclaimed. "Clock's stopped. What time d'you make it?"

The specialist glanced at his watch.

"Twenty to ten. A clock that stops just about the right time could be a source of real mischief," he added thoughtfully.

"Quite," agreed William. "Was your train late?"

"I didn't catch the express, after all. Lost it by a minute. I came by car, but I stepped on the gas."

He stopped to watch the rain which was pelting against the window. It reminded him of something.

"By the way," he said, "when the rain came on, I couldn't stop to put up the hood. And, as I didn't want the seats to get soaked standing outside, I took the liberty of running the car into your garage."

William's face turned grey.

"The garage?" He spoke with an effort. "But—it was locked."

"Not locked. A bar across the staples."

"I know."

William leapt to his feet.

"Hurry, man!" he cried. "*You've let Waring out!*"

As he dashed through the door, his eye fell upon the clock, and he reflected bitterly, that had he been waiting at the gate, as had been his intention, the tragedy would have been averted.

For a stopped clock—the most harmless object in its futility—can, on occasion, become potent with the powers of life and death.

WHEN the two men reached the shed—which served for garage—the double doors were wide open and the car had gone.

They stared at each other, in stunned horror.

"Didn't you see him when you ran your car in?" asked William.

"No. It was dark and he was possibly hiding behind the door. *Why*—in Heaven's name—didn't you lock the door?"

"Key was lost, and I hadn't bothered about it, because no one would want my old stinkpot. And the garage seemed the safest place for Waring, as it was without windows. I'd warned my housekeeper and the surgery-boy—and there was no one else."

"But why didn't you truss him up?"

William shrugged wearily.

"What with? I keep bandages in my surgery, not rope. We had the devil of a dust-up. By sheer luck, I knocked him out, and when he was groggy, managed to drag him to the garage."

"But—later?"

"Later? I was all in. Think I'd risk a second fight in the garage, and probably get knocked out myself? I thought I'd wait for you and your men to tackle him. The chances were a thousand to one against anyone letting him out, and he'd be there now, but for that infernal clock."

Dr. Perry shrugged his shoulders impatiently.

"Well, there's no time to waste. We can trace him through the car. That is, if he's not too cunning to dump her, once he's got clear away."

SUDDENLY, William's mind recovered from its shock. He had a ghastly recollection of his letter to Kay shaking in the fever of Waring's clutch.

"My God!" he cried. "He's gone after the girl!"

It taxed Dr. Perry's specialised training to calm his frenzy, and restrain him from riding off on his old push-bicycle, in pursuit. He was still shaken by his brain-storm, when the car—hired, by telephone, from the nearest garage—splashed over the muddy road, on its way to the bungalow.

The sky was blotched with heavy clouds, which travelled over the heavens and burst in local storms, like slanting black wires. Sometimes, a white gleam of light would pass, like a searchlight, over the fields. The scene was unearthly and foreboding as a bad dream.

William sat in dumb agony, wrenching his thoughts from the fear that they might be too late. Yet he was stung by the irony of the rescue. They two were responsible for the situation. They had unloosened a ravening Waring upon a defenceless Kay. One had supplied her address and the other had given him liberty and a car.

At last, they reached the bungalow, set amid its cropping chicken-coops and pens.

William rose up in his seat and then gave a shout of joy.

"They're safe! Hullo!"

He pointed to a rising slope, where two figures were outlined against a livid sky; one, in trousers and incongruous dangling green earrings—the other in short wine-red skirt and sweater, facing the wind with the vigour and radiance of youth.

Dr. Perry gave them but one glance.

He, too, had risen in his seat and his keen eye had espied a far-off object in a tributary lane.

"The car. Ditched. Look out, Tree! He must be somewhere near."

"If he is, we'll soon have him out," responded William cheerfully, leaping from the car.

"What's that?" asked Dr. Perry sharply, as they passed through the gate.

William laughed.

"Took you in, too? That's Kay's scarecrow."

"A mighty realistic one." Dr. Perry gave it a longer look. "Come, there's not much cover here."

It was the work of a few minutes to search the chicken-houses, although William stopped in the middle, to greet Kay and her mother and to explain the situation.

Fortified by daylight and the presence of two men, both remained calm.

"He might have slipped into the bungalow, while we were out," said Kay. "It's plain he's nowhere here. Come and look!"

Dr. Perry, however, lingered. His eye swept over field and low hedge. There was no ditch or furrow, and hardly cover for a fox.

Then his glance was once again caught and arrested by the scarecrow.

He touched William's arm and spoke in a low voice.

"I'd like a closer inspection of that gentleman."

The two men advanced warily: but, as they drew nearer the scarecrow, the illusion of humanity faded.

Dr. Perry laughed.

"A fine take-in," he confessed. "Your young friend has some idea of anatomy. Studied art, you say? Well, now for the bungalow."

The scarecrow hung mute and lifeless. It had played its part in the grim conspiracy. It had held the eye and distracted the attention of those who might have made a closer search.

Directly the voices had faded behind the closed doors of the bungalow, there was a stir, followed by a disruption, in a large pile of leaves, rotting into mould.

From under the heap, emerged an earth-stained figure, which writhed its way swiftly over the grass, to its ally—the scarecrow.

A MINUTE later, the scarecrow hung again on its supporting poles. The collar of its weatherproof met the brim of its hat; its hands and legs looked no more lifelike than the padded gloves and breeches, which were buried with the rest of the straw, under the leaf-mould.

There was only one difference. A button—wrenched off, in the mad haste—was missing from the middle of the coat.

But the scarecrow was content. It had only to wait. It must not stir a muscle, lest someone should be watching from the bungalow. Its two enemies were there. And to hang from the pole, like a bat, was easy, for while the body was slack, the mind could wander.

The scarecrow knew that she was here. It had heard her voice as it lay under the pile of leaf-mould. But there was another voice beside, and he wanted her—*alone*.

It knew it had but to wait, and she would come. On the ground, beside it, lay a key. She was always dropping keys. Once, she had dropped the key of her flat in the scarecrow's studio, and, because it had grasped the obvious implication, she had made a terrible scene.

She would fool men no more. The scarecrow was waiting for her to come. Two minutes would suffice—and then, its enemies might come.

They would find nothing left of any use to them.

INSIDE the bungalow, voices were raised in discussion and laughter. Only Dr. Perry chafed at the delay, for he was anxious to pick up the trail. Milly—who had donned femininity with high-heeled French shoes and a long red cigarette-holder—tried to charm him in vain.

"Waring can't be far off," he asserted. "You and I'd better move on, Tree."

William shook his head.

"If he's lurking around, I'm not going to leave Kay."

"Oh, I feel quite safe now." Kay laughed happily. "But I'll own up, I simply can't face another night."

"You shan't," declared William. "If he's not caught by then, I'll sleep in the sitting-room. But it will be safer to catch him. Perhaps, I'd better look around for about half an hour."

Dr. Perry clinched his decision.

"Wisest course, Tree. We're bound to get him if we're systematic. I'll follow the road in the car, while you beat the fields."

"In this rain, and without a coat?" protested Kay indignantly. Then her face cleared.

"I have it. The scarecrow is wearing Roly's old Burberry. You'd better have that."

"Righto. That's a clinking dummy of yours, Kay."

She gurgled.

"I loved making it. And I feel a worm to strip it, when it protected us so nobly through that horrible night."

William walked to the door, but turned, on the threshold, at Kay's voice.

"I just want to see you, one minute, in the kitchen."

He knew what she meant. He had not kissed her yet. With a sheepish beam on his face, he hastened to follow her into the adjoining room.

Fate must be blind, for how otherwise, could she deliberately fight against the helpless? Even while the lovers lingered—Kay's cheek pressed against William's tweed shoulder—the wind shook the last drop from the inky cloud.

William—self-conscious but aloof—appeared from the kitchen, in obedience to Dr. Perry's hail.

"Sorry to keep you waiting. Kay wanted something nailed up. Hullo! It's stopped raining. Good egg! I won't bother about that coat now, Kay. Sooner we're off the better."

Milly kissed her hand to the men, and then called to Kay.

"When you've seen them off, just take these eggs to the egg-house, angel."

"All right."

Kay picked up the basket and then turned to the empty nail on the wall.

"Now, what have I done with that blessed key?" she cried, "I know I had it yesterday."

"Always losing keys," laughed William.

"Think back," advised Milly.

Kay proceeded to think back, to Dr. Perry's ill-concealed annoyance. But, suddenly, she gave a cry of triumph.

"I know. I was just going to date those eggs, yesterday, when I heard William's stinkpot. I must have left it in the orchard."

She walked with the men to the orchard, and the scarecrow heard her voice. At the sound of her laughter, it tensed its muscles. The waiting was nearly over.

HER hand on the gate, she turned to wave farewell to the two men. She felt happy in William's presence, and in the warm glow of her relief. The night held no more terrors for her. William would be there. Even the sun was going to shine for her.

Her joy was visible in the radiance of her smile. The brightening light bronzed her brown hair. William thought he had never seen a sweeter picture.

"Do look at my scarecrow," she said with a chuckle. "It's waiting to make love to me. Wouldn't you like to touch it and see if it's alive?"

Both men laughed as they shook their heads.

"You don't get us twice," said William. "We've been had, both of us."

"I'm not surprised," said Kay. "He scared me, and I made him. Good-bye—and don't be long!"

The men turned away and she opened the orchard gate, just as the sun broke through the cloud.

It travelled over the field and fell upon the scarecrow. As it did so, a spark of fire glinted from the gap in its coat, where the button was missing.

Kay only noticed her key. She was running towards it, when she felt William's hand upon her arm.

"Come back!" His voice was low and tense. "Perry, make ready! That scarecrow's wearing a watch-chain."

CLUE IN THE MUSTARD

Leo Bruce

Leo Bruce was the pen-name of Rupert Croft-Cooke (1903–1979), whose life was so eventful that he felt moved to produce no fewer than twenty-seven volumes of autobiography. Barry Pike, compiler of *Murder in Miniature*, a collection of Bruce's short stories, points out that only two of those memoirs make any reference to his detective fiction. Similarly, Croft-Cooke's obituary in *The Times* failed to mention his work as Leo Bruce. It is ironic, Pike notes, that it is Leo Bruce the crime writer, rather than Croft-Cooke, prolific author of mainstream novels, plays, and non-fiction, who is celebrated in the *Dictionary of Literary Biography*.

Bruce created two major detective characters, Sergeant Beef and the history teacher Carolus Deene. Beef made his debut in *Case for Three Detectives* (1936), an entertaining novel in which caricatures of Lord Peter Wimsey, Hercule Poirot, and Father Brown are outshone by the plebeian, darts-playing Beef. This account of Beef's first important case has also been published under the alternative title of "Death in the Garden".

* * * * *

"My first important case?" said Sergeant Beef. "Yes, I can tell you about that. I shouldn't hardly call it a who-done-it, though, because everybody knew that if old Miss Crackliss had been murdered, there was only one person it could be. All the same, it was an interesting case. What you'd call mackayber..."

"Mack…?"

"You know, gruesome," explained Beef impatiently.

"Oh, macabre."

"That's it."

I knew better than to underrate Sergeant Beef because of a little eccentricity in pronunciation. Large, crimson of cheek, a hearty eater and a good public bar man whose ginger moustache had refreshed itself in many a pint glass, he looked what he once had been, a village policeman. But his insight and common sense had enabled him to solve a number of murder cases, and now he had retired from the Force he was gaining a reputation as a private investigator.

The case he described to me happened twenty years ago or more, when Sergeant Beef was a constable stationed in a small village called Long Cotterell, in one of the home counties. His passions were gardening and darts; when it was too dark to continue the one he settled down nightly to the other. Then old Miss Crackliss, who lived at the Mill House, died suddenly.

He knew Miss Crackliss well. In fact, he confessed, he used to put in a few hours at the week-end helping her gardener.

"Pay wasn't so plentiful in those days," he explained, "and I wanted a bit extra to get married on. Besides, she let me put odds and ends in her greenhouse, and *that* was handy, too."

Miss Crackliss was in her sixties, a frail and shrunken old lady, who suffered from heart trouble. To look at her, Beef said, "you wouldn't have thought she'd have taken much murdering." She was reputed to be excessively rich.

Her nephew lived with her, and in the eyes of the village here was a ready-made suspect. Ripton Crackliss was the least popular resident of Long Cotterell, a tall, gloomy man in his thirties, powerful and slow-moving; he had a way of ignoring the greetings of others.

It was understood that Ripton Crackliss would inherit everything on his aunt's death.

The Mill House stood well away from the village, a pleasant red-brick house with a walled garden beside it, in which were two large greenhouses. It was in this garden that Beef was working on the last occasion on which he saw Miss Crackliss alive, a Saturday afternoon in May.

"I was off duty," he explained, "and I'd come up to do a bit of planting out for her. Besides, I had a couple of boxes of mustard and cress in the conservatory and I wanted to see how they were doing.

"I went in to look at my boxes and found the seedlings coming through nicely, then I went over to get on with her work.

"Presently the old lady came out to settle down in her garden chair for the afternoon.

"She had one of those metal-framed chairs with canvas seats and backs to them, because she liked sitting upright and not stretching out as you would in a deck-chair. I went and said good afternoon to her.

"She was all wrapped round with rugs because, although there was sunshine, it was none too warm. She seemed quite cheerful, sitting there with her book and looking up to see what I was doing. Her own gardener finished midday Saturdays. The next day I heard she was dead."

At first there seemed nothing unnatural about this, for the local doctor, a great friend of Beef's, had long been prepared for a fatal heart attack. He was a keen, conscientious man, this Doctor Ryder-Boyce, and he was upset by the event because he liked old Miss Crackliss.

It appeared that when tea-time came she had not returned to the house and the housekeeper, a stern Scotswoman called Mrs Craig, had gone up to the room which Ripton called his study and told him that his aunt was still outside.

Ripton had got up and said he would go across to the walled garden and bring her in to tea.

There was nothing unusual in this. The old lady loved her garden and was apt to stay far too long in it when the weather was not really warm enough. Besides, she frequently dozed off to sleep. So Mrs Craig made the tea. Then Ripton Crackliss came hurrying into the house.

"You must go to her at once," he said. "She's had one of her attacks, I think. I'm afraid she's dead."

Mrs Craig set out for the walled garden while Ripton telephoned for the doctor. She found Miss Crackliss dead, sitting in her chair with the blankets round her. There was a look almost of horror in the dead eyes and the features seemed somehow twisted as though with fear.

"Poor thing," thought Mrs Craig. "She must have died in pain after all. One of those terrible attacks of hers."

But she noticed something else. The dead face was flushed as she had rarely seen it.

The doctor arrived and ordered Miss Crackliss to be carried up to her bedroom. He made his examination and asked both Mrs Craig and Ripton Crackliss a number of questions. She had said nothing to lead either of them to suppose she was unwell. She had lunched with them. As Mrs Craig said, there could be nothing to upset her in anything she had eaten or drunk because all three of them had had the same.

The doctor went home, but later that afternoon he telephoned to Beef and suggested that he should come round.

Beef found the doctor silent and abstracted.

"Know what they're saying in the village?" he asked. "They think Ripton Crackliss did for his aunt this afternoon."

"What makes them think that?" asked the doctor.

"Well, you know what gossip is. They don't like the fellow and they know he gets her money. Besides, he was up at the house all the afternoon. Think there's anything in it?"

"I don't see how there can be," said the doctor. "I've examined the old lady and she certainly died as a result of her heart trouble. It might have come at any time, as you know. The fact that she seemed well to-day means nothing."

"Then what are you so worried about?" asked Beef.

"I simply can't say. Yet there is something I don't like about it. She *looked* strange, for one thing. As though she'd had a shock— from the outside, I mean. And there were a couple of points..."

"Go on," said Beef.

"They may mean nothing at all. Probably they don't. But I'm not quite happy."

"What were these points?"

"Just above her upper lip was a tiny smudge. At first I thought it was dirt, but it was sticky. Only a very small smudge. But she never ate sweets."

"And the other one?"

"When the three of us went out to carry her in, Ripton Crackliss got there first and seemed to be trying to drag her to her feet. He'd got hold of her forearms and was pulling quite hard. When I examined her later I found that he had been so violent that it had left marks on the skin. It seemed such an extraordinary thing to do when we were all on our way to carry her properly."

"Yes," said Beef. "There were no signs of violence?"

"None at all. Not even an abrasion anywhere."

"And she could not have been poisoned?"

"That, of course, we shall find out if I'm not satisfied. But I see no signs of it at all."

"I think I'll go and have a look round that garden, though," said Beef. "It won't be dark for another couple of hours yet."

Beef cycled off to the Mill House. Putting his cycle into the hedge, he went straight to the walled garden. The chair in which Miss Crackliss had sat that afternoon was still there, and he examined it carefully. Then he made a minute inspection of the rough stone paving on which it had stood.

"There was nothing," he said, telling me the story. "Nothing at all in the way of a clue. I decided to pack up and wait for the post-mortem, if there was going to be one."

Before he started for home he thought he would go and have a look at his mustard and cress, and switched the light on in the greenhouse. This brought Ripton Crackliss over from the house at a run, and he asked Beef what the hell he was doing. Beef remained calm.

"I'm just having a look at my seedlings," he said. "Come on wonderfully, haven't they?"

Ripton Crackliss seemed to control his anger.

"I understand that you had permission from my aunt to use this place," he said. "But my aunt died this afternoon. In future, if you want to come here please call at the house first and see if it's convenient."

"Very well, sir," said Beef, and followed him out.

He went straight back to the doctor's house and the two talked seriously for half an hour. Then they got into the doctor's car and drove off to the nearby town. Here they went to the police station and another conference took place. Within forty-eight hours a warrant was out for the arrest of Ripton Crackliss on a charge of murdering his aunt.

"Caused quite a sensation at the time," said Beef, "and I won't say it didn't do me a bit of good in the Force. 'Murder in the Garden', the papers called it, but that was wrong, because the murder hadn't taken place in the garden at all."

"No?"

"No. It was in the greenhouse. You know what that fellow had done? He'd waited till his aunt was in her chair, tucked up tight in her rugs so that she couldn't move in a hurry, then he'd come out to her.

"Must have been about two o'clock that Sunday afternoon when Mrs Craig was having her nap and nobody would have seen him going across from the house. All of a sudden he'd put a piece of plaster, like they use for bandages, over her mouth and held her arms to the chair.

"What could she do? She was a frail little thing and couldn't even struggle enough to leave any traces. Then he'd tied her arms to the framework of the chair and she was powerless.

"Of course, it needed more than that. Doesn't matter how weak and old people are, they don't die easily. He lifted the chair with her on it and took it across to the greenhouse. He had the furnace stoked up and the heat in there was the maximum.

"That's what killed her. With her heart she was dead an hour later—or sooner, let's hope."

"Good Lord," I couldn't help exclaiming.

"I told you it was gruesome. But ingenious, too. She really had died of a heart attack and there might have been no evidence of anything else.

"He'd thought about the marks of where her arms were tied and covered that up by pretending to try to pull her out of her chair when we went across with the doctor.

"We got quite a lot of evidence, but I doubt even then whether he would have been hanged if he hadn't confessed.

"There was the mark of the sticking plaster, and the fact that a whole sack of coke had been used after the gardener left on Saturday. And he was the only one on the spot. But he might have got off for lack of medical evidence. You see, the way he had chosen left no trace at all. Murder by heat, you might call it."

"But what gave you the idea?" I asked him. "What really led you to see what had happened?"

He smiled slowly.

"It was that mustard and cress of mine," he said. "I told you I said to Ripton Crackliss that it had come on wonderfully. Well, it had. It had shot up. And there had been no sun that day.

"As soon as I saw those long, thin stalks I knew there was something wrong. That was my only clue."

OUR PAGEANT

Gladys Mitchell

Gladys Mitchell (1901–1983), for many years a pillar of the Detection Club, was a schoolteacher who published *Speedy Death*, an extraordinary first novel featuring the formidable Mrs Bradley, in 1929. The last Mrs Bradley novel, *The Crozier Pharaohs*, appeared 55 years later – her career was, therefore, astonishingly long, even by the standards of fictional detectives.

Like many of Mitchell's short stories, "Our Pageant" originally appeared in the *Evening Standard*, which for a few years in the Fifties was an excellent market for crime writers capable of fashioning short tales with a twist. This story, from which Mrs Bradley is absent, reflects an enthusiasm for British customs which is reflected in many of Mitchell's novels.

* * * * *

You remember our pageant, of course – the Roman Legions supplied by the Youth Clubs, the rather remote Saxon saints portrayed by the Girl Guides, the Normans led by William the Conqueror (our Town Clerk distressed because his nose-piece pressed more heavily than the Pageant Master had intended), King John and his barons all signing Magna Charta like mad whenever they got any applause, and all the rest of it.

And did you notice the Morris Dancers? There were just the six of them. They could do Bean-Setting, Trunkies (not very well – the Capers are the difficulty there), Blue-Eyed Stranger and Laudnum

Bunches. Teddy Pratt could do a Morris jig, too, rather nicely, but, unfortunately, so could Cyril Clark.

Women did not enter into this – rather, they should not have done, but you know how it is. Five good men and true do not make six good men and true, and so our stout-hearted Miss Galley from the Bank had to be pressed into service, and a certain Miss Johnson was to act as Jack in the Green.

Jack in the Green comes down to us from the Middle Ages. You don't have to be able to dance, you just play the fool and collect the money. It is a man's job, but we hadn't got a man to do it.

If you've ever taken part in a village pageant, you'll remember that rehearsals begin at least a month too soon.

It is not too soon, considering the amount of practice involved, and it is not too soon when one considers that scarcely ever is it possible to obtain a full rehearsal until about a week before the day. There are always unavoidable gaps because of people who've got something else important to do just when the Pageant Master needs them most. But it is too soon because of all the quarrels that begin.

We had the usual crop, but the most obstinate one was that between Teddy Pratt and Cyril Clark. It was a cut-throat rivalry over which of them should dance a Morris jig.

Well, week followed week, and both fellows practised for all they were worth, but still there was really nothing to choose between them.

Then a new factor entered into the situation. Pratt and Clark fell out about Miss Johnson. The girl was to impersonate Jack in the Green and go with the Morris dancers, so it mattered all the more to the two men which of them should be chosen to perform the Morris jig.

As the great day came nearer, bets were being laid at six to five on Clark for the Morris jig, eight to three that Parson St. George would fall off his horse, and ten to one that the financial result would show a deficit. (We were taking a silver collection from the crowd to defray expenses.)

Those that had betted on Clark lost their money, for the Pageant Master, having to make up his mind at last, picked Pratt. Clark, he thought, was rather small, being no bigger than Miss Johnson, the Jack in the Green.

The first intimation we had of something amiss was when a message came from the Pageant Master to say that Clark had withdrawn altogether from the Morris dancing. This put everybody concerned in a stew, because, Morris jig or not, it was a plain impossibility for five men – that is to say, four men and one woman – to perform dances intended for six.

Well, much against our feeling of civic pride – if the word civic can be applied to a village – we had to ask a fellow called Fathing from Peascod to come in and dance sixth man.

Meanwhile the expected had happened. The rehearsals had gone on for so long that before the pageant, and before he withdrew from the dancing, Clark had had the banns cried three times and had wedded the Jack in the Green right under Pratt's nose, as you might say.

The great day came at last. The band came first, and then the procession followed. The Romans led, and the cavalcade from the

Hall followed the Morris dancers, because we could not think of anything much to put in between.

It was at the end of the dance called Bean-Setting that the tragedy happened, and it happened right in the middle of the village green, just before the big tableau was due to move into place. There was a lot of noise during the All In and Call, and a bit of horseplay with Jack in the Green in the middle of it, and suddenly Pratt fell down dead, so we had no Morris jig after all.

Nobody could believe it at first, and then the police took over – not just Nimmett, but the real police from Hurstminster. Pratt had been stabbed to the heart, and the weapon had been about five inches long.

That was all we knew for a long time, and then they got a London chap on to it from Scotland Yard. He didn't know any of us, and that was a good thing really, because he could not be biased, although we could have told him of the bad blood between Pratt and Clark.

Suspicion would naturally have fallen on Clark if he had been one of the dancers, but, of course, he had taken himself out of it. Nevertheless, the Scotland Yard man got really inquisitive, because when he compared the prints he had got on the Morris sticks, not one of the sets fitted with prints he'd found on the weapon.

Then the Scotland Yard man noticed something else. On the end of the weapon was a loop so that it could be hitched on to a belt. He examined all the Morris-men's belts, but none of them had a hook to have taken the loop on the sword-stick.

The chap was very bright. He put two and two together all right. He asked Clark's wife if she had any objection to being measured round the waist. She had to say no, and a woman police officer was brought along to measure her. Then Clark was measured, and the Scotland Yard man knew he had solved his problem.

"You took her place as Jack in the Green," he said to Clark. "You're much the same height, but her waist is much smaller than yours. How comes it, then, that two distinctly different tag-holes have been used? See?" He showed Clark the rubbings on the belt where, some distance apart, it was obvious that the belt had been fastened in two entirely different places. There was a hook on it, too, where the lethal weapon had been hung. Easy to hide it, with all that greenery about him.

"And you married the girl so that, when it came to the murder you'd planned, she couldn't give evidence against you," the detective said in conclusion.

Clark's prints were on the sword-stick, of course, and that settled his hash.

Still, it spoilt our pageant, and we'd taken all those weeks to get it ready. It did seem rather a pity, and the silver collection was negligible, but that was only what we'd expected.